DEATH
IN THE
CRYPT

BOOKS BY FLISS CHESTER

THE CRESSIDA FAWCETT MYSTERIES SERIES

1. *Death Among the Diamonds*

2. *Death by a Cornish Cove*

3. *Death in the Highlands*

4. *Death on the Scotland Express*

THE FEN CHURCHE MYSTERIES

1. *A Dangerous Goodbye*

2. *Night Train to Paris*

3. *The Moonlit Murders*

THE FRENCH ESCAPES ROMANCE SERIES

1. *Love in the Snow*

2. *Summer at the Vineyard*

3. *Meet Me on the Riviera*

DEATH
IN THE
CRYPT

FLISS CHESTER

bookouture

Published by Bookouture in 2024

An imprint of Storyfire Ltd.
Carmelite House
50 Victoria Embankment
London EC4Y 0DZ

www.bookouture.com

ISBN: 978-1-83525-101-0
eBook ISBN: 978-1-83525-100-3

It was late October and drifts of golden leaves were falling from the great beech and chestnut trees that stood imposingly in front of the eighteenth-century house. The only thing that rivalled the trees was the even more monumental west front of Winchester Cathedral, just beyond them.

The Honourable Cressida Fawcett had arrived at the ancient city to visit her favourite aunt, her mother's sister. As much as she loved driving her bright red Bugatti motorcar, it had been a long journey after an early start. Her pampered pug, Ruby, had been poor company, snoring away in the passenger seat. But no sooner had Cressida stretched her long limbs, smoothed down her shingled blonde hair and walked into the parlour of Priory House, than she was enveloped by the welcome smell of freshly brewed coffee along with the arms of her aunt.

'Darling girl! Welcome, welcome!'

'What ho, Aunt Mary!' Cressida said, her voice muffled against her aunt's olive-green cashmere shawl, which was securely swathed about her shoulders.

Of course Cressida's Aunt Mary would be dressed perfectly

for the chilly weather. She was the epitome of prudent behaviour. If a sensible shoe was needed, Aunt Mary would already be wearing it. If a chill to the air was expected late on the day of a picnic, Aunt Mary would have made sure extra jumpers were packed and warming drinks provided. It was this foresight and planning that made Aunt Mary, tall and slim, like her niece, such a wonderful hostess, and all-round good egg. Cressida had always tried to emulate her, though knew herself to be far too hot-headed to ever truly match up to her favourite aunt.

Yes, Lady Mary Dashwood-Howard was in all things a paragon of common sense, except when it came to decor. But with trends all around her changing, and her skirting boards in need of a touch-up, she had realised it was time for something new in her beautiful home. She'd invited her niece Cressida, who was well known in their society circles for her talent for interior decoration, for some much-needed moral support in the matter. It was also a welcome excuse for a visit; different though they might be, the women loved each other dearly, as could be seen in the long, warm embrace they shared now in the parlour.

Once the coffee was poured, courtesies and family gossip exchanged, and they were both seated comfortably by the fire, the conversation turned to what Aunt Mary wanted to change about her beautiful home.

'You can see I became entranced by William Morris and the Arts and Crafts Movement,' Aunt Mary said, waving the hand that wasn't holding her coffee cup in the direction of a botanical wallpaper that adorned one of the walls in her elegant parlour. 'But it's all wrong for this sort of house. These high ceilings and elaborate cornicing and whatnot, they don't work with this cottage-style print. Morris obviously thought that everyone with taste lived in some Sussex hovel with panelled walls and cat-slide roofs...' she trailed off, realising perhaps that she had all but described Mydenhurst Place, the sixteenth-century manor where Cressida grew up, and home to Mary's own sister, Cressida's mother, Rosamund.

'It's a handsome print,' Cressida interjected, as she slipped a buttery piece of bread under the table to Ruby, who greedily snaffled it from her fingers. 'But you're right, Aunt Mary, it's not the sort of thing for a Queen Anne room like this one. Too busy, too tight.'

'Quite, quite. I knew you'd understand.' Aunt Mary's enthusiasm had returned. 'And that's why I'm now quite intent on redecorating in the Art Nouveau style.'

Cressida almost spat out her coffee and clattered her delicate china cup back into its saucer.

'Careful, dear. Those are Limoges,' Aunt Mary gently reprimanded her.

Cressida carefully placed her cup and saucer back on the table.

'Aunt Mary, I hope you don't mind, but I've already made a start on what I think might look simply perfect for this room. I took the liberty of going to, well, Liberty, and have found some rather beautiful silks and papers that would update the room but keep it looking perfectly Queen Anne too. I adore this house, always have—'

'I like to think of it as your second home, dear girl,' Aunt Mary said indulgently.

'And that's exactly why I couldn't bear to see it turned into some Art Nouveau experiment.' Cressida looked at the gracious proportions around her and held back a shudder at the thought of false ceilings and inset lights.

Aunt Mary sat back in her chair. 'Well, if you insist, though I thought those new motifs rather jazzy.'

Cressida raised an eyebrow. 'Jazz is the word for it, Aunty M. And I can't see it syncopating here. And if you don't believe me, you might listen to my friend Maurice.'

'Oh, that nice chap you recommended to your mother? She said he was simply marvellous with her drapes.'

'Yes, Maurice Sauvage, he's the big cheese at Liberty as far as fabrics are concerned. And I hope you don't mind, but he's arriving on the lunchtime train, armed, I hope, with all the swatches and prints I picked out for you last week.'

'Oh, splendid, splendid. Nothing like cracking on. Now,' Aunt Mary handed Cressida a plate of ginger biscuits. 'Do try one of these. My new maid rustled them up. Simply delicious.'

Cressida took one, and, as if on cue, Aunt Mary's maid entered the room with a steaming pot of hot water with which to refresh the coffee pot.

'Ah, Nancy. Thank you, thank you.' Aunt Mary beckoned her over and made space for the pot on the tea tray. 'Nancy, this is my niece, the Honourable Cressida Fawcett. Cressida dear, this is Nancy Biddle, my new girl.'

'Good day to you, ma'am.' The maid bobbed a curtsy.

'Hello, Nancy.' Cressida met her gaze with a smile as she stood back upright again. 'And this is Ruby, my pug.'

Ruby, on hearing her name, sauntered out from under the low table and blinked up at the maid with her black, globe-like eyes.

'Hello, Miss Ruby,' Nancy said, a look of pure delight on her young face.

'Nancy dear, will you telephone the dean and tell him that I'd like to show Cressida around the cathedral. This morning would be as good a time as any, help her stretch her legs after her long drive. And I believe the bell-ringers will be practising.'

'Yes, ma'am.' The maid bobbed a curtsy again and left the room.

'I'm really awfully glad to have her. After Elspeth upped and left with that man from the circus, well it's been a relief to have a decent girl again,' Aunt Mary said, then sipped her tea.

'And I hope she won't find it macabre contacting the dean on our behalf.'

'Why would she? Is he a particularly macabre man?'

Aunt Mary settled herself into her chair and held her coffee cup and saucer to her chest. She shook her head and her well-set chestnut curls swayed as she did so. 'Well, those long black cassocks the clergy insist on wearing. It *is* like something from Dante. Other than that, he's a very nice man really. But, you see, along with a few other cathedral houses, Nancy did for him and the late Mrs Sitwell, his wife. Alas, recently departed.'

'Oh, I see.' Cressida's hand hovered over another ginger biscuit, but she pulled it back. 'How did she... I mean, was it an illness?'

Aunt Mary raised an eyebrow. 'Drowned, the poor thing. She had never been a strong swimmer, apparently.'

'Oh dear. How terribly sad. And the dean released Nancy from his service? Surely he needs a good maid now more than ever, a man on his own and all that?'

'He's moving into cathedral lodgings. There are small houses that come with laundry services and meals included and that sort of thing. You see, without Mrs Sitwell, who was so active in the life of the cathedral and would entertain visiting bishops and all the clergy and whatnot, well, the poor man said there was no point maintaining the Deanery with her gone. It really is a substantial house, quite something. I know baronets with smaller homes. I believe the precentor might be in line for it. He has a charming wife and two small boys. So much more apt, having a family in such a large home, rather than the dean rattling around there all on his own.'

'Quite. And forgive my ignorance, but what is a precentor? Sounds like some Roman army general. Hail Caesar and all that.'

Aunt Mary gave her niece a look that was both withering and affectionate and smoothed down her checked tweed skirt as she explained. 'A precentor is in charge of the musical life of a cathedral, dear. All the organ music and various concerts. He's really quite a moderniser this one. Wife's a friend of mine, though she does rather fancy herself better than she ought. She'll be mightily happy to be in the Deanery now – next stop a Winchester College education for the boys. Ah, Nancy.' Aunt Mary welcomed her maid back into the parlour. 'Was the dean amenable to our little tour?'

'Yes, ma'am.' Nancy bobbed again, and Cressida looked at her properly this time. She was young, barely out of her teenage years, and very thin. Wiry almost. Her skin was fresh though, and her cheeks flushed, almost to the extent that Cressida wondered if Nancy had just dashed across to the cathedral to ask the dean face to face, rather than using the telephone. 'Mind how you go though, my lady,' said the maid, 'and you, Miss Fawcett. There's been another sighting in the graveyard.'

'A sighting?' Cressida asked.

'Pay no heed, Cressida dear,' Aunt Mary said, glancing to the heavens, but Cressida looked at Nancy again and nodded.

'Go on, Nancy, what sighting?'

Nancy paled, though perhaps it was just the weak autumn sun disappearing behind a cloud outside the parlour window. Still, there was a tremor in her voice when she replied.

'The Silent Friar.'

The name rang a bell in the distant recesses of Cressida's mind. 'Are there still monks here? Why the excitement over a sighting?'

'Oh, he's not a monk, ma'am. Not anymore in any case.' Nancy made the sign of the cross over her chest. 'He's dead, ma'am. The Silent Friar is a ghost.'

'Oh, the old ghost.' Cressida sat back in her chair and pulled Ruby onto her lap. As cool as she played it, she had to admit that the hairs along her arms prickled. But then she looked over to her aunt, who was shaking her head as if hearing nonsense for the umpteenth time.

'Pish posh. Pish posh. Ghosts, I tell you. All a figment of your young and overstimulated imagination, Nancy.'

'But I saw him, ma'am.' She stood up straighter, determination clenched in her jaw. Then, as if remembering her place, she bobbed a curtsy and poured some more coffee for Cressida and Aunt Mary.

'I think I remember the stories about him from when I was a child. "Be you saint or sinner, pauper or prior, no one can hide from the Silent Friar." Funny how these things just come back to you.' Cressida laughed, though there was a touch of nerviness to it. She remembered being terrified of seeing the spectre as a young girl. 'And he's been seen around the graveyard, you say?' Cressida asked Nancy before Aunt Mary could tut again.

'And in the cathedral itself, ma'am. Tall as a lamplighter he is, and he just disappears into the ether.'

'Or mist. He could just disappear into the mist. It is the season of those after all,' Aunt Mary sighed.

'Aha, so you do believe in him, Aunty M?' Cressida grinned at her aunt.

'Oh, fiddlesticks. No... it's all silly talk. Ghosts and what have you.' Aunt Mary put her coffee cup down and pulled her shawl around her shoulders a little tighter. 'What we need to worry about more is that robbery. Now that was a real-life mystery.'

'A robbery?' Cressida was even more intrigued by this than talk of old ghosts. But then she was suddenly worried about her aunt, who had lived alone since her uncle's death in the Great War. 'Where, Aunt Mary? Here?'

'No, dear, the cathedral archive. It was broken into several weeks ago now, though the burglar didn't have to try very hard as the padlock had all but rusted off. Though, as I believe your father always says, Cressida, a padlock only keeps out an honest person.'

Cressida nodded thoughtfully. She had heard her father say that phrase and it had always struck her as odd, but she understood it now. If someone was determined to get in somewhere, a rusty old padlock would hardly be a deterrent.

She looked back at her aunt. 'And what was stolen from the archive? Anything valuable?'

'Urgh, battered hymn books and ledgers full of old bishop's laundry lists,' Nancy muttered under her breath, then bobbed an apologetic curtsy to Aunt Mary, who had raised an eyebrow. 'All I mean to say, ma'am, is that it's just full of dusty old books and papers and the like, my old pa says so anyway.'

'Quite the opposite, Nancy,' Aunt Mary frowned. 'The archive is chock-full of all sorts of valuable documents. And not just documents, but paintings and blueprints and registers and the like. Very valuable to historians. Oddly enough though, with all the truly valuable items in there – I believe some of the illustrated manuscripts are priceless – it was one of the old record books that was taken, along with the burglar making a terrible mess of the place. Dear Mrs Sitwell was quite upset by it all, especially as she'd undertaken the huge task of reorganising all the books and records. All in all, very odd, very odd.'

'Mrs Sitwell, the dean's late wife?' Cressida asked. She glanced at Nancy, who looked glumly at her hands, held neatly in front of her. 'Was she the archivist?'

'No, but as I said, she was very much part of cathedral life and she kept in with Mr Flint, the archivist. She would sit for hours with him going through what was what. And yes, she was quite upset by it,' Aunt Mary confirmed.

'And was anyone caught?' Cressida asked.

'No,' sighed Aunt Mary. 'Not a sausage. No one owned up, of course, and the police had nothing to go on really.'

'It'll be the Silent Friar, ma'am, mark my words,' Nancy murmured, glancing at Cressida.

Cressida twitched a reassuring smile at her without her aunt noticing, but moments later, Aunt Mary was hurrying the girl out, saying that it was time for them to visit the cathedral.

Cressida put Ruby down and followed her aunt back out to the hallway. Nancy was holding out her camel-coloured cashmere coat for her, along with her smarter set of hat and gloves that had already been unpacked.

Cressida shivered as Nancy opened the door and showed her and Aunt Mary out, before announcing that she too had some errands to run. A gust of wind swirled a handful of leaves down the pavement beyond the garden, and Cressida watched, her thoughts whirling like the leaves as they barrelled down the lane, this way and that, caught up in their autumnal dance.

A robbery, a ghost and a drowning... What next?

As Cressida and Aunt Mary crossed the small park between Priory House and the cathedral, they could hear the pealing of many bells. The sound reverberated around them and Cressida fancied that it made the trees shimmy and give up a few more pieces of their golden treasure to the ground. Ruby toddled along next to them, investigating every pile of leaves, as they approached the vast west front of the cathedral.

The original stone was all but stained black from coal smoke, but the carvings were still as sharp as they had been all those hundreds of years ago when the cathedral was built. Three great gothic arches formed the base of the west front, and Aunt Mary guided Cressida towards the one to the left.

Before they entered, Cressida picked up Ruby and held her close to her chest. Another peal resounded from the tower and made Cressida jump. She laughed to herself, though once she'd regained her breath, she gasped as a sudden movement caught her eye among the few remaining graves of the old priory churchyard next to the cathedral.

The Silent Friar?

No, she shook her head and turned back to smile at her

eminently more sensible aunt. It wasn't the ghost, it was just young Nancy going about her errands, her dark woollen coat fluttering in the breeze behind her.

Cressida bent her head down and planted a kiss on Ruby's head. Her aunt smiled at her indulgently, then walked briskly under the arch and in through the old oak door to the cathedral.

'Ah, Lady Dashwood-Howard, how are you?'

'Very well, Geoffrey, very well indeed,' Aunt Mary greeted the man in the black cassock, his bald head round and shining, a smattering of white hair edging the sides. The dean, Geoffrey Sitwell, wore wire-framed glasses and was moderately over-weight; noticeable, Cressida thought, despite the slimming powers of black cloth. Otherwise, though, he looked reasonably sprightly, the sort of man you'd trust with your bag if you came across him in a first-class rail carriage.

At the correct moment, Cressida accepted the dean's hand-shake and returned his smile with one of her own. She listened as he and Aunt Mary chatted about the bell-ringers and the verger, the late Mrs Sitwell's missing hairbrush, and the choirboy who'd left a boiled sweet under a kneeler and now ants were infesting the chapter house. While she did so, Cressida took in the soaring stone as it swept up towards the vaulted ceil-ing. As she looked, the peals of bells filled the void with the most glorious sound, and she felt somewhat foolish having jumped so much at them earlier.

Ruby sat cosily in her arms, and Cressida felt, rather than heard, her gentle snores. After all the scrapes Cressida had found herself in recently, from country house diamond heists to murder on an overnight train, perhaps she could find some peace here, despite rumours of ghosts and all too real robberies and drownings. She looked over to her aunt, who was dressed in practical wellington boots under her thick tweed skirt, her brown curls set closely to her head, and her hazel-coloured eyes looking intelligently at everything the dean was saying. Aunt

Mary was the last person who would serve her a side dish of murder along with lunch. She was far too sensible for that.

The dean did an admirable job of showing them the highlights of the cathedral, and Cressida could sense that the building was able to give him a huge amount of solace in the wake of his wife's death. Though she did have to offer him her handkerchief as they paid homage to the grave of Jane Austen, as the similarity of two such society-loving women, cut down in their prime, was almost too much for him. Aunt Mary suggested drawing the tour to a close, but Mr Sitwell shook his head and announced that they simply must visit the crypt.

'It's rather damp, I know, as we held a simple Mass down there this morning, but I think we'll manage. You can't leave without seeing the Canterbury candlesticks.'

'Well, I do have a penchant for chandlery, do lead on.' Aunt Mary swept a hand out to chivvy on the dean, then clasped both of hers behind her as they headed along the north aisle to the crypt.

Cressida held Ruby tight to her chest with one arm, and trailed her other hand along the cool stone wall as she descended the uneven stone steps down into the very depths of the cathedral. Narrow, deep-set, plain-glass windows let in a touch of natural light, and the pale daylight was spread thin as the shadows dominated the corners of the gothic arches and vaulted ceiling, exaggerating the curving stone. She was grateful for her stout and sensible driving shoes as she waded through deep puddles, though she wished she'd had Aunt Mary's foresight to wear wellingtons. When one particularly deep puddle threatened to dampen Ruby's undercarriage, the dean offered an explanation.

'It's the rising water table. A problem we thought had been fixed by my predecessor, Dean Furneaux, back in 1911. The cathedral was sinking and listing, you see, the foundations not strong enough to support the vast weight of stone above us.' He gestured up and Cressida could well imagine the tonnage of sandstone bearing down on them, here in the depths of the dank crypt.

'I remember, it was a very worrying time,' Aunt Mary shuddered.

The dean carried on: 'It's all in the records, how they sent a brave man down for months in a diving bell to shore up the foundations. He was submerged under the water as he single-handedly removed the soft peat soil and replaced it with bags of cement to stop the groundwater from washing away what little foundations we have. Well, it worked for a while, but here we are. Still damp at times when the River Itchen breaks its banks.'

The dean pulled up his cassock an inch or two and stepped through the puddle, gathering the cloth in one hand as he pointed out more architectural details to Cressida and Aunt Mary.

Cressida watched where she stepped, and in some ways quite liked the oddity of sloshing through water, finding the sound rather relaxing along with the dean's gentle voice. But then, as another deep puddle swamped her shoe, she thought of the dean's late wife, poor Mrs Sitwell, and her untimely death by drowning. *I wonder where it happened?* Cressida thought to herself, and it made her shiver.

'Are you chilly, dear?' Aunt Mary said, reaching a hand to Cressida. 'I have a spare scarf here somewhere...'

'No, no. I'm all right,' Cressida reassured her. Her thoughts didn't stray far from the dean's late wife, though, and she added, 'I remember seeing a river with broken banks on my drive down here. That must have been the Itchen?'

'Yes, it would have been,' agreed the dean, a pensive look on his face. Then he carried on, 'Of course, our ancient ancestors couldn't have imagined this happening. The worst of it was that the poor chap in the diving bell – Walker I think his name was – was a changed man after he'd done his job. I still pray for him.'

'Why?' Cressida asked, holding Ruby tighter lest she fall into the ever-deepening puddle around them.

'The things he saw.' The dean shook his head. 'The cathedral was listing to one side, great cracks had appeared. But, of course, churches aren't built in isolation. They come along with graveyards.'

Cressida looked at her aunt and then back to the dean. 'Do you mean to say the graves were flooded too?'

'Yes. And the soft soil had shifted so much over time that Walker had to do his work, hard enough as it was, with foetid bodies and old bones floating past him.'

'Oh, Geoffrey, really,' Aunt Mary exclaimed. 'You'll give the poor girl nightmares.'

'I'm sorry, Lady Mary, but that's the truth of it. A nightmarish task undertaken by the bravest of men. And it's how this great cathedral is still standing.'

'Gosh,' Cressida said, but Aunt Mary was having no more talk of it.

'Come, come, show us the altar and these candlesticks on loan from Canterbury. Jewelled and whatnot? And Canute, isn't he around here somewhere? Let's stop talking about bodies and go and see something jolly.'

Cressida was in total agreement with her aunt, though she debated in her head if a tomb to a long-dead Saxon king could be described as jolly.

But as they splashed around the inch-high water in the crypt, they came across a sight even more ghastly than the bones of yore.

For around the next corner, raised up out of the water, was an altar, resplendent in gold embroidered cloth.

And in front of it, mere yards above the centuries-old bodies that lay beneath, was one that was clearly very newly deceased.

A young man – a clergyman at that – was lying face down several steps from the altar. His blonde hair was matted with blood and the water around the body was gradually turning a reddish pink against the pale sandstone.

But the most shocking thing, the most awful sight of all, was that kneeling beside the body of the dead clergyman was none other than Nancy Biddle, Aunt Mary's maid.

And in one of her bloodied hands, she held aloft the glistening gold of a jewelled candlestick.

4

Once the dean had used some words that weren't usually in the liturgy, and Aunt Mary and Cressida had released their clasp on each other, they gradually moved towards Nancy, who was pale with shock.

'Nancy, my child, what have you done?' the dean asked, falling to his knees in the bloodstained water beside his dead colleague.

'It wasn't me, it wasn't, it wasn't...' Nancy's voice disappeared into sobs as the candlestick clattered from her hand and fell down the steps in front of the altar.

'Who is he?' Cressida whispered to her aunt, who was silently praying.

She stopped and whispered a reply. 'Anthony Preston, the verger.' She glanced at the body, then quickly averted her gaze. 'I must go and fetch help. The police. Cressida, will you stay here with Geoffrey and Nancy?'

'Of course, Aunt Mary.' Cressida felt her aunt squeeze her shoulder and then she left, as quickly as she could through the inch-high water. Cressida watched as she trailed a wake behind her and listened to the exaggerated sound of splashing footsteps.

The walls of the crypt loomed over her and she felt entombed, almost, by the heavy-set stone around her. She took a deep breath, grateful for the reassuring weight of Ruby in her arms, and turned back to where the dean was now standing over Nancy, holding her by the shoulders.

'Control yourself, child,' he said sternly. 'Tell me what happened.'

'I... I found him... lying there, so still... Oh, Mr Sitwell, it reminded me so terribly of your poor wife,' Nancy sobbed. 'Then I saw... the blood.' Her words were hidden in her tears again, yet the dean held her shoulders firmly.

Cressida, still in shock herself, moved towards the stricken maid. Poor Nancy, for whatever reason, *must* have killed the verger. She had been, literally, caught red-handed.

A motion behind her made Cressida turn around and she saw to her relief that Aunt Mary was back, businesslike and above all sensible, with a cathedral security guard and another clergyman.

'This way, this way!' Aunt Mary could be heard saying as they splashed towards them. She returned to Cressida's side. 'I've called for the police. And I found Michael, the precentor, hovering by the door, so I thought he had better join us.'

Cressida glanced at him and couldn't help but recoil from his gaunt frame and high, domed forehead. She observed him for a moment more before turning back to witness the security guard grab Nancy by the shoulder. He heaved her away from the murdered man and she squealed in anguish.

'Get off me, I didn't do it!'

'My good man, do unhand her!' Aunt Mary exclaimed, her hand outstretched towards her maid, though she was quite a few yards away. 'She says she didn't do it.'

The precentor had come to stand the other side of Cressida and she felt his tall presence next to her. The elbows of his robes were covered in dust and he had let his cassock hem fall to the floor, allowing the water to seep up the cloth; yet he didn't seem to notice as he quietly whispered prayers. As comforting as this was, it wasn't the practical sort of resolution to a problem that Cressida, or indeed her aunt, favoured.

She reached out for her aunt and clasped her arm. 'Aunt Mary, what can we do?'

Before her aunt could answer, there was another squeal as Nancy was marched away from the dead body. The security guard held onto her tightly, though she was squirming in his grip. It took Cressida a moment to realise that they had to pass them to leave the murky waters of the crypt.

Was there only one way in and out of this ancient tomb? she wondered as she felt Aunt Mary's hand clench around her arm.

Nancy and the guard were walking past them now and Nancy was sobbing. Yet she was saying something through the tears and Cressida listened as best she could.

'There were people after 'im... selling the bones, you see,' she managed to get out between sobs.

'What's that, girl? Speak up, speak up.' Mary reached out a hand again, hoping to stall the guard in his march through the water, but he didn't let up.

Nancy now craned her neck back to look at Aunt Mary and Cressida. She gulped in some air, then spoke again. 'It wasn't me, ma'am. I didn't do it. Someone else must've found out about the bones.'

'Come on, you,' the guard pulled her on toward the narrow staircase that led in – and out – of the crypt.

Nancy had stopped struggling quite so much, but tears now coursed down her face as she was dragged away. She looked as fragile as a ceramic figurine compared to the bulk of the guard.

'Tell me, Nancy, honestly, did you do it?' Aunt Mary called to her, and Cressida noticed her own eyes were glistening with tears.

'No, ma'am, I didn't do it. I could never kill 'im. Not my Tony.'

'Your Tony?' Aunt Mary asked, and Cressida could feel her hand tighten on her arm.

'Yes, ma'am. I didn't kill 'im. How could I? I loved him, ma'am. And 'im me. Um, well, you see, we were to wed, ma'am...'

Her voice faded into the narrow staircase that led up from the crypt and suddenly the underground tomb felt hollow, quiet, empty. Cressida could feel her heartbeat pounding in her chest, and the fingers of her aunt's hand still clenched around her arm.

'She loved him,' whispered Aunt Mary. 'And I know her. She wouldn't kill him. I'm sure of it.'

A sloshing sound made them turn around. Geoffrey the dean and Michael the precentor, who had been praying over the body of their fellow clergyman, were walking back towards them, their heads bowed and their expressions grave. Cressida could hear their murmured conversation.

'She used to do for you and the late Mrs Sitwell, didn't she?' the precentor was saying.

'Yes, yes. Young Nancy. It really doesn't seem like something she'd do.' The dean shook his head. 'Clara was always very fond of her, advising her on life and the like. Right up until the end.'

'Well, I'm afraid the evidence does seem damning. Caught in the act. I expect Anthony came across her trying to make off with the candlesticks,' Michael said, plainly.

'I'm afraid you must be right. May God forgive her.' The dean shook his head.

'Yes. We must pray for her soul, Geoffrey. Anthony would have wanted that.'

The two cassocked figures walked past Cressida and Aunt Mary, and the dean nodded at them. Cressida saw Aunt Mary raise a hand, with what looked like great effort, to wave politely back. Then they were alone, with the sloshing water left in the two clergymen's wake. And, of course, the body of the verger.

Aunt Mary, with a comforting hand on Cressida's back, turned them both around and started to walk towards the entrance to the crypt. 'If Nancy says she didn't do it, I'm inclined to believe her. Except that—'

'That all the evidence points to her killing him,' Cressida finished her aunt's sentence for her.

'Indeed, indeed. But if she loved him, like she said?' Aunt Mary stopped and turned to Cressida, a pleading look in her eyes. 'Then why would she kill him? She seemed utterly distraught. Maybe she found him like that?'

'And picked up the murder weapon?' Cressida mused.

'Yes, yes. And picked it up in a Shakespearean tragedy sort of way. She has a dramatic streak to her, does Nancy. All that talk about ghosts and ghouls. That's exactly the kind of thing she'd do.'

Aunt Mary was more animated now, her grip on Cressida's arm even tighter than before. Cressida held the warm lump of Ruby and nuzzled the dog as Aunt Mary continued, almost conspiratorial.

'It makes more sense to me that, instead of completing her errands, Nancy followed us here and snuck past us to rendezvous with her lover – the morals of that, of course, to be withheld from judgement until a later date—'

'Of course. And I did see her, on the other side of the grave-yard, just before we entered.'

'Well, there you go. She found him here, coshed and clot-ting on the altar steps.'

Cressida admired her aunt's turn of phrase, but nonetheless grimaced at the image. 'Poor thing, if indeed that was the case. Imagine finding your beau brained on the floor of the crypt?'

Aunt Mary nodded. She withdrew her arm from Cressida's

and crossed both of hers over her chest as she thought. Finally, she said, 'We simply must help Nancy. The police in these parts are rather simple chaps, used to schoolboy high jinks from the college and sorting petty rifts between market traders. They'll not cope with a murder. And if the dean – as much as I respect him – and the precentor, have made their minds up, then I'm afraid the police will probably just follow suit and there'll be no chance for poor Nancy. She'll hang before Christmas.'

Cressida gripped Ruby tighter in her arms. 'She'll get a fair trial though, won't she?'

'I'm afraid I'm not so sure. What chance would you give a young maid brought before the beaks? It's a gentleman's club with added wigs, and the fact they're all in matching robes – clergy and judges alike... they'll gang up on her. Easy prey. Poor Nancy.' Aunt Mary shook her head. 'No, we must do something.' She narrowed her eyes, and looked at her niece. 'If your mother is to be believed, you've discovered a nascent talent for this sort of thing. An eye for design means you have an eye for a crime? Isn't that what she said?'

Cressida blushed, feeling the hot prickle over her cheeks. She *had* uncovered a few murderers recently, not to mention thieves and adulterers too. And yes, she did put it down to her eye for design details and the like, as she was prone to spotting things others would miss. But she never did it on her own, despite what her mother had led her aunt to believe.

'Mama is rather overstating my prowess there, but...' Cressida stroked the soft velvety fur between Ruby's ears as she thought. Could her acquaintance and ally DCI Andrews be persuaded to come to investigate this grisly murder? Supersede the local bobbies? She'd solved several cases alongside him, and he was a good egg who didn't mind, after a fashion, her helping out. And, after all, it *was* a man of the cloth who had been killed, and Winchester *was* one of the great cathedrals. This could become a national scandal... and so perhaps it *would* fall under Scotland Yard's remit.

Cressida looked up at her aunt and smiled.

'... I'll do what I can to help,' she sighed, 'and I think I might know just the chap who can lend us a bit of Scotland Yard-sanctioned muscle.'

'That's the spirit,' Aunt Mary said, clapping Cressida on the back.

Cressida hoped she wouldn't let her, or Nancy, down, but the evidence was damning. Still, Aunt Mary was convinced Nancy didn't do it and, except for design choices, her aunt was rarely wrong.

Cressida had planned on a peaceful Winchester holiday without a side order of murder, but how could she not try to clear the girl's name? With Nancy all but caught red-handed, the devil really would be in the detail... and Cressida did, after all, have quite an eye for detail. And more than that, she hated the mess of an unsolved mystery. She only hoped she could unravel it all in time to save the young maid from the hangman.

5

'Do you really think this detective chap of yours will come, then? All the way to Winchester?' Aunt Mary asked as she and Cressida left the dankness and tragedy of the crypt.

'I believe so, he's rather game for this sort of thing usually,' Cressida replied as several young constables, who had responded to the whistle, clattered down the stone steps. Once they'd sploshed through the deep puddles and seen for themselves the body of the verger, they'd asked Cressida and Mary to leave the crime scene. And as they stood in the north transept of the cathedral a movement caught Cressida's eye.

For a moment, she thought it might be the Silent Friar, but to the benefit of her heartbeat she realised it was simply the dean, Geoffrey Sitwell, who was walking towards them, his floor-length cassock still weighted down with the water from the crypt.

I hope he didn't soak up any of that poor man's blood too, Cressida thought to herself with a shiver as the dean approached. She held on tightly to Ruby, who had now finally woken up after all the commotion.

'Geoffrey dear,' Aunt Mary reached out a hand in comfort.

'Mary,' he patted her hand, which was resting on his arm. 'Such a terrible thing to have happened.' He looked pale, and Cressida noticed a sheen across his forehead, which he wiped away with a spotted handkerchief.

'I simply can't believe it.' Aunt Mary shook her head. 'I know the evidence is damning, but Nancy is such a pleasant young girl. A little on the superstitious side, I'll grant you, but not a killer.'

'I don't want to believe it either, but how can she not be?' The dean sighed. 'Standing there, the candlestick in her hand. A crime of passion, perhaps? I didn't know there was any sort of romance between them, but from what she said as she was led away...'

Aunt Mary nodded sagely.

Cressida let Ruby down as she'd started to squirm. It could indeed have been a crime of passion, she thought to herself as she watched Ruby sniff around the base of one of the cathedral's vast columns. But then she remembered the look of pure horror, disgust and desperate sadness on Nancy's face as she had knelt over the body of the verger. She hadn't looked like someone with blood on her hands, even though this was the literal reality.

A terrible accident then, perhaps? A lovers' quarrel gone horribly wrong? But then what was that comment she'd made about the bones? It was as if the verger's death hadn't been wholly out of the blue, even if Nancy hadn't expected it. And not to mention shrewd Aunt Mary's character reference...

Cressida mulled all this over as she corralled Ruby back from disappearing under a set of chairs. When she returned to her aunt and the dean, they were talking about DCI Andrews.

'He's a detective apparently. Approved of by my brother-in-law, Cressida's father, Colonel Fawcett,' Mary was advising the dean.

'Well, if he can spare the time, I dare say the local chaps will be all right with it,' the dean sighed, then wiped the tip of his nose with his handkerchief. He turned to Cressida. 'Miss Fawcett, would you care to call this detective chief inspector from my office? I have a small cubbyhole near the vestry. You can use the telephone we recently had installed in there.' He looked back at Mary. 'It's only been you, Lady Mary, and the Archbishop of York, who have ever called us on it before.'

Cressida nodded, hoping DCI Andrews would be available and not tangled up in some London case. She'd do everything she could to clear poor Nancy's name and catch the real killer, but with all the evidence stacked up against the maid, and the outrage that was sure to explode as soon as people knew a man of the cloth had been murdered, she knew she would need all the help she could get.

'Lead on, Dean, please,' Cressida agreed, and the three of them, and Ruby, crossed the nave in front of the great screen made of ornate sculpted stone.

Once in the south transept, they found themselves facing an old wooden door, set within a panelled wooden wall. The dean turned the wrought-iron ring handle and pushed it open.

Aunt Mary paused before entering the vestry. 'Cressida dear, if you don't mind, I'll go home. We're expecting Mr Sauvage from Liberty for lunch, you said? And Dorothy and Alfred Chatterton, aren't we? It's been a while since I had a viscount to stay. I'd better check that Nancy had made up the bedrooms for them; I know Dorothy loves the Peacock Room. If not, I'm afraid we'll all be rummaging in the linen cupboard. Not sure I can even remember where it is. Oh dear.'

Cressida closed her eyes for a moment. In the shock of finding the verger dead she'd quite forgotten that her dear friend Dotty and her brother Alfred were joining her here in Winchester. Opening them again, she nodded at Aunt Mary and thanked her. Aunt Mary bid her farewells and left them hovering by the hobnailed door of the vestry. A moment later, the dean ushered Cressida and Ruby in and closed the heavy door behind them.

The first thing Cressida noticed was the smell. A staleness in the poky room compared to the vast airiness of the cathedral. Did dust have a smell? Old leather-bound hymnals perhaps did. And beeswax polish. The second thing she noticed was the long black robes hanging from the back of the door. Ruby had plonked herself down in front of them and Cressida furrowed her brow. *The Silent Friar... a spectral monk who roams the cathedral in robes just like these...* She reached out to touch them as the dean unlocked another, less heavy, door across the room.

'This one leads to my office,' he said, then noticed her looking at the robes. 'Ah, those were Anthony's spares.'

'Oh dear,' Cressida pulled her hand back. 'Poor Mr Preston. And I'm sorry for your loss too, Mr Sitwell. You must have known him well?'

The dean ahemmed. 'Yes, well enough. Poor chap, as you say. Very rum all of this. Very rum indeed.' The dean heaved a sigh and turned back to opening his office door.

Cressida reached out for the robes again and ran her hand down the cassock. This time, her finger caught the edge of the pocket, and without thinking, she slipped her hand inside.

By Jove, she thought as her fingers found a piece of paper. Her eye caught those of Ruby, who was sitting, frog-like, looking up at her and blinking. Cressida raised an eyebrow at her little pup.

'Miss Fawcett?' the dean enquired, still standing by the now open door to his office.

'I'm sorry, Mr Sitwell, I was just...' She pulled the paper out of the pocket along with some red thread.

'Whatever have you found?' the dean asked, and to Cressida's relief, he didn't sound angry or at all miffed at her terrible manners.

'I'm not sure,' she murmured as she unfolded the paper and turned it the right way round. 'It looks like a page from a record book. You know, the sort you use for accounts that have blue lines and the occasional column formed by a red line.'

'And what does it say?' the dean enquired further, taking a step towards Cressida. His presence, whether he intended it or not, made her feel a little hemmed in in this dusty, oppressive room and she felt rather awkward as she pressed in closer to the dead verger's robes.

'There's something here about "findings after the flood" and "Walker's good deed that saved the cathedral but caused other problems to quite literally arise; in this case, St Swithun." What can that mean?'

The dean, perhaps sensing her awkwardness, hadn't got much closer to her than the cluttered desk, on which the hymnals were piled high along with sheet music and Books of Common Prayer. He leaned against it and shook his head. 'That's very interesting. St Swithun, eh?'

'The local saint? He was a bishop here, wasn't he? In medieval times?'

'Yes, glad you were listening to my talk earlier.' He paused to take his glasses off, giving the lenses a good rub with his handkerchief. He slipped them back on and continued. 'He was indeed a bishop, and a pious and good man. So much so that when he died, he was beatified by Rome and made a saint. So many people from around the counties made a pilgrimage to his bones that he was given a special tomb, or what we might call a reliquary, by the entrance to the cathedral.'

'A reliquary? For his bones?'

'Yes, and it was moved as time went on, from the early medieval church to this comparative new build.' He waved his hand as if to indicate the mass of stone and stained glass of the cathedral beyond the solid wood door. 'Until, of course, the Church broke with Rome.'

'Henry VIII, and the dissolution of the monasteries.' Cressida remembered her schooling, even if saying that ancient king's name also reminded her of the time Emily Johnson-Humphries had snuck her a sip of gin from a hidden hip flask in the middle of a lesson and they'd both hiccupped their way through the famous rhyme about his wives. 'Henry had agents take all sorts of valuable items from the churches and monasteries, didn't he?'

'Yes, and the bones of St Swithun were among them. Or so we think. The records from the time aren't very complete. Well, they're almost non-existent, to be exact. Some believe the monks of the priory that stood on this site concealed their most holy of relics from the king's agents.' The dean sighed. 'What we do know, and have written down, is in the cathedral archive. But it's not like Anthony to tear a page from one of our cathedral record books. No wonder Mr Flint was so cross with him.'

'Mr Flint?' Cressida asked, recognising the name but not quite able to place it. Whoever he was, though, he had been upset with the verger. *Upset enough to kill him?*

'Samuel Flint, our archivist. He makes sure our modern records are better kept than those of King Henry's day. We may have lost St Swithun's bones back then, but nary a Book of Common Prayer can leave this cathedral now without Flint knowing about it.'

'Why was he cross with Anthony?' Cressida asked. 'You think it was because he tore this out from one of the archived records?' She held the page up.

The dean took his glasses off again and rubbed his wrinkled brow with his thumb and forefinger. 'I don't know. Perhaps. Or it may have been to do with the break-in that we had at the archive a few weeks ago. I saw them having a bit of a set-to about something the other night.'

'Did anyone else see them? Could anyone have overheard? I would have thought sound would carry rather well in a cathedral.' Cressida said the last few words almost to herself, but the dean responded.

'Oh, they weren't here in the cathedral. They were in the Wykeham Arms. Rather good local hostelry. Frequented by gown and town alike, as they say.'

'Though the gowns in this case aren't academic, they're religious,' Cressida added, pausing to touch the verger's spare robes again.

'Quite. Anyway, Anthony and Samuel were in a crowded saloon bar. I'm afraid I didn't catch any of their conversation. Not that I would be listening, of course.'

'Of course. So they might not have been arguing about the break-in then?' Cressida thought for a moment. 'Do you think Mr Flint knew about Anthony's secret engagement? And that's why they were arguing? Did you know about it, Mr Sitwell?'

The dean puffed out his cheeks. 'This romance with Nancy?' He shook his head, and the answer came with another sigh. 'I did not. They must have been keeping it very quiet. Anthony never mentioned anything to me, and Clara, my late wife, never said anything either and she would have known, I'm sure. She was like that. Awfully good at knowing what was going on. She had a way of finding out things from the people... I never knew how she did it.' A sadness crossed his face as he remembered his late wife.

Cressida crossed her arms in thought. 'Nancy must be heartbroken.' She thought again of the look of absolute devastation on the maid's face as she'd held that bloodied candlestick aloft. Then she remembered that what she was holding in her hand might be evidence that could help Nancy. 'Can I keep this?' Cressida held up the torn piece of paper and was relieved when the dean nodded.

'I assume your policeman friend will be interested in it.'

Cressida smiled at the dean and pocketed the torn page. *Of course* Andrews would be interested in it, but it was hers for now. Aunt Mary had asked her to help Nancy, and she wanted to. There was something that wasn't making sense about all this, and there seemed to be more to unravel about this supposedly mild-mannered verger. More than met the eye, at least. Andrews would, of course, chastise her about taking evidence away from the crime scene and getting her fingerprints on it, but she needed to read it properly and find out what Anthony had found so intriguing that he'd tear it out from the archive and pocket it.

With Ruby on the promise of staying put in the vestry, the dean led Cressida through the door into his office, and towards the telephone. She hoped DCI Andrews would be able to join her; he was always useful and, unlike her, had the full might of the law behind him. But, in any case, she was determined to do what she could. And she had the first clue in her very own pocket.

She might not be a policewoman – though she did momentarily admit to herself how smashing she'd look in a natty uniform – but she was investigating this murder.

Then a thought flashed through her mind, and memories of falling alabaster busts, coshes to the head and guns being fired at her made her tense her whole body.

Yes, she was going to investigate this murder, and as she picked up the receiver, she just hoped deadly danger wouldn't come calling for her again.

6

Cressida replaced the earpiece back on the hook of the candlestick-style telephone receiver. She'd not been able to speak to DCI Andrews directly, or indeed Sergeant Kirby, who was usually at his side. But the helpful receptionist at Scotland Yard had promised to relay her message, and Cressida had given her Aunt Mary's exchange code. If she were a more normal society heiress, this would have been where it ended; Scotland Yard were summoned, end of involvement. But, of course, she wasn't a normal society heiress, *and* she had a head start.

She felt in her pocket for the torn page from the archive and was about to pull it out and study it again when the door opened. Cressida looked up to find the dean poking his head around it, with a small canine face doing the same at more like floor level.

'Are you finished? I didn't want to disturb, but the local police are here and they need to use the telephone. Anthony had some family who are connected to the telephone exchange and it seems the most expedient way to contact them.'

'Of course. I've left a message with Scotland Yard. I think

that's all we can do.' Cressida stood up, two fingers of one hand crossed behind her back.

'Will you wait one moment while I put in a quick telephone call myself? Then I'll walk you both out,' the dean asked, pointing down to Ruby's panting little face, and Cressida nodded.

Despite her usual gung-ho-ness, she was glad of the offer of being accompanied out of this warren of small rooms and the cold, stone emptiness of the cathedral itself. She couldn't help remembering the bloodied water around the murdered man, whose body still lay beneath them, below all this stone, in the flooded crypt.

Cressida waited for the dean to go into his cubbyhole and close the door, then she looked around the vestry. She was drawn again to the verger's spare robes and ran her hand down them. Something clunked on the opposite side from where she'd found the torn-out page and instinctively she slipped her hand into that pocket. Her fingers clasped around some cold metallic items and as she brought them out, she realised it was a bunch of keys.

A sound from the cubbyhole office alerted her and just before the door opened and the dean appeared, she slipped the keys into her own pocket. As she walked with him to the door, she could feel the dead man's keys weigh heavy in her coat. Keys, of course, were only useful if one knew which lock to use them in, so Cressida tried as subtly as possible to gauge where that might be.

'Will someone be able to collect Mr Preston's belongings? From his lodgings or house. When death is so unexpected, one wonders how this all comes about.'

The dean nodded thoughtfully. 'That was the reason for my telephone call. I had to let the bishop know, of course, and he can make arrangements for Anthony's small house on Symonds Street to be dealt with.'

'Symonds Street, that's the one that leads onto Aunt Mary's road, isn't it?'

'Yes, the cathedral owns numbers five and seven. I'm in one of them myself, now Clara isn't with me anymore.'

The mention of her death reminded Cressida of her manners and she offered her condolences to the dean as they walked.

'Mr Sitwell, I'm awfully sorry to hear about your wife.'

His pace slowed. Then, after a moment, he turned to speak to her, stopping altogether. 'Thank you, Miss Fawcett. It was a terrible shock. Clara and I were most happy. Most happy indeed.'

'I'm so very sorry,' Cressida repeated, wanting to reach out a comforting hand to the grieving man, who was now pinching the top of his nose between a thumb and forefinger. She waited until he had composed himself and added, 'I should imagine the whole community here misses her, too. Aunt Mary said she was very much part of things.'

'Your aunt is astute as always. Clara liked to know what was going on.' He chuckled to himself over some memory. Then his face became sombre again. 'She had her pet peeves though, as we all do, and I'm sad to say she had rather a lot of stress in the lead-up to her death. The bell-ringers rota for one. She was often complaining about our head bell-ringer, Mr Havering, not listening to her, and how he *never* listened to poor Anthony.' The dean shook his head. 'And, of course, she was terribly rattled by the robbery at the archive.'

'Yes, Aunt Mary said she'd had quite a bit to do with sorting out the records before the break-in. She must have been so upset by it all.'

'Devastated. She didn't seem the same since it happened to the day she died.' They had arrived at the door. 'Well, here you are.'

'Here I am. Thank you, Mr Sitwell. And again, my condolences.'

'Thank you.' He sighed. 'However much I miss her, I'm glad in a funny sort of way that she's not here to see this. She was fond of Anthony. And Nancy. I wouldn't wonder if she knew about the secret engagement. She was always so good at knowing what was going on. She'd be terribly upset about Nancy being arrested and would be the first to champion her and try to clear her name, and not just because a decent maid is hard to find. She saw a lot of good in that girl. Yes, she'd have been in a real pickle about all of this. Oh, dear Clara.' He shook his head. 'Dear, dear Clara.'

'I wish I could have met her,' Cressida said, and meant it. As she clicked her fingers to try to bring Ruby to heel, she realised that along with it being a tragedy that she had died so young, Mrs Sitwell would have been a very useful person to talk to about all this. It was a shame, indeed, that she was dead.

The sharp air hit Cressida as she left the cathedral, and she pulled her leather gloves out of her pocket. In so doing, the page she had found in the verger's robe fluttered to the ground and drifted along a few paces ahead of her, whisking away further in the breeze each step she took towards it.

'Oh, darn it,' she mumbled as she hurried along the flag-stoned pathway, not taking her eye off the fluttering paper as it whipped along with the horse chestnut leaves. 'Ruby, fetch!' she tried fruitlessly, but Ruby paid no attention whatsoever.

Cressida was just about to lunge for it herself, in a most unladylike way, when she bumped into a short, but well-dressed woman in a tweed suit with a natty hat covering a stylish chestnut bob.

'Oh gosh, I'm terribly sorry,' she blurted out, before she could stand upright.

'Cressy!' The lively voice was exceptionally well known to her, and to Ruby, who was now panting happily, her bulbous little eyes sparkling up at the young woman who had been Cressida's greatest friend since their schooldays.

'Dot! Oh Dot...' Cressida was now caught between embracing her darling friend and dashing off after her runaway piece of paper, which was, frustratingly, nowhere to be seen.

'Cressy, what is it?' Dot stood in front of her friend, pushed her tortoiseshell-rimmed glasses up the bridge of her nose and then clasped the tops of Cressida's arms in her gloved hands. 'You look utterly flustered. Are you all right?'

'Yes. Well, no. Oh, darn it. That piece of paper I was chasing. Did you see—'

'You mean this piece of paper?' A rather handsome chap with wavy chestnut brown hair and dark, conker-brown eyes appeared behind Dotty, holding, to Cressida's utmost relief, the runaway page.

This was Lord Alfred Delafield, Dotty's brother and a long-term friend of Cressida. Alfred had been occupying quite a few of Cressida's waking, and sometimes dreaming, thoughts of late. Unlike Dotty, or Lady Dorothy Chatterton as she was more formally known, Cressida was not a romantic. She adored her independence, almost as much as she adored her pug, her shining red Bugatti motorcar and her wonderful little pied-à-terre in Chelsea. She had often been known to argue that marriage would only tie her down, or tie her up. Yet, Alfred, who looked incredibly dashing today in his three-piece, olive-green tweed suit, had after all these years, been causing quite some strange new sensations within her recently. And now, as he stood before her, holding up the first clue in her latest investigation, her stomach did all sorts of somersaults.

She took a deep breath. *Steady on, Fawcett*, she thought to herself.

'Hello, old thing,' Alfred said, seemingly oblivious to the

gymnastics in her gut as he passed her the paper. 'You did look funny then as you walked around, nose to the ground. Like a veritable bloodhound, old thing.'

'Oh, thank you very much, Alfred,' Cressida replied, pretending to be affronted, but she couldn't help smiling at him. The notion did also cross her mind that Alfred, and especially Dotty, might be super-useful in helping her solve this case. Then she looked at them both and noticed something was missing. 'Are you both travelling extraordinarily lightly, or have you lost your bags?'

'Don't be silly, Cressy,' Dotty said, grinning. 'You know I can't go anywhere without at least a hat box—'

'Or two,' murmured her brother, who raised an eyebrow at Cressida as he did. Dotty put her hands on her hips and stared at him, but before she could defend herself, he added, 'And one of them is empty! Can you imagine that, Cressy? Travelling all the way from London with an empty hatbox?'

'It's in case I find something I like in one of the boutiques, Alf. Cressida's aunt would understand. She's always telling us to be more prepared.'

'That's true,' chuckled Cressida. 'So where are your bags and hatboxes and whatnot?'

'We enlisted one of the porters to bring them along to the house in a bit,' Alfred answered. 'Nice chap. At least he won't struggle under the weight. Not on this leg of the journey, anyway.'

Alfred ducked as his sister threw a conker at him.

Cressida thought she better change the subject. She waved the torn-out page she'd been chasing between them. 'Well, thank you for this. Phew!'

'What is it, Cressy?' Dotty asked, taking the piece of paper from her friend.

Cressida sighed. She knew Dotty was still recovering from their last brush with murder, and she had so been looking forward to a jolly little shopping jaunt in Winchester. Cressida picked up Ruby from the flagstones and did what she so often did when she needed to impart something difficult to her friend, offering the warm pup to her to hold.

'Oh, hello Ruby,' Dotty said, smiling, but she was never one to miss a trick. 'Now, why has your mistress thrust you upon me? What does she need to tell me?'

Cressida exhaled slowly.

'Well, chaps, I'm afraid I do have some rather shocking news for you. And I'll tell you all about it on the way to Aunt Mary's.'

Dotty raised an eyebrow at her friend, but followed her, with Alfred too, nonetheless. Cressida hoped that luncheon would be served when they got to Priory House; for one thing, she was famished, and for another, well, murder was never best discussed on an empty stomach.

7

While Cressida had been speaking with the dean and bumping into Dotty and Alfred, Aunt Mary had rushed home and set in motion The Protocol. The Protocol was a plan that society ladies hoped they'd never have to action, but, today, Operation The Maid Has Been Arrested was rolled out at Priory House. Lady Mary Dashwood-Howard was fortunate enough to employ a cook as well as more casual staff, such as a gardener for the neat topiary at the front of the house and the lawn and small orchard behind, a chauffeur for when London trips were necessary and, of course, a charwoman, who helped with the cleaning. But without her maid, The Protocol was necessary.

Cook had luckily already started on luncheon, which, to Aunt Mary's relief, could be served buffet-style from the side-board. Cook, understanding they were now operating under The Protocol, would help clear and would then spend the next few hours preparing easy cold cuts that would see Lady Mary and her guests through the next few days while a new maid was recruited. Dressing, of course, would be an issue, especially with house guests of an age who insisted they didn't need ladies' maids, travelled without them and then always invariably nabbed one's own. With that in mind Lady Mary had put through a call to an agency almost as soon as she'd entered the house. She was expecting some nice young woman to materialise before evening.

The materialisation of Lady Dorothy Chatterton, her brother Lord Alfred Delafield, and respected London interiors expert Mr Maurice Sauvage for lunch was just one more thing to be coped with and adapted to along with The Protocol. Lady Mary Dashwood-Howard didn't gain her reputation for being prepared for all things, at all times, for nothing, however. She took it all in her galoshes-donned stride and welcomed her guests with aplomb.

'Dorothy, my dear girl. Look at you.' Aunt Mary held Dotty by the tops of her arms and smiled at her indulgently. 'You know I never can look at you and not think of your dear mother and how we used to have such larks.'

'She sends her love to you, Lady Mary,' Dotty replied, then gestured to her brother. 'And do you remember Alfred? My brother. Though I think he was only small the last time we came to stay.'

Aunt Mary let Dotty go, and she moved into the hallway, while Aunt Mary sized up Alfred. 'Short trousers and sticky fingers. That's what I remember about you, Alfred. Or are you going by Delafield these days?' She arched an eyebrow.

'Alfred is just fine.' He stuck out his hand to his hostess. 'Spiffing to see you again, Lady Mary. And don't worry, no sticky fingers this time.'

'I remember Cook had an awful trouble prising you away from the treacle sponge, but you've grown up so much since then. Quite handsome you are, too.' Lady Mary guided him in but couldn't help but raise an eyebrow at her niece.

Cressida blushed and glared at her aunt, willing her not to say anything else embarrassing. Aunt Mary simply chuckled to

herself and elbowed her niece in the ribs as they followed their
guests into Priory House.

And, as expected, another guest was waiting for them.
Maurice Sauvage was standing by Aunt Mary's fireplace in the
parlour when Cressida and her friends walked in.

'Mr Sauvage! Maurice...' Cressida put Ruby down as she
approached him and took his outstretched hand in both of hers.
'I'm so glad you're here.'

And she really was. Not just because of his prowess with
prints and patterns; Maurice was an interesting man and
Cressida was very fond of him. He was dressed smartly, in a
neat, dark pinstripe suit, yet Cressida knew that the back of
his sombre-looking waistcoat was no doubt a floridly fuchsia
pink or some ragingly chaotic pattern. He also had slick oiled
hair, and the most neatly twizzled moustache, one end of
which he liked to twist between a finger and thumb as he
concentrated on something. And he *was* concentrating on
something – namely what Cressida was saying as she
recounted the terrible tragedy of what had happened that
morning in the cathedral. And this was another thing that
made him so interesting; Maurice worked at Liberty of
London, one of the capital's foremost department stores. He
was well-regarded by his peers and clients, so much so that he
often found himself privy to outrageous conversations in
Mayfair drawing rooms, while also picking up titbits of information from the railway porters at Euston station as they
unloaded packets of Manchester cotton from the northern
trains.

Cressida knew all this thanks to the time she'd spent at his
cutting table in the upholstery fabrics department at Liberty. It
was little wonder that she'd sought him, his wisdom and
network of informants out during her murder investigations in
the past. So perhaps he might be of use again now, here in
Winchester, with poor Anthony lying dead in the cathedral, the

killer at large and potentially innocent Nancy carted off to the nick.

If only his visit could still be confined to its primary purpose, that of guiding her aunt away from whatever garish pattern or dubious stripe she might choose without Maurice and Cressida's help. Cressida had had such lovely times here at Priory House, having stayed often as a child, especially when her parents had been away travelling, as was often the case. And her aunt had frequently extended the invitation to Dotty, who had come to adore the house almost as much as Cressida did. It was this fondness for the place – and of course her indomitable aunt – that had made Cressida so determined to help with the decor. If she picked up some more tips from her aunt on how to prepare oneself for any eventuality in the process, well, that would be the icing on the well-organised cake.

With all of this in mind, and dark thoughts of dead bodies and wrongly accused maids put to one side for just a moment, she brought the topic to her aunt's attention.

'Aunt Mary, Maurice has brought some silks for you to see, fresh off the boat from India, I believe. Don't you think that weave would look simply wonderful here with the light coming in from the windows and catching on it?'

'It's not terribly modern, though, dear,' Aunt Mary said, looking distracted as she stood with her hands clasped behind her back, staring out of the window. She turned back to face Cressida, Dotty, Alfred and Maurice. 'I do apologise. I'm simply finding it hard to concentrate on silks with everything that's been going on this morning.'

'That's very understandable, Aunt Mary.' Cressida walked over to her and put a reassuring hand on her shoulder. 'But I find concentrating on something else for a little while can really help calm the mind.' She meant it too, but what she didn't add was that it was often parallels in the decorating world that gave her the key to unlock the mysteries she'd solved. Sometimes she compared it to pulling a thread at a hem of a fine fabric, slowly unravelling it, but often it was more obvious – she could just spot things that were out of place or simply looked wrong. Perhaps discussing the decor in this beautiful house would also serve to help her untangle the mysterious case of the body in the crypt. So, she gently nudged her aunt again. 'We only have Maurice for a few hours before he heads back to London, Aunt Mary. Do come and look at these fabrics. The paisleys are quite superb and I could definitely see the ikat patterns working on some new occasional cushions.'

Aunt Mary nodded and smiled warmly again at Maurice, remembering that, above all things, he was her guest and she couldn't ignore him. Cressida encouraged her to look at the fabrics and was relieved when she noticed that Aunt Mary was really getting quite into it. Cressida stepped back to allow Maurice to flounce a luxuriously woven woollen throw out to its full size so Mary could admire the pattern.

Dotty caught her eye, and Cressida showed Dotty her crossed fingers under Ruby's warm belly. Dotty giggled and Cressida smiled at her. They both knew how brilliant Aunt Mary was, how she could cope with most anything life threw at her, from losing her husband to terribly missing her two sons who now both worked abroad. In many ways, Cressida modelled herself on her aunt. Vivacious, independent, and above all practical; three excellent characteristics in Cressida's eyes. But when Aunt Mary started describing some geometric prints that she'd seen in Biarritz and telling Maurice how jazzy and avant-garde they were, Cressida swallowed her exasperation, rolled her eyes and was pleased when Cook finally rang the bell for luncheon.

8

'I'm afraid to say that Nancy hadn't prepared one of the spare bedrooms before today's unfortunate events,' Aunt Mary said, as her guests tucked into the chicken in a cream sauce that the rather harried-looking cook had left on the sideboard of the dining room. 'She'd made up yours, Cressy dear, and then just one other.' Aunt Mary glanced between Dotty and Alfred, a pained look on her face.

'Don't even think of it, Lady D-H,' Alfred said, raising his hand in a nonchalant wave. 'I shall find myself a local inn. Nothing could be better for a young man than lodging for a night or so in some fine hostelry. The camaraderie of my fellows at the bar, a few ales to finish off an evening, some japes with the locals. I shall hear no more about it, and take my bags off to...' He paused, cocking his head on one side, then carried on, 'In fact where shall I take them?'

'The Wykeham Arms is very good,' Aunt Mary said, relief writ upon her face.

'The Wykeham Arms?' Cressida asked, recognising the name from her conversation with the dean. 'It's close by here, isn't it?'

'Yes, just around the corner. Not that I frequent it, of course, not since that time I needed a brandy after...' Aunt Mary paused, a smile glimmered briefly on her lips, then remembering she had guests, she continued, 'But I think it's suitable enough for the clergy to pop in for a light ale or two.'

'The Wykeham Arms it is then,' Alfred said, popping another potato into his mouth.

'Alfred, that's awfully good of you,' Cressida told him. 'And that means you can have the other room, Dot.'

'Well, if you're sure you're happy with that, Alf?' Dotty looked over to her brother, who still had his mouth full, so he just nodded and gave her a thumbs up.

'Are you on the afternoon train, Mr Sauvage?' Aunt Mary turned to Maurice.

'Indeed, Lady Dashwood-Howard. I need to be back in town before Liberty closes for the evening, see what the department have got up to in my absence. Last time I left Mildred in charge, there was a debacle with the bouclé.' He gave a little shudder. 'Let's hope she's not so wayward this time.'

'Sounds intriguing, Mr Sauvage.' Aunt Mary shook her head. 'Still, I do hope you get to see some of our beautiful city before you have to leave?'

Maurice nodded with a smile.

'I was very much looking forward to seeing some more of Winchester, too,' said Dotty, putting her knife and fork down. 'Especially that nice hat shop by the Buttercross. But it doesn't seem right, gallivanting around and enjoying ourselves now there's been a murder.'

'You're right, of course. And poor Nancy is behind bars.' Aunt Mary neatly laid her knife and fork together on her plate. She pulled her napkin off her lap, touched the corners of her mouth with it, and laid it by the side of her plate. Then she sighed. 'I just don't believe it of her. She was a little unpolished around the edges, I grant you, but a kind girl with a good heart, I thought. Not a murderer. She was devoted to Clara Sitwell.'

'The lady who died quite recently?' Dotty had been rapidly caught up on Winchester's latest news by Cressida before lunch.

'Yes, the very same. Another tragedy. And Clara would never have been able to bear the possibility of Nancy... Well, we all know the outcome of a guilty verdict. And what if she didn't do it?' Aunt Mary looked at Cressida imploringly. 'It just doesn't make any sense to me at all. A nice girl, with a good job with yours truly. And she was in love, it seems. Why on earth would she kill him?'

Cressida shook her head. It made no sense to her either. 'A lovers' tiff, a quarrel gone horribly wrong I could understand, but... it really did seem as if she was distraught, and not just in a shocked-at-what-she-had-done way. Then she said that thing about the bones, almost as if...'

'What Cressy?' Dotty asked.

'Yes, what's caught that eye of yours?' Aunt Mary added.

'More my ear in this case, Aunt. Just that it almost seemed as if she was expecting it, like she'd been afraid for him.'

'Expecting it?' Alfred questioned, able to join the conversation now most of his plate was clear.

'No, not *expecting* it. That's the wrong word. But she had a reason that came straight to mind as to why he would be so horribly killed. *The bones.*'

'Could that not have been some simple nonsense made up on the spur of the moment to throw doubt into the police's minds?' Alfred furrowed his brow, which made Cressida feel very strange. But Alfred's words also reminded her that her friends, though darned useful at times during her investigations, weren't always as keen as mustard on her dashing head first in among possible murderers and suspects.

She closed her knife and fork together on her plate, in case it had been a surfeit of green beans that had caused these stomach-based somersaults. Though she rather hazarded that it was that look of kindness and concern on Alfred's face.

He carried on in the same vein as before. 'Look, old thing, is there really much of an investigation to be had here? I'm terribly sorry, but it does sound like this maid of Lady D-H's here was caught in the act, bang to rights and all that.'

'And you know what happens when you start investigating murders, Cressy. People get shot, or alabaster busts of my ancestors fall on your head and that sort of thing,' Dotty interjected, though Cressida could see just the tiniest glint in her eye.

Cressida grinned at her. She would have winked, but she believed winking was frankly deplorable, mostly because it usually happened after far too many cocktails and by someone totally unsuitable.

'Is this true, dear? I know you've been investigating murders and whatnot, but I didn't realise you'd been in danger yourself.' Aunt Mary interrupted Cressida's musings with an anxious look in her keen hazel-coloured eyes.

She fiddled with her napkin, folding it more neatly, and then sat back upright in her chair. 'Well ... there *has* been an alabaster bust aimed at my head—' Cressida started, but was interrupted by Dotty.

'Lady Adelaine came off the worst though,' sighed Dotty. 'Which says a lot, I suppose.'

Cressida mouthed a 'thank you' to her friend. She didn't want Aunt Mary to regret asking for her help, even though, jokes aside, Cressida had indeed almost been killed several times. But each of those times, it was because she had been so very close to finding out who had truly been responsible. And, as Dotty had just helpfully pointed out, most importantly, she *had* survived, even if the alabaster bust had not.

She smiled to herself, realising that after so many years it was about time Dotty got fully on board with her hot-headedness. And Dotty had been terribly useful when poor DCI Andrews had been shot in the summer... Well, perhaps she wouldn't mention *that* to Aunt Mary. The truth was, sometimes investigating murders could be rather dangerous and land one with a splash in the hottest of soups.

'That piece of paper we found you chasing after, that was something to do with this cathedral murder business, wasn't it?' Alfred asked, and Cressida snapped back out of her thoughts. He closed his knife and fork on his plate, though Cressida did notice his hand slip under the table with one last piece of chicken and she knew there would be a small, rasping tongue greeting it within moments.

'Yes. Well, maybe. The dean only let me keep it as I promised I was going to give it to DCI Andrews when he arrives.' She kept quiet about the keys she had also found. Something told her that owning up to taking those without the dean's permission was possibly a stretch too far, even for her indulgent friends' forbearance.

'I didn't realise you'd telephoned the chief inspector. That is good news,' said Dotty. It seemed nursing DCI Andrews through a particularly nasty gunshot wound back in the summer had made her rather fond of the older policeman.

'Good thing too. Andrews is a sensible man, what?' Alfred agreed. 'He'll take things in hand and that will hopefully leave us to just enjoy this lovely autumn stay in Winchester. Cressida, I was wondering if you might fancy a jaunt out to the New Forest while we're down here, I—'

'I'd love to, Alfred,' Cressida found herself saying, almost to her own surprise, and very much to Dotty's excitement, as evidenced by her dear friend shifting around in her seat as if she had the proverbial ants in her pants. But both Dotty's and Alfred's grin faded when Cressida continued. 'But we can't. Not now anyway. That poor verger clonked over the head in the coldest of bloods... well, if it wasn't Nancy, who is responsible?

Someone here in Winchester, I'd wager, and we'll not find them, or any clues, jaunting around the New Forest.'

Alfred and Dotty nodded in resigned acceptance. Cressida was grateful for their understanding, and had meant what she'd said too. All of it. She would love to go out for a drive with Alfred, but she also very much wanted to find out what Nancy had meant when she'd said 'it's all about the bones'. Was the murderer still loose in the cathedral? Or lurking somewhere among Winchester's cobbled streets?

And if the murderer wasn't Nancy, and Cressida didn't find out who it was, would they strike again?

9

'So, that piece of paper?' Alfred asked as he, Cressida and Dotty walked across the pretty little park in front of the cathedral. 'You'll hand it straight over to Andrews, yes?'

'Yes, of course,' Cressida replied, throwing a stick for Ruby, who gamely chased off after it.

Cressida, Alfred and Dotty had decided to take a little walk, following on from not only a rather good lunch, but also a heated discussion about modern interior trends afterwards in the parlour. In the end, Cressida believed that she and Maurice had got through to Aunt Mary about the benefits of sticking to a relatively traditional decor style for her beautiful Queen Anne house. Maurice had offered to consult the local upholsterer about Indian damask for the dining-room chairs, and they had just waved goodbye to him as he'd pulled his coat collar up and headed off.

Cressida continued, 'But Andrews won't be here for hours. The telegram that arrived just after we'd eaten said he'd received my message and would be down on the afternoon train, which means he won't be here until teatime at the earliest,

I think. Don't you think we should try to get a few facts straight for him before he arrives?'

'As Alfred said earlier, Cressy, I'm not sure what there is to get straight.' Dotty sighed. 'Nancy was caught red-handed.'

'Candlestick to the skull. QED,' Alfred pointed out, as he reached into his pocket and fetched out his pipe.

'Oh, Alfred!' Dotty blanched, then ticked off her brother. 'You do have to make it all sound so sordid.'

'He's right, Dotty, I suppose. Murder is a dreadful old business. But doesn't it make you wonder? What would drive someone like Nancy to do something like that, something so violent? She was, by all accounts, a rather sweet young girl. Aunt Mary certainly rated her, and we all know Aunt Mary doesn't suffer fools, and she's an excellent judge of character. I've always rather admired her for that, along with her practicality and—'

'But not her sense of style,' chuckled Dotty.

Cressida sighed good-naturedly. 'There are some things my dear aunt and I will never agree on, that's true. And some of those colour matches of hers are amongst them. But back to Nancy... Would she have even had the strength to wield a candlestick like that with such deadly force?'

Dotty picked up the stick that Ruby had returned to them, grasped one end in her gloved hand and gave it a swing. Once, twice, she swung it, then, as if surprised at her own brutality, she dropped the stick to the ground. Cressida and Alfred looked bemused.

'Pretending to murder someone?' Cressida asked, picking up Ruby and holding her to her chest.

'Yes, watch out, George. If that proposal doesn't come quick, I worry for the poor man,' Alfred joked, then jammed his pipe in between his back teeth and bit down on it so it stayed at a sort of rakish angle coming from the side of his mouth.

'That's what I was doing,' Dotty replied. 'Obviously I would never hurt George, proposal or not, but I was trying to imagine...' Dotty shivered.

'It's a horrible thought, isn't it, Dot. But *crimes passionelle*, or crimes of passion, I think they're called, well, they do happen. Do you remember Pinky Frostick was so upset at Humphrey Littlejohn during their engagement that she pelted a whole sack of coconuts at him at the Lower Benchley village fete?'

'Poor chap had only suggested they not invite Bobby Finchampton to the wedding,' said Alfred, a serious look on his face despite how comical the scene in question had been at the time. 'And that was only because Pinky had been engaged to him at the same time last year.'

'This is different though.' Cressida stroked Ruby's ears as she thought. 'As far as we know, poor Mr Preston had done nothing of that sort, and Nancy just seemed *so* genuinely distraught. Honestly, if you'd seen how she looked, you'd agree with me.'

'I'm rather glad I didn't,' Dotty grimaced. 'It all sounded so ghastly. And I for one am still in the camp that believes that one doesn't go about braining one's fiancé.' She paused. 'If only one did have a fiancé.' She kicked a pile of falling leaves.

Cressida could see that Dotty was still pining deeply for George. George Parish had been at a rather fateful party with them down in Cornwall earlier in the summer and had taken a fancy to Dotty, and she to him. This had been a relief to Cressida, since Dotty had been engaged before to an utter bounder who had cheated on her and bruised, if not actually broken, her heart. But George, as lovely as he was, was an archaeologist and had spent much of the summer away on digs in Egypt. He and Dotty had written though – lengthily and often, if the passages that Dotty had read out to Cressida over a coffee at Lyons or a cocktail at the Ritz were anything to go by. Still, letters weren't quite the same as having one's beau in town for the season, and

Cressida hoped George realised how lucky he was to have captivated the heart of such a fan of letter writing. Dotty seldom
complained, though over several martinis one evening, she had
admitted to wanting 'fewer missives and more kissives'... Still, at
least when those missives did come, from the heat of the desert,
they said all the right things.

Cressida reminded Dotty of this and the two of them shared
a secretive smile, much to the horror of Alfred, who 'ahemmed'
in a brotherly way, then took his pipe out of his mouth and used
it to gesticulate as he brought the subject back to the murder in
hand.

'Less of that, you two,' he frowned as Dotty tried to keep a
straight face. Then he continued, 'So you really don't think your
aunt's housemaid would kill her fiancé then, Cressida?'

'No, I don't. As I said, not if you'd seen how distraught
Nancy was. And Aunt M thinks she's a good egg, so—'

'So, let's assume she didn't do it,' posed Dotty. 'That it
wasn't a crime of passion and all that. That she loved Mr
Preston very much, even though she was clearly aware of something mysterious that he was up to regarding those bones.'

'Yes, the bones,' Cressida agreed. 'I must say, that bones
business really does add to the argument that she didn't do it.
Something else was clearly going on.'

'Well, if she didn't do it' – Dotty crossed her arms – 'then
who did?'

Cressida looked from her friend, to the handsome eyes of
her brother, and then to the more frog-like, but equally inquisitive eyes of Ruby. 'That, Dot,' she said with a sigh, 'is exactly the
question.'

'Right,' Dotty agreed. 'And now we've established that, can
we talk about me and George again, please?'

. . .

Once Dotty and George's latest correspondence had been discussed (between Cressida and Dotty, since Alfred had stalked off to 'go and look at some graves' as soon as the first few lines of romantic letter writing had been quoted), the conversation returned to the gruesome murder in the crypt. Cressida and Dotty met Alfred outside the cathedral's great west window, while Ruby snuffled around their ankles.

'So, this piece of paper you found, Cressy?' Alfred tried for the third time.

'It was a page from one of the cathedral's record books, I believe,' Cressida replied, pulling the page out of her pocket, careful not to let it get caught in the breeze again. Another gust had just sent a swarm of leaves spiralling around the park, so she kept a firm grip as she carried on talking. 'You know the sort of book, one of those that housekeepers use to tally up payments to the butcher, baker and so on. But this one wasn't used like that, it looks like some sort of diary entry.' She showed Alfred the page and, once he'd read it, he passed it to Dotty. 'I suppose there goes our chance of a fingerprint from it.' Cressida sighed, taking it back.

'You didn't find it at the murder scene though, did you, Cressy?' Dotty asked. Cressida shook her head, so Dotty carried on. 'Well, it mentions the water rising, with all those bodies in it, which just sounds grim, and the cathedral foundations being fixed, so that's got to place this as being at least twenty years old. I should imagine any fingerprints that were on it would be so jumbled up with others from over the years that they would be inadmissible in court,' Dotty said matter-of-factly.

Cressida looked at her. 'Inadmissible in court? You sound like you've been called to the bar, Dot! And not our usual type of bar at that.'

Dotty raised an eyebrow at her friend. 'I found a rather juicy collection of detective fiction books while I was in town the other day. After what happened to us on the Scotland

Express, I couldn't help but buy them and, of course, I devoured one on the train back to Chatterton Court. What with the strange things that have been going on recently, I thought it might help if I knew a bit of the lingo and whatnot about how to solve a crime.'

'Excellent idea, Dot,' Cressida grinned at her friend.

'Very sensible, sis.' Alfred squeezed her shoulder. 'And top thinking about the fingerprints. But back to that bit of paper. From a record book you say, Cressy?'

'I think so, yes. The dean said there were more volumes just like this one, here in the cathedral in the archive, and... Oh...' Cressida paused.

'What is it, old thing?' Alfred asked.

'The dean said that Anthony, the verger, had been seen having an argument with the archivist, a Mr Flint, in the Wykeham Arms. Just the other day, in fact. He thought it had something to do with the break-in. But perhaps there is a link between this page being torn from one of the records in the archive – possibly the one that was stolen – and Anthony and Mr Flint's argument?'

'Sounds like we need to go and find this archivist then?' Alfred said, and Dotty nodded enthusiastically too.

'Most definitely. But look, I think it might come across a bit heavy-handed if we all go and find him. Nothing could shut someone up quicker than being mobbed by three, albeit charming, aristocrats.'

'Point taken, Cressy,' Alfred agreed. 'And I need to get myself over to the Wykeham Arms and see if they have a room available for the old bonce for a night or two.' Alfred knocked his pipe against his head.

'It's only until Aunt Mary has fathomed where her linen cupboard actually is,' Cressida reminded him, her tone soft. 'It seems her preparedness for everything doesn't extend to the top floors of her house. But it was very gallant of you not to make a fuss.'

Cressida wondered if Alfred was blushing, but didn't mention it as he blustered something about 'not a problemo, old thing'.

'I suppose even just the two of us might be too much for one man,' Dotty agreed, pulling her coat around her to fend off the chill in the wind that shook the boughs of the trees around them. 'You can do the legwork, Cressy. But do take Ruby with you just in case. I'm going to go and sit in your aunt's splendid library and see what else I can garner from my detective fiction.'

With that, the decision was made. And Cressida turned away from her friends and once more entered the vast, stone-encased space that was Winchester Cathedral, Ruby at her heels.

A shiver crossed her shoulders. The last time she'd walked through this door, a man had been killed while the bells had pealed. And the killer was still at large, of that she was sure.

10

Ruby obediently trotted alongside Cressida as she walked the length of the nave. She remembered seeing a similar door to that of the vestry, close to it in the southern transept. The cathedral was quiet, and she couldn't help but think of the poor verger, still lying dead in the crypt.

'At least he has company down there,' Cressida whispered to Ruby. 'There are heaps of dead bodies in this place.' She shivered again. 'But I suppose it's only human of us to get so upset about another one, particularly one so recent.'

Ruby stopped in her tracks and gave Cressida a quizzical look, before rolling onto her rump and licking an itch on her tummy. Cressida crossed her arms and chewed the inside of her lips. She stared down at her little dog as she thought. It wasn't only that Anthony's death was recent. *We're upset because he was murdered.*

The image of his bloodied head flashed back to her, and she blanched in horror. The cathedral was full of dead bodies it was true; but Jane Austen, who was buried the other side of the nave, had been taken by what must have been the nastiest of chills. Terrible, of course, but at least she wasn't clobbered over the head with a candlestick.

And St Swithun himself was at least allowed deathbed requests, Cressida thought to herself, *if what the dean said earlier was anything to go by.*

'Can I help you?'

The voice gave Cressida a start, and she jumped again when she turned and saw a figure clad all in black robes. She relaxed when she recognised the tall frame and gaunt face of the precentor.

'Oh, hello... I'm sorry, in the horror of what we discovered downstairs this morning, I didn't make your acquaintance.' Cressida could take in more of him now though. Tall, hollow-cheeked, but with a full head of mousey-brown hair. He wore glasses with thin, almost perfectly circular frames, which sat at the top of his long nose.

'You can call me Michael.' The precentor stuck his hand out.

'Cressida Fawcett.' Cressida took his hand and shook it, and she was impressed by his strength. An image flashed across her mind of him swinging a candlestick... he certainly had the height and power to do it. But a man of the cloth? Surely not.

She blinked the scandalous image away and hoped he hadn't noticed. She had to remember that, despite almost everyone being a suspect, they were also innocent until proven guilty.

Plastering one of her winning smiles on her face, she kept talking. 'And this is Ruby, my pug. She's allowed in here, isn't she?'

'Well, there's a policy—'

'The dean didn't mention one earlier. And it's just that we're trying to find the archive,' Cressida interrupted him, forgoing manners for expediency. *What would her mother say?* 'Would you be able to show me where it is?'

The precentor, who perhaps wasn't used to being cut off so short, paused for a moment before answering.

'And what would your business be in the archive, Miss Fawcett? It holds many precious, ancient tomes, and we don't allow members of the public, or their' – he looked down at Ruby, who stared back at up him with her frog-like eyes agog, then carried on – 'familiars, to go in without a member of the cathedral staff with them.'

'Well, I was hoping to find the archivist, rather than just the tomes themselves. Not that those old record books aren't very interesting and all that, I'm sure.' *Especially to whomever stole one, and possibly tore this page from it,* she thought to herself, smiling again at the precentor, while slipping her hand into her coat pocket to check she still had the torn-out page she'd found in Anthony's robes.

'In that case, let us see if he's in, shall we?' The precentor spread out one arm in the direction of the southern transept and Cressida clicked her fingers and beckoned Ruby to follow her, grateful for her safe and comforting presence. Despite wanting to give the precentor the benefit of the doubt, there was something unnerving about being followed by a tall man in jet-black, floor-length robes. Cressida tried hard not to shiver, but she could feel the hairs on the back of her neck prickle, just as they had when Nancy had mentioned the ghostly figure, dressed all in black and as 'tall as a lamplighter' – the Silent Friar.

'Here we are then.' Cressida broke the silence as they turned into the transept. She noticed something that reminded her of a phrase Aunt Mary had said this morning over coffee. *A padlock only keeps out an honest man...* The door in front of her had a very new and very shiny bolt across it, one that could support an extremely bulky padlock. Of course, it had only recently been broken into. She pointed to the door. 'I take it this is the archive, Michael?'

'Indeed,' he intoned, and knocked twice upon the door: two loud, sharp knocks.

They waited, with Cressida pretending to be deeply interested in the stone carving next to her rather than lock eyes with the precentor. She found it hard to believe that this was the man with the charming wife and two small children of whom her aunt had spoken. Why some women married at all really did baffle her at times.

After what seemed like hours, the door opened and Cressida snapped to attention in time to see a middle-aged man peer through the gap.

'Ah, Michael, it's you. Oh, and, this is?'

'Miss Fawcett. Cressida Fawcett.' Cressida stuck out her hand to him, and waited as he cautiously opened the door wide enough to allow his hand to come and greet hers.

Now she could see him better, she noted his mousey-brown hair, and that his tortoiseshell glasses were doing a grand job of hiding dark, hollow circles under his eyes. Had recent events in the archive taken their toll on him, or was the stress of planning a murder leaving him sleepless instead?

'And how can I help you, Miss Fawcett?' His reedy voice jolted her back from her suspicions.

The precentor cut in before Cressida could speak: 'I shall be leaving, now you have found the person for whom you came.' He gave a grave nod and swept around, his hem barely touching the cold grey stones of the transept's floor.

Cressida gave him a weak sort of wave and turned back to the archivist, not entirely unhappy to have the precentor's haunting presence gone.

'Mr Flint, I presume?' Cressida continued greeting the archivist. 'As I said, I'm Cressida Fawcett, Lady Dashwood-Howard's niece. Oh, and this is Ruby, my pug. Don't mind her, she's awfully well trained.' Cressida crossed the fingers of one hand, hidden from view behind her back, remembering the various indiscretions the small dog had committed since first having her as a puppy last summer. She was pretty sure chewing books wasn't one of them, so carried on confidently, 'But I was wondering if I could come in and have a look at the archive, and indeed, talk to you about something.'

'Something? That sounds rather ominous. On today of all days. Haven't you heard about our verger?' Flint looked peeved, and it showed in his furrowed brow.

'I have indeed. In fact, that's why I'm here: I wanted to talk to you about poor Mr Preston. May I come in?'

'I suppose you may.' Flint opened the door wider and ushered her in.

Cressida didn't need to click her fingers this time, as Ruby walked, nose and tail both proudly raised, into the archive in front of her. The room itself was dark, with only very high, very narrow windows that were crosshatched with leaded lights and were not particularly good at letting in much sunlight.

'The books and documents prefer it this way,' Flint said, reading her mind, though it was easy enough as she'd been blinking to refocus her eyes in the dim light and looking up at the near-pointless windows.

'I suppose that makes sense,' said Cressida, and took a seat offered to her by Flint as he sat back down at his desk. The old oak chair, like those found in schools since Victorian times, creaked under her and gave a little wobble. Flint didn't seem to notice, and Cressida didn't make a fuss, instead turning to him and engaging him in conversation. 'It's terrible what happened to the verger. I'm very sorry for your loss. Did you know him well?'

'I did, yes. We'd worked together for several years now,' Flint said sadly, as he shuffled papers around on his desk.

'All my heartfelt condolences then. It's awfully hard to lose a friend,' Cressida said, genuinely feeling saddened for the man.

Flint stopped moving the papers around and looked at Cressida. 'Friend. Yes, I suppose he was. He was a young, ambitious priest of course, but a nice man too. Gentlemanly, you know.'

'From what I hear of him, I do, yes. Tragic.' Cressida met the archivist's eye, trying to glean what she could from his inscrutable expression. But no, there was nothing in those grey eyes, except a steeliness that she couldn't interpret. 'I also heard you had a burglary here in the archive. What a shocking time for you recently.' She looked around her. There was no sign of any disturbance now; black cloth-bound journals took up four shelves of an oak bookcase, and various other leather-bound volumes were nestled into the mismatched array of other book-cases. Some were stacked up on the top of shoulder-high cupboards, but although the filing seemed haphazard, it wasn't a mess.

'Yes, a burglary. How do you know about that? And indeed, how can I help you, Miss Fawcett? What is it that you want?' Flint's eyes bored into Cressida, and she hoped she hadn't been too blunt and got off on the wrong foot with the archivist. Andrews would be horrified if he knew she was investigating and, what's more, doing it so badly.

She sighed, and dug around in her pocket for the torn page. Honesty perhaps, was the best policy. 'I found this in... well, I think it belonged to Mr Preston.' She handed the page over to the archivist, having stopped worrying about fingerprints, thanks to Dotty's excellent points.

As he was looking at it, with his brow furrowed once again, she asked another question.

'I heard that one of the record books was stolen. Do you think that this page might have been torn from it, or indeed from any of them?'

Flint looked back up at her, pinched the top of his nose between a finger and thumb and took another deep breath. Cressida couldn't help but feel that her presence was vexing him greatly, and she felt rather guilty for questioning the poor man so soon after the death of his friend. But she also knew that he was the only lead she currently had, and if a murderer was still out there – or indeed in here with her, perish the thought – there was no time to lose.

'I'm sorry, Miss Fawcett, but who are you again? And why are you asking these questions? The general public aren't really supposed to be in here.'

Darn it, thought Cressida, studying the archivist's face. Was he peeved at her or just tired and finding it hard to grasp why she'd be here? She smiled at him, hoping it was the latter and explained again. 'My aunt, Lady Dashwood-Howard, well, she was a good friend of the late Mrs Sitwell.'

Flint's eyes flickered at the name. 'Oh yes?'

'Yes. She said her friend had spent many hours helping you in here and was distraught when the burglary happened. Aunt M is terribly upset about Mrs Sitwell's death, and of course she was with me this morning when we found Anthony, and so I want to do what I can to help. I thought you might be able to answer some of my questions.'

'You were the one to find him?' The archivist turned his piercing grey eyes back onto Cressida.

'Y... yes. Well, I was with Mr Sitwell, the dean, and my aunt,' she replied. 'And as I'm rather pally – long story – with a Scotland Yard detective, I went off and telephoned him and asked him to come and help the local bobbies. And while I was in the vestry, I found this page in Anthony's cassock.'

The archivist nodded, obviously appreciative of Cressida's honesty, and rewarded her with a reply of his own. 'Anthony, as verger, would have had access to any number of these books. There's nothing to suggest that this page you found came from the one that was stolen, or even from one of the ones here in the archive at all.'

'But the mention of the flood, the bodies and all that, on this page,' Cressida pointed out, as a thought suddenly occurred to her. Could the mention of those bodies in the flood also have something to do with what Nancy said about the bones? *Old bodies decayed and some bones could easily have been found around that time... Even St Swithun himself.* She pushed the archivist further. 'I thought records like this would have been just the sort of thing to have been kept in the cathedral archive?'

'Not necessarily.' Mr Flint peered at the page that Cressida had shown him. 'It might have been notes Anthony took himself. I don't recognise the writing, but that's not to say it's not his, since I never paid much attention to that. He may have been scribbling notes for a sermon. He takes... *took* some services in the north chapel when the dean and bishop couldn't attend. He came here, to the archive, often to research the cathedral's history, and he always came armed with his own notebook.'

Cressida took the page back from the archivist. She wasn't entirely satisfied with his answer, but one thing was certain. He had just confirmed what had been taken in the robbery. Aunt Mary was right, it *was* one of the cathedral's record books.

And if her suspicions were correct and the torn-out page was indeed taken from the stolen volume, how did Anthony come to have it in his pocket? Was it a coincidence that the robbery had taken place just weeks before his murder? Or were the two crimes somehow connected?

As Cressida folded up the piece of paper, she wondered if Mr Flint was really as friendly with the murdered verger as he said he had been. They'd recently argued, after all, and she found it hard to believe that a skilled archivist wouldn't recognise whether or not the handwriting on the ledger page belonged to a colleague. Was the archivist, with his steely gaze and endless tomes of books, hiding something from her? Could he have had motive, opportunity and indeed access to the crypt just before Anthony was killed?

She had to find out more.

11

'Now, if you don't mind, Miss Fawcett, I really must be getting on,' Flint said, pushing himself back in his chair and thwarting Cressida's plans to start asking some more punchy questions. The sudden move startled Ruby, who snortled in disgust. 'You really shouldn't bring dogs into the cathedral, you know.' Flint frowned at the small dog.

Cressida took her chance to get the conversation back to the murder. 'Oh, I don't know, Mr Flint. I think worse things have happened in this cathedral lately than my small dog being allowed in.'

'Well, that's as it may be, rules are rules.' Flint stood up and gestured for them both to leave, but Cressida stayed obstinately sitting for just a while longer. Ruby, as if on cue, toddled away from her mistress and started pawing at some piles of loose sheath paper on the floor. Then she sat herself down in them and turned around and about, scrunching up the paper under the rolls of her pudgy tummy.

'You see!' Flint raised his hands in frustration, then pointed to where Ruby was making herself a little nest in the paperwork. 'We've only just had those prints done. Dogs should not be in here. Can you stop her?'

'Ruby!' hissed Cressida, clicking her fingers and desperately trying to get her dog's attention. This wasn't what she'd planned. She'd wanted to keep Mr Flint onside so that she could ask him about the argument and subtly find out if he had an alibi for the time of the murder, but Ruby wasn't helping. She leapt up from her chair and scooped up her small dog from her papery perch. 'I am sorry,' Cressida apologised, though she had to give Ruby credit for making such beautiful prints into her bed. They represented medieval figures, haloed and crowned, holding out offerings and gifts to the Virgin Mary. Apologising again, Cressida asked about them. 'This is a beautiful painting, where does it come from?'

'It's the Romsey Triptych, printed for the first time so that we can bind it into folios for the universities. It shows King Canute, you see, and the ghostly form of St Swithun offering his own bones to the Virgin. One of the best examples of late-medieval church art we have. And not dog bedding.'

Cressida had the grace to look embarrassed. And apologised again.

'I think it's time you left. Now, good day, Miss Fawcett.' Flint gestured towards the door, coldly.

Cressida felt her shoulders sag. This man had been her very best lead, and she had failed to get anything out of him.

As she walked through the door, she saw the brand-new latch and shining padlock.

'I see you've improved security after that robbery,' she commented. *One more try...*

'Yes.' Flint reached out and fingered the lock, his annoyance at her fleetingly passed. 'Funds were eventually found where previously there had been none. Anthony always said it was my responsibility, but I disagreed. It's the verger's role to look after the fabric of the church.'

'Oh, he liked fabrics, did he? Poor man.' Cressida felt even more sorry for him, especially now she knew he was a fellow material lover. Then she felt rather stupid as Mr Flint corrected her.

'No, the fabric of the church refers to the stone, the wood, the windows. The whole building. There's a fabric committee, of which the verger is the chair.'

'And Anthony didn't sign off on a new latch for you, then? Not until after the robbery, when it was too late?'

'Exactly so. Even though I'd given him a piece of my mind about it. Vestry gets a proper lock.' He pointed over to the hobnailed door with the large iron ring handle and Cressida saw the large cast-iron keyhole just next to it. 'I suppose it does contain the safe. But the archive, well, apparently that was my responsibility.'

'I see. So, Anthony argued that securing the archive was your responsibility, but you thought it was his, along with all the rest of the fabric of the church. You didn't by any chance have this discussion over an ale at the Wykeham Arms, did you?'

Mr Flint looked aghast. 'Certainly not. It was a light amontillado sherry.'

Cressida almost laughed but caught it in a cough. She didn't want Flint to stop talking now, and her laughing at him might do just that.

'Of course. One of my favourites too. How awful, though, that the shoddiness of the lock meant you were broken into.'

Flint exhaled and rolled his eyes. 'I told Anthony that we needed a better lock, as we have some real treasures in here, which he knew about all too well. And I was proved right! The old lock was forced, and the archive turned over. What use had my warning been? Nothing was done about it and there you go, lock broken and archive ransacked.' Flint was getting worked up again now. Locks were obviously as triggering to him as small hounds who made nests in his paperwork. He stood with his hands on his hips, huffing and puffing with the memory. 'And the records themselves, I had to rearrange them all, which was most difficult with Mrs Sitwell no longer with us and the 1910 one lost...'

Aha, thought Cressida, *now we have a date.*

'... I said to Anthony, "If we lose any volumes, I know exactly who I'll go and see."' He looked at Cressida as if she should know, too. She didn't, but she nodded in encouragement, hoping he'd elucidate. 'Well, that bookseller on St Swithun Street, of course. I've seen some very nice volumes there, centuries old some of them, and he never says where he gets them from. Says he has contacts on the Continent, but I think some of those books of his are from archives like this, right here in England. He was there the night I was giving Anthony a piece of my mind about the security of my archive, and then, just days later, we were broken into.'

Flint had built up quite a head of steam now, and Cressida took a step back. He was most certainly capable of losing his temper, she thought. And this mention of a bookseller was interesting. Very interesting indeed. Now she had what she had come for: confirmation of what Anthony Preston and Samuel Flint had been fighting over. And, more importantly, she had someone who could tell her all about the argument he'd overheard – the bookseller.

Mr Flint calmed down and looked down at the lock once again. Then he said, 'Do excuse me, Miss Fawcett, I really must be getting on. And those triptych prints need flattening before they can be used.' He eyed Ruby suspiciously.

'Of course. Good bye, Mr Flint. Thank you for your time.' Cressida watched as the archivist turned around and headed back into his small, dimly lit library. She caught her breath as his elbow caught a set of long black robes that were hanging up just inside the door. They swayed with the motion of it and

Cressida remembered Nancy's words; the Silent Friar had been spotted again recently.

The likelihood was that he wasn't a ghost after all, but someone who had access to robes just like this. Someone trying to keep out of sight, lurking around the cathedral and the grave-yard in such a way that they might be mistaken for a ghoul?

Deep in thought, Cressida walked back along the nave, and another black-robed figure caught her eye, swiftly moving between the great columns. She stopped and waited, but no one materialised; what's more, she heard no footsteps on the cathedral's old flagstone floor.

She'd seen a figure. But no one was there.

12

Cressida followed the path around the side of the cathedral. Ruby, who obviously had no idea why she'd been pulled from such a comfortable nest on the floor of the archive and then shouted at, walked with a rather peeved attitude some steps behind. Cressida merely rolled her eyes at her miffed pup and continued, knowing that from here she could slip onto St Swithun Street by heading across the Cathedral Close and going under the medieval arch.

The wind rustled the leaves in the trees and Cressida pulled her caramel-coloured cashmere coat more firmly around her. Had she really seen the Silent Friar among the colossal pillars of the cathedral? She shook her head. She didn't believe in such things, not since school, where she'd spent years waiting for the legendary ghostly nun to haunt her in the dorms, yet never saw anything more ghostly than Minty O'Hare looking pale as a sheet after discovering matron's gin stash. No, it was far more likely that she'd just seen the quite frankly spectral-looking precentor. But Nancy had been so insistent that a ghost had been responsible for the break-in at the archive. Could a sensible girl really believe that? When a lock, whether it be rusted to ruin or stout and firm, wouldn't matter to a ghost? And yet the archive *had* been very definitely broken into.

No, Cressida didn't believe a ghost had been responsible for that burglary. And she couldn't honestly bring herself to believe one existed at all. Though she had to admit that the towering buttresses of the cathedral and the whistling wind through the boughs of the great horse chestnut trees did lend an eeriness to the cathedral and the grounds around it. It wasn't surprising that a young girl like Nancy, with an avid imagination perhaps, saw things in such an atmospheric place that just weren't there. *Or were they?*

Cressida shivered, and surprised herself by thinking of Alfred as a way to conjure up happier thoughts. She thought back to bumping into him earlier that day, and her stomach gave that little somersault again. The idea of marriage was anathema to her, always had been, despite Dotty's best attempts to convince her otherwise. She'd told her best friend that the thought of a pretty dress and a nice bunch of flowers did nothing for her, or at least *they did*, but she could buy both for herself any time she liked, thanks to her substantial allowance. No, she'd seen too many young women of her social circle lose all their freedom by marrying – why would she want that? Marriage, she'd decided, wasn't for her... But love...?

She shook her head again and looked instead at the wonderful wooden beams that made up the buildings closest to the old medieval arch. They reminded her of her favourite shop, Liberty, and she wondered how Maurice was getting on with tracking down upholsterers. She'd been awfully glad that he'd accepted her invitation to lunch with her aunt to help with choosing some new decor for Priory House, and she was even more glad he was here now, albeit only for a brief few hours more. He might not be a detective, but Maurice, when called upon, had been terribly useful in her investigations. And with a murderer on the loose and an innocent young woman soon to be headed for the gallows, she needed all the help she could get...

She was pondering this as she heard the great bells of the cathedral chime three o'clock, and then Alfred hullooed her from further along the street. When he got closer, he carried on. 'Well met, and all that. How did you get on with the archivist chap?'

Cressida smiled at him and crossed her arms, trying to ignore the now-familiar flips her stomach was doing. Then she felt that that was a bit stand-offish and uncrossed them and shoved her hands in her coat pockets.

Alfred seemed to find this all very amusing and grinned at her. 'Some sort of new dance? One I haven't seen before. Not like that one we did the other night with Beatrice Kirk-Huntington at Brooks. I had no idea she could get a leg—'

'Oh, I remember all right. Looked painful. And no, sorry, I'm just feeling all at sixes and sevens. I must admit it was a bit of a shock to stumble across another dead body this morning.'

'Yes, quite.' Alfred stopped grinning and reached into his pocket for his pipe. He took it out, shook out some old tobacco and clamped it in his back teeth, then carried on talking. 'Not fun for you, old thing, not fun at all.'

Cressida looked at his wavy, brown hair and was mesmerised for just a second at how a few stray strands were caught in the breeze. Suddenly very self-conscious, she brought her eyes back to his, which was almost worse, as she felt the prickle of a blush across her cheeks.

'Look here, old thing. Perhaps you should come back to the Wykeham Arms with me? Have something restorative? I've managed to get a room for a few nights and I met the landlord, very friendly chap. It's not such a bad place, nice saloon bar, we could set you up with a balloon of brandy or some such?' Alfred really did look concerned, but as he spoke, Cressida pulled herself together.

'As lovely as that sounds, no thank you, Alfred.' Cressida bent down and picked up Ruby, who had started to wander off towards some compelling-looking drain cover. 'By the way, I've just had a very interesting talk with Mr Flint, the archivist, and he admitted to arguing with Anthony. But I don't think you'd kill someone over what they had disagreed about.'

'Which was?' Alfred asked, then chomped down on his pipe again.

'Just whether a padlock should be fitted to the archive's door,' Cressida shrugged.

'Definitely not a head-clonking offence, quite right,' Alfred agreed.

'But he did say that the bookseller had overheard them, so I thought I might go and see him, get his perspective. Just to corroborate Mr Flint's version of events, or not. It'll save Andrews some time, you see, if I've already managed to rule out Mr Flint from the—'

'You don't need to justify yourself to me, Cressy.' Alfred, who had taken his pipe out of his mouth to speak, smiled at her, and she noticed the delightful little crinkles at the corners of his eyes. 'But you do need to take me with you this time. Can't have you having all the fun on your own.'

Cressida grinned at him and, with Ruby in her arms, she walked companionably by his side down St Swithun Street. Despite having found a dead body this morning, and despite being terribly worried about Nancy's fate, and despite swearing that marriage was definitely not for her, in that moment she felt very, very content.

13

'... And then Dickie Tratham said to Larry, "Not like that, you fool, it shoots from the other end," but it was too late and Larry had given himself a nasty shock, which only goes to show that gunpowder and Welshmen don't mix...' Alfred wrapped up his tale, and Cressida, who had wiped away a tear only a few moments ago as she'd laughed at the previous story about a chap in the army who'd lost a finger opening a tin of custard, elbowed him in the ribs.

'Honestly, Alfred, you should go on the stage,' she said.

'Oh no, Welly Watson-Wells tried that and got the full rotten tomatoes treatment. I suppose that's what you get for starting your career at the Lower Witheridge Horticultural Show, but still, it is a warning to us all.'

'Oh Alfred.' Cressida shook her head, then set down Ruby, who had started squirming in her arms. They were under an archway belonging to an old cart stable that was now open at each end, with buildings either side and above it. To one of the sides, behind a colonnade of old wooden struts, was the anti-quarian bookshop that Cressida remembered from her many previous visits to her aunt's house.

As soon as she'd been old enough to venture out along the cobbled streets on her own, her aunt had sent her with a couple of pennies to treat herself to a book. That Cressida had almost always spent the money at Angelo's Ice Cream Parlour instead seemed to have gone unnoticed by her aunt, though, as an adult now, and one who had no doubt inherited some of her observational skills from her aunt, Cressida smiled to herself as she realised that Aunt Mary had undoubtedly known exactly what young Cressy had been doing.

Latterly, though, when Dotty had started joining her on some of these visits, they'd really and truly headed to this bookshop, to quench Dotty's near limitless thirst for the printed word. And Cressida hadn't minded, as H. T. Bell and Co was a gem even among the other beautiful Winchester shops. It had a hand-painted sign with white lettering on a glossy black background, which hung on two hooks over the door of the shop. Despite being under the colonnade of the old coaching arch, the shop had a bay window which jutted out just like a Dickensian sweet shop, and inside it were volumes and volumes of old books, interspersed with hand-drawn or limited-edition prints and maps.

'Good thing Dot's not here,' Cressida noted. 'We'd never get any sense out of the bookseller as he'd spot an easy sell a mile off.'

Alfred took his pipe out of his mouth and replied, 'Too right. She'd spend half her inheritance before the poor chap could properly ring up the till.' He smiled as he said it, knowing full well that his sister's love of books had actually been rather helpful in some of their recent adventures.

'Although at least Dotty would insist on us having a plan before we go charging in,' Cressida said, admiring as ever of her friend's good sense. She tapped her chin with her finger before saying 'hey ho' as she pushed the old wooden door of the shop open, to the tinkling of a bell.

'Good day to you,' the bookseller said, looking up from behind a counter, behind which he seemed to be folded, his long legs concertinaed against it as he sat on a low stool. The counter itself was chock-full of rolled-up maps and scrolls, plus piles of books, some of which were in desperate need of repair. Cressida noted their purple suede covers as they reminded her of a pair of shoes she'd seen in Dickins & Jones recently, though, unlike those pristine shoes, these books were ragged, with the suede worn down past the nap to the leather, bald in places where they'd been well-used.

'Good day,' Cressida and Alfred said in unison. Then Cressida approached the counter. Without Dotty's foresight to come up with a plan, she improvised an idea on the spot and hoped that it would lead into something. She caught the eye of the bookseller, who had pulled himself up a bit straighter and run a hand through his grey-dashed light-brown hair. 'I'm not sure if you remember me, Mr Bell. Lady Dashwood-Howard's niece. I've been in before with a great book-loving friend of mine, Lady Dorothy Chatterton.'

'What a shame *she's* not here then,' the bookseller said, in the most deadpan voice she'd ever heard.

Cressida carried on regardless. 'Right, well... I was wondering if you could help. I'm after something decorative. Something like one of those old record books, full of Victorian-style writing if possible, so I can add it to a room I'm decorating. Do you stock that sort of thing?'

'Decorative items?' The bookseller, though seated, was somehow still managing to peer down his nose at Cressida through his pair of thick horn-rimmed spectacles.

'Yes. It's a bit nouveau, I grant you, but that's the thing with trends, always popping up and surprising one.' Cressida could feel herself waffling, so she stopped and let the bookseller sneer at her if he liked.

'The only decorative items I have are these maps.' He

pointed up to the framed maps on the wall; each of them very decorative, to be sure, but not what Cressida was looking for.

'No, I'm afraid I was really after an accounts book or ledger, something more utilitarian, you see. I'll have a browse though, if you— Oh Ruby, stop that!' Cressida was suddenly distracted by her blessed little dog, who had decided that the bookseller's chair was as good a place as any to rub her back. 'I am sorry. She's just being affectionate. I think.' Cressida moved around to the side of the counter and bent down to pick Ruby up, who had uncharacteristically started growl-snorting. 'She's usually very well behaved,' Cressida muttered, though, as she stood up, with Ruby in her arms, she noticed a long black cloak hanging in a half-open cupboard, just the other side of where the book-seller was sitting.

That's odd, she thought to herself. *He's not a clergyman, is he? Though with legs as long as that he could be 'as tall as a lamplighter'...*

Cressida was about to ask him about the long, black cloak when Ruby squirmed from her arms and dropped, inele-gantly, to the floor. Then, with a wag of her curled, little tail – if such a tail could be said to wag – she confidently stalked across the floor behind the bookseller's stool to where the cloak was hanging and bit it, then tugged it until it tumbled to the floor.

'Oh gosh, I'm terribly sorry.' Cressida pulled Ruby away from the cloak, secretly rather pleased with her pup's naughti-ness as it allowed her to notice that it was indeed a cassock such as the clergy wore.

Henry Bell was up and off his stool in a moment and swiped it away, bundling it up, and pushing it onto a shelf in the cupboard among the other bits and bobs there: paintbrushes in a jar of turps, old books that needed rebinding, tins of paint and what looked like a lunch box.

He mumbled something about 'keeping dogs under control'

and Cressida, with a now satisfied-looking Ruby safely back in her arms, went to join Alfred at the other side of the shop.

'Blood from a stone, old thing,' he whispered through clenched teeth, his unlit pipe jammed in between them.

'Not helped by Ruby here,' Cressida sighed, then perked up when she noticed something just over Alfred's shoulder.

'What is it?' Alfred asked, peering at his shoulder and dusting off whatever offending article was there.

'No, not you, Alfred.' Cressida reached past him and pulled out an innocuous-looking book from the shelf behind him and flipped it open. 'Aha. Thought I saw something sticking out of it. Look at this,' Cressida whispered as she did her best to manoeuvre the book between her hands while still holding Ruby. In the end, she gave up and passed Ruby over to Alfred, who held her rather stiffly, if exceptionally carefully, while Cressida surreptitiously fished out the note she'd spied sticking out of the top of the book, and read it.

You must stop this silly behaviour, it's illegal for one thing, and not befitting someone in your position for another. I will give you a day or two to return the record book, but if I find out you still have it, then I will have to call the police. What you're planning is illegal, not to mention immoral and ungodly. If you sell them, there will be severe recriminations...

The note didn't look as if it carried on over the page; it just stopped. Not signed and not addressed either.

Cressida turned it over, but there was nothing on the other side except the ink of the pen that had seeped through. She slipped it as subtly as possible into her pocket, then flipped the book over. *An Anthology of Modern Poetry.* Cressida opened the front cover, wary of harming the already decrepit dust jacket.

A handwritten dedication caught her eye on the frontispiece, neat copperplate in brown ink. A shiver ran down her forearms making her hairs stand on end as she read it again.

To Clara Sitwell, Christmas 1902.

This book that contained a most interesting letter had once belonged to none other than the dean's wife.

The dean's very recently deceased wife.

14

'Look,' Cressida nudged Alfred. He'd read the letter over her shoulder, and nodded as he took on board the dedication in the book's jacket.

'Who do you think the letter's from?' Alfred whispered, still carefully holding Ruby.

'Clara, I suppose. Or maybe it was a warning received by Clara from someone else—'

'And she kept it in her book until she... died.'

'A severe recrimination if ever there was one,' Alfred murmured, both keeping their voices low and their heads turned conspiratorially towards the shelves.

'But Mrs Sitwell's death was an accident,' Cressida reminded him. 'She was a poor swimmer and drowned.'

'The verger then?' Alfred suggested. 'Did she write this letter to him, threatening him, before he ended up dead?'

'But then why would it be in her book? And, anyway, she was dead long before Anthony was murdered. And now this book is here, in Mr Bell's shop.'

Cressida's musings were interrupted by a cough from the

bookseller. She took a deep breath, then turned around and headed back to the counter with the book in her hand.

'Found a decorative book, have you?' the bookseller asked, a heavy dose of sarcasm in his tone.

'Well, all books can be decorative, don't you think?' Cressida replied, then thought a bit more about how important the book in question might be to solving the mystery. She would have to buy it from Mr Bell. 'I know I said I wanted a ledger, but actually this rather lovely poetry anthology would do just fine, I think.'

'I can't take any money off for the state of the dust jacket.' Mr Bell took it from her and turned it over in his hands before passing it back to her.

'No need. I think it's perfect. Beauty is in the eye of the beholder and all that. And, of course, you more than most people should know that one should never judge a book by its cover. You don't happen to know where this one came from, do you?'

The bookseller peered at it through his glasses and poked his tongue around his cheeks as he thought. 'Ah, yes. That one I sourced from the monthly auction over in Billingshurst.'

'Interesting,' Cressida said, turning the book over in her hands. 'I'll take it. And, Mr Bell, could I trouble you for one more thing?'

Mr Bell looked at her, and then to Ruby, who was sitting panting in Alfred's arms, with a look on his face as if to say 'haven't I suffered you all enough', but he nodded and Cressida carried on.

'Mr Bell, do you ever go to the Wykeham Arms?'

'Rarely. Why?' he asked, and Cressida wondered if there was a note of caution in his reply.

'Oh, well, my friend here,' she pointed to Alfred, who was still cradling Ruby, while also trying to look nonchalant with his pipe sticking out of his mouth at a rakish angle, 'he needs a room for a night or two and was thinking of the Wykeham Arms. And as it's just a stone's throw from here, I thought you might know it?'

'Oh, I see. Well, it has the best rooms in this part of town, but then there's the Cross Keys and, of course, the Chesil Inn too.'

'But you've been to the Wykeham Arms, of an evening?' Cressida pursued. 'I've heard some of the clergy go there. In fact, I heard that the poor man who died this morning was there the other night. Someone said he was having cross words with another man, and, well, I wouldn't want my friend here caught up in any bad behaviour, if that's the kind of thing that goes on there.'

Alfred, who was unable to say much due to not being able to take his pipe out of his mouth in time, just grinned out of half of his mouth and nodded. Cressida wanted to laugh, but she kept a straight face and turned back to the bookseller.

'I don't think I was there that night.' The bookseller found some papers to shuffle. 'But, as I say, it's a good enough establishment and the landlord will look after your friend here.' In a quieter voice, he added, 'He's very amenable to the simpler sort.'

Cressida really had to try hard not to laugh at that, but she did her best, biting down on her lower lip until she almost made it bleed.

'Thank you, Mr Bell. I was worried, as Alfred here is prone to get into trouble. I heard a rumour that some bones had resurfaced the other day too, and I don't think we should get mixed up in that sort of thing.'

'Bones?' Mr Bell asked, his voice harder now. 'What sort of bones? Where did you hear that?'

'Oh, you know, old bones and the like.' Cressida remembered what the torn page in her pocket had said about St Swithun. 'Saint's bones, perhaps. Relics. Now where did I hear it? I can't remember...'

'Bones and relics are strictly forbidden items to sell in this country. If you hear anyone speak of it while you're at the Wykeham Arms...' He turned to Alfred, who was trying to look serious while holding a chubby little pug and sucking on an unlit pipe. He raised his voice and spoke clearly and slowly, 'You, sir, if you hear of anything, you let me know.'

'Aye aye,' Alfred said, it being the easiest thing to say as his pipe was less clenched than it usually was.

'How much is the book?' Cressida asked, trying very hard to keep a straight face.

'That'll be two shillings and eight pence, Miss...?'

'Fawcett, Cressida Fawcett. As I said, I'm Lady Dashwood-Howard's niece. And here you are, two shillings and eight pence. Thank you, Mr Bell.'

At that, Cressida turned around and raised an eyebrow to Alfred, who nodded a goodbye and followed Cressida out of the door. She closed it behind them, the bell tinkling once more.

Alfred looked to see if any carts or bicycles were thundering past, then put Ruby down and took his pipe out his mouth. He shoved it rather unceremoniously into his pocket and crossed his arms. 'Dash it all, Cressy, that man must have thought I was an imbecile, nodding like a donkey and rendered speechless due to my pipe.'

Cressida giggled but couldn't help reaching out to straighten Alfred's collar as she did. She noticed him blush and felt her own cheeks prickle again too. 'It was rather funny, Alfred,' she said. 'But ever so charming.'

'Well, in that case...' Alfred reached up for his collar and their hands brushed as she pulled hers away. 'No harm done, eh?'

'No, none at all. And do you know what else we found out that's awfully interesting?'

'That he lied about where that poetry book came from. He

gave us some cock and bull story about an auction in Billing-shurst, when it's obviously from the Deanery.'

'Yes, that was fishy. There are plenty of auction houses closer to here than Billingshurst. I can imagine Mr Bell might go far and wide sourcing books for his shop, but would Geoffrey Sitwell go all the way to Sussex to consign a book to auction?'

'Exactly. Fishy is the word.'

'So, we think he was lying about where he got this book from. And then there's this note.' She reached into her pocket and pulled out the letter, placing it back between the pages of the book. 'This is what prompted me to ask about the bones.'

'It doesn't mention bones or relics though,' Alfred pointed out. 'It says the recipient took the record book—'

'No, but read it again, Alfred, it clearly relates to someone selling "*them*". And "ungodly behaviour" and all that. And did you notice that when I mentioned the bones—'

'And made him think I was a simpleton who might get mixed up in that sort of thing,' huffed Alfred, though good-naturedly.

'Yes.' Cressida giggled again, then became more serious, 'But, listen, all I said was that I'd heard a rumour about some bones. Saintly bones to be fair, as perhaps that was what Nancy was referring to, but I never mentioned anyone buying or selling them. He leapt to that conclusion all by himself.'

15

'Much to tell Dotty, don't you think?' Cressida remarked as she and Alfred walked the rest of the length of St Swithun Street, its high-sided wall on one side, and modest terraces on the other.

'And see if your aunt's cook has anything for tea. I'm famished.'

'You're as bad as Ruby, always thinking of your stomach, Alfred,' Cressida teased, then ran a few steps ahead to stop Ruby, who had darted between the railings of one of the terraced-houses' gardens, her nose straight into the flowerbed. Cressida leaned over the fence and pulled her out, her paws and face covered in soil, but a satisfied look on her rumpled face.

A group of passing gowned schoolboys from the nearby college walked past and burst out laughing, pointing at Cressida and her mucky pup.

'I say, rum chaps,' Alfred exclaimed. 'Still, one could never trust a Wykehamist.'

'I dare say you were just as bad as a schoolboy, Alfred,'

Cressida taunted. 'Weren't you once caught straining a home-made cider through your sports shorts?'

Alfred smirked. 'Spiffing stuff it was too, though it made my rugger matches darn itchy occasions for the rest of the Michaelmas term.'

Cressida smiled and they walked on in companionable silence. Another group of schoolboys walked past, this time without a dose of the giggles, and Cressida remembered her aunt once saying that everyone locally, and even those from further afield, aspired to send their sons to Winchester College. Despite Alfred's aversion, born no doubt from simple sports field rivalry, to be a Wykehamist – a pupil or old boy of Winchester College – was a most coveted thing. She was roused from this pondering as they passed two women who appeared deep in conversation. Cressida and Alfred nodded a 'good day' to them, but they barely looked up. Cressida did hear a snippet of conversation, though, and she strained to catch what one of the tweed-clad women was saying to the other.

'... say he killed her. And now with poor Anthony dead, and him so against the...'

'Did you hear that, Alfred?' Cressida grasped his arm and whispered into his ear.

'I did, yes.' Alfred stopped in his tracks and looked down at Cressida with a furrowed brow. 'What did they mean by killed "her"? It's a chap who's been done in, not a lady.'

'I wonder if they meant Mrs Sitwell?' She shook her head and bit her lip. 'No, it can't be. As we were just saying, she drowned. No one has implied it was remotely suspicious.'

'Rum stuff again.' Alfred took his unlit pipe out of his pocket and clamped it in his jaw. 'Rum stuff indeed. Dare I say it, Dot's got a good head on her. She might have a thought or two about all this.'

'Too right. Especially now she's brushing up on gumshoes

and private investigators. Speaking of which, we must see if there's any news on DCI Andrews' arrival.'

Alfred nodded, but it was clear his thoughts were still on his sister. 'I wouldn't be surprised if she's given up on the books and is mooning about that Parish chap again. He sent a letter quite recently, but the poor stooge is on some far-flung archaeological dig in deepest Mesopotamia or somewhere. Can't expect him to be writing letters every five minutes, but Dot does worry that he's not interested.'

'I know, she said as much the other night when we were at the theatre,' Cressida sighed. 'I'm sure he is very much enamoured of her, and he's much, much nicer than that dratted Basil Bartleby. I do hope he is serious about her. You know, she's even started thinking about life out in the desert, sand-swept vistas and camels and all that. And you know how much Dot usually hates the outdoors. So for her to be shopping for safari suits and sun hats really is something. In a funny way, I think I can imagine her swathed in linen, looking all romantic by the perfectly white canvas tents.'

'Sounds rather fun to me,' Alfred said, raising an eyebrow as they reached the fine iron gates of Aunt Mary's house on Cloister Close. 'Perhaps we'd have to go out and join her?'

'Tea looks good, and, by jingo, proper macaroons. Well done, Lady D-H,' Alfred said as he and Cressida had joined Dotty and Maurice Sauvage in the parlour. They had been looking at fabrics and Cressida was pleased to see that Maurice was back from his mission to find an upholsterer.

'Where is Aunt Mary, Dot?' Cressida asked, accepting a cup of tea from Dotty, who seemed to have been left in charge.

'She's headed off to the agency to place an advertisement for a new maid. Already.'

Maurice was by the window poring over the fabric samples

and Cressida smiled at him, slightly embarrassed that he'd come all this way to help with the decorating only to find her aunt had rather more pressing things to handle.

'She's instigating The Protocol, I suppose. I'm afraid it doesn't bode well if even Aunt Mary doesn't think Nancy will have her name cleared any time soon.'

'Poor Nancy. I've been thinking...' Dotty sat back in her chair with her teacup and saucer in one hand and with the other she tickled the soft fur between Ruby's ears. 'What if she's covering for someone? In the books I've read, and they're really rather gripping, well, often someone confesses to cover up for someone they love. Or someone they're threatened by.'

'I don't know, Dot,' Cressida nursed her tea. 'She didn't confess, it's quite the opposite. She claims she didn't do it, even though we caught her with the candlestick in her hand – her raised hand at that.'

'I know. But what if she found Mr Preston, her "Tony", like that.' Dotty stared into the fire and Cressida fancied she could practically hear her brain working away. Dotty turned back to face her friend and continued, 'And she saw the murderer running away, but was then found in that compromising position, having wrangled the candlestick off him. She might have seen the real killer, but she doesn't want to say, because she's protecting them. That would explain why she was caught holding the weapon, and perhaps she's sending you off hunting after bones and ghosts to distract you from the truth of the matter?'

Cressida thought about this. It would fit with her conviction that Nancy was innocent, but then it would also mean she knew who the murderer was. And if she loved Anthony so much, why would she protect the person who killed him?

Maurice caused them all to look up as he swore under his breath while a pile of fabric samples slipped off the chaise longue and onto the floor. 'Pardon me, Miss Fawcett,' he apologised as she got up and went over to help him. 'The problem is we have too many samples here.'

'Yes, too much choice for Aunty M, perhaps,' agreed Cressida. 'But they're all so beautiful. It's funny isn't it, how my aunt, who I adore and respect in so many ways—'

'And take after too,' added Dotty.

'Yes, I suppose I do,' admitted Cressida with a grin. 'Who wouldn't aspire to be like the woman who has a cocktail named after her in not one, or two, but *three* European hotels?'

'Thought I might live to regret the Bathing Mary I had in Baden-Baden,' Alfred chipped in, then shook his head as he recounted. 'But it was the Mary's Flush in Monte Carlo that really undid me.'

'Exactly. Plus she's always so practical and knows what's what. But, unlike me, I'm afraid she can't decorate for toffee.'

'And, as far as we know, she hasn't solved any murders.' Maurice raised an eyebrow at Cressida as he took over re-sorting the samples.

'Well, I wouldn't put it past her,' Cressida said, a wry smile crossing her face as she sat back down. 'And I haven't got her brains for playing bridge. Do you remember, Dot, how she tried to teach us that Easter and had to give up as we both kept getting our trumps in a twist.'

'That's another cocktail I regret drinking,' murmured Alfred.

'I wonder if the police would let me in to visit Nancy and have a chat with her,' Cressida brought the conversation back to the case in hand. 'I could claim it was a welfare visit on behalf of her employer, or something like that?'

'Oh, speaking of police, I have news of dear DCI Andrews,' Dotty said, putting her teacup down, disturbing a sleeping Ruby as she did so. 'He put a call through to us here.'

'Oh yes? Is he on his way?'

'Rather, and quickly too. Not even waiting for the afternoon train but motoring down with Sergeant Kirby as we speak.'

'Jolly good,' Cressida rubbed her hands together. She was worried that she was already exhausting her list of suspects and it would help to have Andrews' input on what was turning out to be a rather tricky case.

But Andrews' wasn't the only opinion Cressida respected, and she returned her focus to her best friend. 'But before he gets here, I'll tell you all about what we've discovered so far. But first, one of those teacakes, please, Dot...'

16

'Gosh, so who's that letter from?' Dotty asked, eyes agog as she looked at the *Anthology of Modern Poetry* and its extra page.

'Quite. And who was it written to?' added Cressida, taking the book back from Dotty, who handed it over most unwillingly.

'Sorry,' she apologised, finally relinquishing it to Cressida. 'It's just a rather lovely collection. I do love poems.'

'I know, chum, but this is evidence now.' Cressida put the book down and then fished out the page torn from a records book she'd found earlier. 'And this too.'

'All in all, it was a rather interesting visit to H.T. Bell the bookseller,' Alfred concluded.

Maurice coughed out an 'ahem' and the others turned to look at him. 'My apologies, Miss Fawcett, Lady Dorothy, Lord Delafield,' he said. 'But I wonder if something, or indeed someone, I saw today might be of some interest?'

'Please, Maurice, do go on,' Cressida urged him. Like the flamboyant backside of his waistcoat, she knew there was more than met the eye with Mr Maurice Sauvage. Whatever he had to say would definitely be worth listening to.

'Well, it's just that you mentioned Bell the bookseller, so it seems rather a coincidence that I saw an acquaintance of mine outside his shop earlier today, when I was seeking out an upholsterer for your aunt.'

'Spotted a chum? Who was it?' Alfred properly turned around in his chair to face him.

Maurice shuddered, then carefully laid down one of the fabric samples and picked his way across the parlour to join them by the fire. 'A "chum" he is not, Lord Delafield. I used the word acquaintance with a certain amount of trepidation, for I dislike being associated with him at all. And he is the last person I would expect to see here in Winchester. Or, indeed, at a bookshop.'

'Who was it?' Dotty pushed, as she slipped a macaroon off the plate and started nibbling it.

Maurice perched elegantly on the arm of the sofa and, once his cuffs had been adjusted to his satisfaction, taking his time while clearly quite aware of the six rapt eyes upon him, he replied, 'A certain Pierre Fontaine. He's an antiques dealer, someone I've come across on various occasions over the years. Some of the less reputable dealers in London buy from him, and even Arthur Liberty himself was tempted from time to time, though he thought better of it on each occasion, I'm pleased to say. He's based in Paris and has notoriously bad English, hence why he barely comes here anymore.'

'But he was outside Bell's?'

'Quite so, and he was very much looking like he'd just been inside the shop. The door was just closing with that little tinkling bell it has.' Maurice looked as if this coy charm of a parochial shopkeeper was an affront to his sensibilities. Once his moustache had stopped twitching, he continued. 'I hailed him good day, of course, and he recognised me, but looked, as my young friends at Euston station would say, "as shifty as hell". Still, I felt I should greet him properly, so I crossed the road under that funny little arch and said hello.'

'Did he continue looking shifty?' Dotty asked, pushing her glasses back up her nose.

'Incredibly so, Lady Dorothy. He looked all about the place except at my face, it seemed. I asked him his business here and he shrugged in that very Gallic way. He was carrying a parcel wrapped in brown paper, so to make conversation I asked him what was in it.'

'And?' Cressida was intrigued.

'He said he'd been tasked with finding some books for a client of his.'

'Well, he was in the right place for that,' Alfred said, as much to himself as to the room.

'What sort of books?' Cressida prompted.

'That's the thing, Miss Fawcett,' Maurice answered her. 'He said "*jolie*" like it was a genre of books instead—'

'Instead of just meaning pretty,' Dotty interrupted. 'Sorry, Mr Sauvage, but that is what *jolie* means, isn't it?'

'It is indeed, Lady Dorothy.' He nodded. 'In a literal sense. I would translate it further in this case to mean ornamental, or perhaps decorative.'

Cressida caught Alfred's eye and he met her gaze knowingly.

Maurice looked at his fingernails as he finished his story. 'I just thought you should know.'

'Thank you, Maurice.' Cressida meant it. 'It can't just be a coincidence that moments later, or perhaps before, Mr Bell very adamantly told me that he sold no such thing as decorative books. I have no idea how that may or may not fit in with anything, but it may indeed be useful, so thank you. What a strange fellow. Worth telling Andrews about, perhaps?' She addressed this last bit to her friends.

'And we can tell him about the bookseller leaping to conclusions about selling relics,' added Alfred.

'Yes, and the archivist who had an argument with Anthony

in the Wykeham Arms, though I still can't see that a spat about a padlock would be something one would kill over.'

'Oh, I don't know. If you love books as much as... well, I would say I do, but I suppose I wouldn't kill anyone over it.' Dotty sipped her tea and tutted to herself. 'No, silly idea, ignore me. No one would kill someone over books.'

'I should hope not, Dot!' Cressida almost laughed, then became more serious again. 'But if not the books themselves, then perhaps what's been inserted in one...?'

A brief knock at the door broke her chain of thought and alerted them all to Aunt Mary standing there, with another sensibly dressed woman behind her.

'Afternoon all,' Aunt Mary said. 'Anything left in the pot? Judith and I are gasping. We just bumped into each other on my way back from the agency, and I said I was sure there would be a pot on, despite the lack of a maid.'

'Of course, Aunt Mary,' Cressida said. 'I'm afraid we started without you, but there's plenty left and some jolly decent macaroons.'

'Thank you, dear, thank you. Yes, I rang through to Mr Cooper the baker and made sure to up the order. I don't think one can have too much in the way of sugared treats during a crisis. And his iced buns are simply delicious. Oh, I'm forgetting myself, let me introduce Judith Ainsworth, one of our bell-ringers here at Winchester.'

With their exemplary manners showing, Alfred, Dotty and Cressida stood up to greet the newcomer, while Maurice quickly slipped off the arm of the sofa and stood behind them.

'I prefer campanologist,' Judith said, and smiled at the four of them. 'But very nice to meet you all, all the same.'

Once Alfred and Dotty had been properly introduced, Cressida shook Judith's hand and offered her a seat, having quickly picked up the poetry book and tattered page from the journal that was sitting next to it on the side table and hidden them behind her back. Her aunt's friend was wearing a sensible tweed suit and had her light-brown hair swept back into a loose chignon. Her low-heeled shoes were plain brown and her stockings a suitable thickness for the weather, much like Aunt Mary's. But there was something else that struck Cressida about Judith Ainsworth, and it had happened when she'd said those first few words.

She recognised her. She recognised the sensible tweed suit, but on top of that, and most of all, the voice. Judith Ainsworth was one of the women they'd passed on St Swithun Street earlier.

The one who had been talking about the dean's dead wife.

17

'Such a shock for us all,' Judith said as she put her teacup and saucer down and chose a toasted and buttered teacake from the plate. 'Anthony Preston was such a nice man, really.'

'And to think, engaged in secret to my maid, Nancy,' Aunt Mary said, eyebrows raised as she gossiped.

'To think, indeed,' Judith concurred, before the teacake found its way into her mouth.

'They fell in love over the feather duster perhaps?' Aunt Mary mused, while Cressida, who had been listening with interest, furrowed her brow. What had Judith just said? ...*Such a nice man, really. Why 'really'?*

'Mrs Ainsworth,' she asked, 'do you think anyone here in Winchester could have had a grudge against Mr Preston?'

Judith put her half-eaten teacake down and flushed slightly in her cheeks.

Aunt Mary answered for her. 'Cressida dear, I'm not sure that's an acceptable question to ask, especially not so soon—'

'No, it's all right, Mary dear,' Judith interrupted. 'There's been something preying on my mind actually and I would appreciate the opportunity to share it. As long as it goes no further, of course.'

Dotty and Alfred nodded, as did Cressida, though she gently crossed her fingers under her tea plate. Andrews would have to know anything of interest that was said, after all. Maurice, used to listening in to conversations in drawing rooms across the country as he measured up for curtains, maintained his silence but gave Mrs Ainsworth a nod to assure her of his discretion.

'Please, do go on, Mrs Ainsworth,' Cressida encouraged her, and the bell-ringer shifted in her seat and then spoke.

'It all started months ago, of course – the "upset", shall we say, between Anthony Preston and our head bell-ringer.'

'Nigel Havering?' Aunt Mary asked. 'What could have been the matter between them?'

'Yes, Nigel. He's a very talented campanologist but somewhat lacking in the other skills one needs to work in a team like ours. His communication can be... shall I say, blunt?'

'Ah,' Aunt Mary nodded as she spoke. 'Yes, I've heard how he speaks to Beryl, the cleaner. Very brusque.'

'Quite. Brusque is the word. Though she does always insist on calling him Mr Have-A-Ring, and finds it exceedingly funny, much to his ire. "Hay-vering," he has to say to her. "Like the horse's food."' Judith shook her head, and Cressida did her best not to make eye contact with Alfred; now was not the time for a mirthful smirk. In any case, Judith continued. 'And Anthony was always such a sensitive soul. One of those quiet men, you know.'

Cressida could sense a motive for murder forming here with this Nigel chap. 'Mrs Ainsworth, what did Nigel do or say to Anthony? Or vice versa. To cause this "upset"?'

Judith shuffled in her seat again. 'Well, Anthony was very cautious about the overuse of the bell tower for tours and the like, and, of course, the annual bell-ringing competition. Oh, and accommodating though he was, he had a view on certain peals and when it was appropriate to ring them. I think he may have had very sensitive hearing, as he never seemed to embrace the sound of the bells quite like the other clergy. Nigel, of course, took the opposite view on almost everything. And they came to loggerheads last week. I'm ashamed to say, that's why the practice was arranged for today.'

Cressida looked at Dotty, who looked equally as bemused, even subtly shrugging her shoulders.

It was Aunt Mary who asked the question.

'Why, dear? What was particular about today?'

'Anthony had asked the dean if he could have a quiet time of contemplation this morning. He was to check on the Canterbury candlesticks, of course, and then do a clean of the Elizabethan silver, and then I believe he wanted to pray. Nigel got wind of this and requested we practise with all twelve bells this morning. It's joyous, of course, and hugely fun to pull, but there's nothing subtle about it. It's very loud.'

There were nods among the tea guests as they understood the pettiness of Nigel's plan. Aunt Mary was the first to add her thoughts.

'Well, I do think less of Nigel now. That's a very silly and spiteful thing to do. Very spiteful indeed.'

'Especially given that after arranging for us all to come in for this extra practice, he didn't even turn up himself.'

'Very bad show.' Aunt Mary shook her head. 'I may have to show solidarity with Beryl and call him Mr Have-A-Ring, too.'

Cressida smiled at her aunt, but the hairs on her forearms had prickled at something Judith had said. 'Nigel set up the practice, but didn't turn up?'

'Not a sign of him. Well, yes, there was a sign. Beryl said she saw his coat hanging over one of the tombs in the retro-choir, but he certainly did not come and join us in the bell tower.'

'How very strange,' Aunt Mary concluded, and Cressida and the others nodded.

It was very strange indeed. To have organised a deafening session of bells at just the time that the verger was trying to concentrate on his devotions was petty. But to organise it at the precise time he was being murdered... and then not have an alibi for that time? Well, that could be a sign of something else.

Something altogether more wicked.

18

A sharp knock at the door caused some of the teacups to rattle in their saucers. It took a few moments for Lady Dashwood-Howard, who had been in deep conversation with Judith about how school fees these days cost a small fortune, to remember that she no longer had a maid, and with an exclamation that bordered on the unladylike, she rose and left the room. Ruby saw this as a chance to jump off Dotty's lap and go and hunt under the low table for crumbs. A few minutes later, Aunt Mary returned, and Cressida beamed at the sight of Detective Chief Inspector Andrews, and behind him, still in the hallway, the ever-reassuring Sergeant Kirby.

'Good afternoon, Andrews!' Cressida called to him, and then made sure that introductions were made.

The elegant parlour was large enough, thankfully, for them all to fit in, even now there were eight of them, and one small hound, in the room. And as much as Cressida was pleased to see them, she couldn't help but notice that Sergeant Kirby did look somewhat out of place, perched on the spindly end of the eighteenth-century chaise longue, recently vacated by Maurice's fabrics. His smart midnight-blue uniform stood out against the faded pink velvet, while his golden buttons blazed under the electric lights that Aunt Mary had turned on to fend off the afternoon gloom. He fiddled with his helmet strap as he sat down, managing to get it off – and relieve Cressida of her fear that one day he would be garrotted by it – to reveal his mop of dark ginger hair.

DCI Andrews was, as ever, dressed in a smart three-piece tweed suit, his neatly trimmed beard and moustache grizzled with the odd grey hair, matching those peppered across his dark hair and greying temples. His stature was always that of a military man, straight-backed and stand-offish, though Cressida knew that his knee often hurt him due to the injury he sustained in the Boer War, and, of course, more recently, he'd been shot in the shoulder. That had been as clean a wound as a bullet could make, and he'd received excellent first aid from Dotty, who had given him a little wave when he'd walked in. But, despite this, Cressida could see that he was favouring his arm in the way that he stood.

'Please, Andrews, sit down here,' Cressida gestured to where she'd been sitting, but Maurice interrupted her.

'No, DCI Andrews, it would be my honour for you to take what was my seat. I fear I must bid you all farewell and travel back to London.'

'Most kind, thank you,' Andrews nodded to him, but before he sat down, goodbyes were said by the assembled guests to the esteemed decorator.

Once Aunt Mary had promised to take a good look at the samples he was leaving in a neat pile by the window, Cressida walked her friend out towards the hall and helped him find his coat and hat in the pile that had built up.

'Never should we take our maids for granted,' she remarked, pulling his neat mackintosh from under Andrews' woollen greatcoat and rescuing his hat from atop the marble bust on the hall table. 'And thank you again for coming, Maurice,' Cressida said, handing him his gloves which had been languishing under Alfred's coat. 'I'm sorry that Aunt Mary and I have been rather distracted.'

'My pleasure, Miss Fawcett, and really, don't mention it.' He nodded, then placed his hat on his head and opened the door. He turned around on the top step and spoke again. 'And don't hesitate to telephone me. I'll be back at Liberty and catching up on the day's notes, no doubt until this evening. I can't help but think there was something strange about seeing Fontaine here, especially after you said something about relics. That's what made him so dubious to most of us here in England.'

'Go on?' Cressida urged, wrapping her arms around her to try to keep out the cold of the doorstep.

'My people descend from the protestant Huguenots – generations ago, of course – but I have enough French in me to know that most of that country's folk are still staunch Catholics, and, as such, much more interested in saints' bones and relics than your average Church of England protestant.'

'You think Fontaine might be the one buying these bones Nancy mentioned?' Cressida shivered at the thought – a shiver made easier by the sharp autumn air.

Maurice merely shrugged and doffed his hat. 'As I said, do feel free to put in a telephone call to the Liberty exchange at any point. I'd be interested to know how this case progresses, and, of course, which Indian silk your aunt ends up choosing.'

Cressida smiled at him, thanked him for his time and samples, and bade him goodbye. His words gave her much to think about. Had Nancy been right in suggesting Anthony was mixed up in some sort of illegal trade in saints' relics? While also being described by almost everyone as a pious, sensitive man? She walked back into the parlour, her head cocked on one side as she gathered her thoughts. One in particular leapt out at her; this Fontaine chap had been able to buy decorative books from Mr Bell, when he had most definitely told her that he didn't trade in that sort of thing. And it was in his shop that she'd spotted the poetry anthology with the strange, almost threatening note in. Mr Bell definitely knew more than he'd been willing to say, she realised. Her next challenge would be working out how to coax more out of him.

She could only hope that what he did say, was the truth.

As she returned to the parlour, Cressida walked in on Alfred enthusiastically talking to Andrews and Kirby.

'Are you fine fellows bedding down at the Wykeham Arms tonight, too?'

'I'm afraid not, sir,' Andrews replied. 'We have simpler police accommodation waiting for us at the station. Speaking of which, I am on my way there now. We have Miss Nancy Biddle in custody, and I need to ask her some questions.'

Andrews stood up abruptly, and accordingly everyone else in the room stood up too.

'Thank you, Lady Dashwood-Howard.' Andrews nodded at her. 'If you don't mind, I'll take my leave now. I just wanted to check in on your niece here.'

'And make sure she hasn't started investigating?' Dotty asked, perhaps a bit too influenced by the sugary cake she'd been eating. 'Well, you're too—'

'Andrews,' Cressida interrupted her friend. 'Would you mind if I accompanied you to the station? I have a few other matters to talk to you about.' Cressida was very mindful of the presence of Mrs Ainsworth, who was clearly a fount of parishioner gossip.

'Of course, Miss Fawcett,' Andrews said, though he gave a knowing look to Dotty as he did so. 'Be my guest.'

With her hat, coat and gloves back on, Cressida was braced for the cool air this time. But she hadn't been entirely braced for the quick peck on the cheek that Alfred had given her as they'd parted ways on Aunt Mary's doorstep. He was on his way to the Wykeham Arms while she followed Andrews and Sergeant Kirby towards the centre of Winchester and the police station. Dotty had elected to stay behind and keep reading her detective novels, but Ruby had an eye for an adventure and so was now gambolling along next to Cressida.

'I didn't want to say too much in front of everyone just now,' she began, 'but the truth is, I have started investigating some things, Andrews.'

'Why does that not surprise me, Miss Fawcett?' Andrews asked, turning to face Cressida, who stopped in her tracks.

'Well, I suppose it shouldn't, Andrews,' Cressida admitted, though she stood as confidently and straight as possible, holding her hands behind her back to iron out her shoulders as she did so.

'And let me guess, Mr Sauvage from Liberty wasn't only here to talk about fabrics?'

'Ah, well, that's where you're wrong. He was invited to Aunt Mary's for the sole task of helping me steer her in the correct direction as far as prints and patterns are concerned, though, of course, right place and right time and all that...' Cressida raised an eyebrow at him.

'Or wrong place and wrong time,' sighed Andrews.

'Well, with or without Maurice, I've already unearthed some interesting things. For example—'

'Miss Fawcett.' Andrews held his hand up to silence her. 'There has been a gruesome and barbaric murder. And, for once, I understand, the victim is not connected to you, has not been found in your best friend's house, was not an old friend of your parents and the murder didn't happen a few rail carriages down from you.'

'Well, no... but Aunt Mary and I were the first on the scene, along with the dean. We saw Nancy Biddle with the candlestick raised above her head as if she'd just cast the fatal blow. And Nancy is my aunt's maid. So, you can see why I've taken a personal interest.'

Andrews sighed again. 'But, Miss Fawcett, you really can't go charging about, interviewing people you think are suspects, ruffling feathers and contaminating evidence.'

'Who says that's what I've been doing?' Cressida pulled her arms in front of her and crossed them. 'So, you're not interested in anything I've found out? Not even one little soupçon of information? Fine.' Cressida unfolded her arms, clicked her fingers at Ruby and made to walk away.

'Miss Fawcett, wait!' Andrews called after her.

Cressida smiled to herself, then changed her expression back to a much more neutral one as she turned back to face him. 'Yes, Andrews?'

'Fine. Tell me what you know already, I'll be pleased to hear it. But, after that, no more investigating. I mean it.' There was an expression on his face that reminded Cressida of one her own father had used on her more than once.

She bowed her head in acceptance. 'Of course, Andrews. Lead on to the station, I'll tell you everything there.'

But as they walked down the cobbled streets of Winchester, the murdered verger's keys still in her pocket, she whispered down to Ruby, who was still trotting along next to her, 'No more investigating, eh? We'll see about that.'

19

Winchester police station was housed within the Victorian Guildhall, a building so elaborate that it quite stood out among the medieval and Georgian buildings of the rest of the city. Andrews had explained to Cressida that the police station had barracks-style lodging for single and visiting policemen, and so he and Kirby would be based there for the foreseeable future.

'So, if you have any urges to go investigating, Miss Fawcett, you must come here and tell me about them first,' he said as they stood on the steps that rose from road level to the highly decorative door.

'I wouldn't call them urges as such, Andrews,' Cressida admonished him, taking a step or two back down to collect a struggling Ruby, who was finding the Victorian architecture just a little too much for her short legs. 'I would say they were inspirations. Shall we go and visit Miss Biddle now and see what she has to say?'

Andrews laughed.

Cressida furrowed her brow and looked to Sergeant Kirby for support, who just clasped his hands behind his back and suddenly found his boots to be of the utmost interest.

'No, Miss Fawcett. There is no "we" at this point. Or, at least, the only "we" is me and Sergeant Kirby, and one or two of Winchester's finest.'

'Oh, dash it, Andrews, be a sport. I've told you everything I know so far. Isn't that usually how we work these things? You do things by the book, and I supply a bit of extra sauce? The mint to your lamb, the horseradish to your beef?'

Andrews shook his head. 'Miss Fawcett, those times have been exceptions to the rule. Which means, every so often, we do actually have to abide by the rules.'

'That's right, miss,' Kirby piped up. 'We've had a talking-to from the commissioner. He's not best pleased with how many investigations you've helped us with.'

Cressida saw Andrews glare at Kirby and assumed the young sergeant had just given away far too much information. 'You mean to say your commissioner doesn't like the fact that you've caught murderers, not to mention done it in a really top-notch way and highly discreetly, with *moi* as your helpmate? How very strange. Who is the commissioner?'

'It's Sir Kingsley Mountjoy, miss—'

'That's enough, Sergeant.' Andrews curtailed Kirby before he could say much more.

'Well, I think it's awfully rummy,' Cressida said, then pointed to her nose. 'See this, Andrews? Very much out of joint, I'll have you know.'

'I'm sorry, Miss Fawcett.' Andrews had the grace to look somewhat sheepish. 'But civilians really cannot be part of police investigations. It was different on the Scotland Express, and up in the Highlands, and in those other remote country houses, but this is Winchester. I have the co-operation of the whole of the Hampshire constabulary, quite literally on our doorstep – this very doorstep, in fact. There's simply no reason for you to be helping us this time. Not to mention the fact that it seems to be, for once, a very clear open-and-shut case. This really must be where I leave you.'

'Au contraire, Andrews,' Cressida replied, and much to Andrews' astonishment and Kirby's wide-eyed shock, she put Ruby down on the top step of the Guildhall's fancy entranceway and then, in one quick motion, slipped a hand under Kirby's chin-strap, pulled it forward and caught his helmet in her other hand. Then, flushed with adrenaline, Cressida threw the helmet over the balustrade of the steps onto the pavement below, right into the path of an oncoming drayman's cart.

Once she'd turned back to pick up Ruby and was standing upright again, Cressida looked squarely into the shocked faces of her two favourite policemen, and grinned. 'I think you'll find, Chief Inspector, that I will be coming into the police station with you. I have committed the heinous crime of stealing a policeman's helmet and wilfully harming it. So, I'm afraid you'll just have to arrest me.'

Cressida's cell was narrow and simple, made of red brick. It contained only a bench to sit on and a rather dubious bucket in the corner. Ruby had it made it plain, in the amount of grunting snuffles she'd given, that she did not approve of this plan, nor did she agree to be an accomplice, but Cressida shushed her and brought out a slice of cheese she'd pocketed at lunch, which went quite some way to consoling her grumpy pup. She was happy that they'd let her keep Ruby with her at least.

The anthology of poetry and the torn page from what she believed was the stolen record book from the archive had been taken from her and catalogued by the desk sergeant when she'd been processed through to the cells. She'd also seen them take the bunch of keys that she'd found in Anthony's robes out of her coat pocket, but they were assumed to be hers and had been kept to one side with her other belongings. She wasn't quite sure why she hadn't owned up to their provenance, but she hadn't.

Sitting on the hard bench, she shivered as a draught caught her. She looked up at the high, gothic-arched window. There were bars across it and nothing else, no glass or shutters.

'No wonder it's so blooming cold in here, Rubes. It's enough to drive a confession from the most hardened criminal. And yes, I realise that I have already confessed. I should imagine punishment will be swift but short. At least I hope so.' In truth, she hadn't had much time to think through the consequences of her actions and she was contemplating this as a voice called down the corridor of cells.

'Miss Fawcett?'

'Hello there!' Cressida called out and, moments later, Kirby appeared in the small, barred window of her door, his reddish hair on show due to his lack of helmet. 'Oh, hello Kirby. Again, dreadfully sorry and all that. How is the helmet?'

'She suffered an indentation to the peripheral, er, perimeter, but nothing that can't be fixed by the quartermaster back in London.'

'Just a dent to the rim. That's spiffing news, Kirby.' Cressida smiled to herself and knew that Alfred would have been amused by the young sergeant's overcomplicated wording too. He was prone to slipping into excess verbosity at times and it always tickled her. Still, she had been at fault and felt she should apologise. 'I am sorry, though, Kirby. It was naughty of me to use you, and your helmet, like that.'

'That's all right, miss. I must say, it's a relief not to have to wear her all the time. The strap was rather tight. I'd been meaning to take her back to HQ and have it loosened. Anyway, I'm to take you to the interview room, miss,' Kirby said as he unlocked the door.

Cressida stooped to pick up Ruby and was waiting ready by

the time the thick, steel door was fully open. 'Interview room? I don't have much else to say. You were the victim and witness. I've confessed.'

'Yes, miss, but the chief inspector would like you to be placed in the interview room, miss. I have my orders.'

'Very well, Kirby,' sighed Cressida. 'Lead on.'

Kirby took Cressida along the corridor of cells and out into a more communal passage, where offices and other bureaucratic rooms were situated. He knocked briefly on the heavily painted door of a room and then entered, but no one else was there. Kirby gestured to one of the chairs on either side of a small table and Cressida sat down.

'If you're cold, miss, the radiator is a good place to stand next to, miss,' he said. Then, with a quick bow, Kirby left and shut the door behind him.

'Well, Rubes. It's an upgrade, I'll give him that. But it's no American bar at the Savoy,' she said as she looked around the whitewashed walls, and the windows that, although glazed this time, were still barred. Still cold from her cell, she got up and perched her bottom on the one, large, cast-iron column radiator, as Kirby had suggested. Resting on it, she leaned back against the wall, which had a copper pipe running up it. And that's when she heard a familiar voice coming from the pipe itself.

'Miss Biddle,' the disembodied voice said, 'you are under caution and charged with murdering Mr Anthony Preston, the verger of Winchester Cathedral. I have a few questions...'

Cressida grinned. *Oh Andrews*, she thought to herself, *you clever, wonderful, man...*

20

Cressida pushed her ear up against the pipe, which was luckily not as hot as the radiator itself. Victorian buildings were stout and thick-walled, but Victorian plumbing was often the cause of what most people thought were hauntings. Spooky vibrations and ringing noises were *de rigueur* with a system like this and Cressida briefly wondered if the Silent Friar could be explained away in a similar fashion. She shrugged away the thought and pressed her ear closer to the pipe.

'You were found holding the candlestick above the dead body of Mr Preston, yet you say you didn't do it?' Cressida recognised Andrews' voice.

'That's right, sir, I didn't do it. Why would I kill Anthony?'

'You tell me, why would you?'

'Well, that's just it, isn't it? I wouldn't.' She paused, then said with quite some certainty, 'He was my fiancé. I loved him, and him me.'

'Engaged? Recently so? Secretly perhaps? There's been no announcement in the newspapers, I see.'

'Secretly, sir, or at least discreetly, like. Too many loose tongues in the cathedral and I know I'm not the sort to usually marry a man of the Church. We kept it to ourselves.'

'Why? If you're in love, why not let the world know?' Andrews asked in return.

'Tony said...' There was a pause, perhaps a sniffle, before Nancy continued. 'Tony knew that people would say I was getting above myself. Marrying him so quick after meeting, and how we met.'

'How did you meet?'

'I cleaned for him. I was employed by the cathedral to do a certain amount of hours and the Sitwells were tidy folks and didn't need all my time, and with Tony being a bachelor who could hardly boil an egg without using every utensil in his kitchen, well, he needed my help. That's how we met and we fell in love so quickly, I can hardly explain it. But Tony, he knew people would talk and make up all sorts of things about me being a – what do they call it? A society... no, a social climber. That's it. He said we needed to give it a bit more time so that the community in the cathedral would see that it was all quite normal. I understood that, though it was hard keeping it to ourselves when we both just wanted to tell the world!'

'I see. And did you ever disagree about keeping it secret? Have a row about it? Lovers can quarrel, fights can escalate...' Andrews pushed her and Cressida listened keenly; she'd wondered this herself.

'Not Tony and me, we never fought. That's not how we were. I know I'm younger than him...' There was a pause again. 'Than he was. But our differences just meant that we had more patience with each other. He taught me about the world he'd seen as a young missionary, and teaching in London, and I made him laugh with stories about old Winchester and locals and that. There was nothing to fight about.'

'So how did you come to be holding that candlestick, which was covered in his blood, above his dead body?'

There was a longer pause and Cressida felt so sorry for Nancy, knowing that she must be crying again. Andrews' questions were direct, but then again, they needed to be, and as a policeman, he could get away with 'ruffling' as many 'feathers' as he liked. But it was the weeping that she could hear through the Victorian pipework that made her surer than ever that Nancy was innocent.

She heard Andrews ask the question again. This time, Nancy answered.

'I slipped into the crypt just before Lady Dashwood-Howard, Miss Fawcett and the dean came down. I was meant to meet Anthony down there, for a little... well, he had sent me a note.'

'I see. Carry on.'

'I knew it was risky. Tony mustn't have realised, see, that Lady Dashwood-Howard, Miss Fawcett and the dean were on a tour and that they would most likely head down to the crypt at any moment. But I also didn't want him to think I didn't want to meet him, or to worry that his message had gone astray. He didn't usually write me notes... but he did this time and I didn't want to put him off doing it again. So I snuck down into the crypt, if only to tell him that I couldn't linger. Then suddenly I saw him, lying there...' There was another pause, and when she started speaking again, her voice had a tremble to it. 'I rushed over and, in my shock, I picked up the candlestick and was holding it up to look at it when Lady Dashwood-Howard and the others found me.'

'And you didn't see anyone leave the crypt as you entered?'

There was a pause. Then, 'Does a ghost count, sir?'

'A ghost?'

'The Silent Friar, sir, he... But no, no, I suppose he could have gone straight through the walls...'

'Did you or did you not see someone enter the crypt, Miss Biddle?' Andrews asked her again.

'No, sir. I saw no one, sir. And I heard nothing either except those bells going hell for leather – excuse my language.'

'Well, I've got the local police looking for witnesses and we'll see if they corroborate what you're saying regarding the timing of your visit to the crypt,' Andrews countered. There was a longer pause than usual and no word from Nancy, before Andrews spoke again. 'You don't think anyone will be able to corroborate it?'

'It's not that, sir,' Nancy said, though Cressida was having to strain her ears to hear her quiet voice through the pipework. 'I just worry that you might not find anyone to say I was there, like.'

'Why would that be? The cathedral was open. The dean was even giving a tour to your employer and her niece. There would be people around and I'm sure the fine fellows here in the constabulary will find someone who saw you enter the crypt just as you say you did. During the bells pealing, wasn't it?'

'Yes, sir, but I've found that no one notices us servants, sir.'

At this, Cressida found herself nodding. It was a theory she agreed with wholeheartedly, though, of course, she didn't agree with the principle of it.

'Can you explain that to me?' She heard Andrews say.

'Well, we're trained to be quiet, sir. Discreet, like. Over the years, it becomes second nature. You walk quickly and quietly, and can enter rooms like a mouse, sir. And the higher-ups, the lords and ladies, are trained in their own way not to notice us. Pretend we're not there. Pretend it's not another human being, no worse than them, cleaning their slops and lighting their fires. If they noticed us, sir, well, their consciences would be so pricked you could sieve flour through them. If you don't mind me saying so, sir.'

'I don't mind you saying it, Miss Biddle, but I'm not sure it's the case here. We'll check witnesses. Is there anything else you'd like to add?'

'Just that *I* had no reason to kill my Anthony.'

There was a pause before Andrews spoke. 'You say that as if there was a reason why someone else would. Is that correct?'

Yes, Andrews! Cressida clenched her fists in anticipation. Now, hopefully, Nancy would tell him all about these mysterious bones, and Cressida had, if not a front-row seat, then at least a warm one.

'Well yes. There must be a reason why someone else would, else they wouldn't have killed him.' Nancy sounded exasperated.

'But the way you said it, it sounded more like "I know there is a reason, and it's not my reason, but I do know it."'

'The bones, sir. That's all I know. There was something happening between him and thems who want to sell the bones. That's all I know, sir.'

'What bones? Who wants to sell them?'

'I can't say any more, sir, I don't know.' There were sobs now and Cressida, with her ear very much as close to the copper pipe as could be, thought she could hear the odd 'now, now' coming from Andrews.

With that, the interview seemed terminated, and Cressida let herself relax away from the pipe. She was, however, still perched on the warm radiator when the door to her interview room opened and Andrews and Kirby walked in. To Cressida's satisfaction, Andrews was carrying what looked like the *Anthology of Modern Poetry* and a separate manilla folder, no doubt containing the torn page from the records book and the letter she'd found in the anthology.

Cressida smiled at him, and then took her seat at the interview table.

'Well, I must say, Andrews, your ingenuity is on a par with my deviousness. Thank you.'

'You can thank Kirby for not pressing charges on the criminal damage sustained to his helmet,' Andrews replied, and Cressida tapped a finger to the side of her nose.

'Yes indeed. Thank you, Kirby. And I understand perfectly, let's keep this all *entre-nous*.'

Andrews opened his mouth as if to say something, then he obviously thought better of it and just sighed. He opened the manilla folder and, true enough, the torn page and the letter she had found in the book were in there. Cressida pointed to them.

'So, what do you think?'

'It's not much to go on,' Andrews admitted. 'A page of some unknown records book found in robes that weren't even on the victim at the time, and a letter you found in a book that could relate to anything.'

'Ah, well, I think that page from the records book *does* relate to something: the bones. And I think the letter is referring to them too. It's annoying that Nancy didn't tell you more about them, as I'm sure she must know more, but I understand you can't heap pressure on a weeping maid, it's not the done thing at all.'

'She's a murder suspect, Miss Fawcett. I could have pressed her further, but my years of experience told me that she had given all she had to give at that point. Mentioning ghosts and then changing her mind. She'd had enough. I'll let one of the locals have a chat to her after her father's been in to see her and then try again myself. We have time, she's not going anywhere.'

'I see. I'm glad she has family nearby. Well, if she does say anything else of interest, will you let me know?'

Andrews frowned and let out a small harrumph.

Cressida pre-empted his answer. 'And, in return, let me tell you what I think these bits of paper mean. This torn page talks about St Swithun. Now, Swithun was the bishop here back in the days of yore and became a saint because he was a generally all-round good egg by the sounds of it. Pilgrims flocked to his grave so they made a – what did the dean call it? Oh yes, a reliquary, for his bones. I saw a medieval portrayal of it in the archive actually, Mr Flint has had some prints made.' She cast her eyes down to Ruby, remembering the awkwardness of her making a nest among the prints, as she carried on, 'But then old Henry VIII and his agents came and dissolutioned the monasteries, and all that, and the bones disappeared, believed stolen. But this page suggests they resurfaced, here in the cathedral, in about 1910.'

'Why 1910?' Andrews asked.

'Simple deduction, Andrews.' Cressida smiled at him, and hoisted Ruby onto her lap in order to stop the small dog from gnawing at the table leg. 'Firstly, the text itself relates to the time when the cathedral was sinking and had to be shored up, and that was around 1910. And secondly, Mr Flint the archivist—'

'You've spoken to the archivist? Miss Fawcett, what have I told you about not conducting your own investigations? I've sent officers off to talk to Mr Flint myself and now they're going to get short shrift if he thinks he's already been questioned.'

'Sorry, Andrews.' Cressida had the grace to look humbled, though that lasted about three seconds before she started talking again. 'But Flint did say that the one records book that had been stolen from the archive during a recent break-in – oh, I suppose your local chaps will fill you in about that too when they report in – well, he said it was from 1910.'

'Miss Fawcett, you—'

'I know, Andrews, I know. I shouldn't go poking my noble old nose into matters while you're here.'

'Or at all!' he said, a level of exasperation in his voice. Then he turned to Kirby, who had been feverishly writing notes as Cressida had been speaking. 'Kirby, can you check in with Duncan on the desk and see if Bert and the boys are back from the cathedral?'

'Yes, sir.' Kirby nodded, put his notebook away and left the room.

Andrews turned back to Cressida. 'So let's say this piece of torn paper describes the same bones that Nancy was referring to.'

'Yes. And that letter too?' She pointed to the one in the folder. 'Talking of illegal practices and the ungodly nature of it. It made me think of selling the bones... that's what Nancy said to us as she was carted off from the scene. And just now in your interview. Something about "selling the bones". And, what's more, today I discovered that a Frenchman has been here—'

'Steady on. I know your family have had beef with the French in the past—'

'Beef? Beef Wellington more like. Waterloo was won for a reason, you know, Andrews, and that reason was Fawcetts. But, anyway, we digress. My friend Maurice, who you met at Aunt Mary's, he saw an acquaintance of his outside Mr Bell's book-shop carrying a package. A certain Pierre Fontaine. Someone Maurice knew to have traded in relics in the past. Catholics, and there are more of them on the Continent than here of course, they love them. Now, it was at Bell's bookshop that I found that anthology, which, of course, had the letter in it. And Fontaine claimed his package was "decorative books", but when, by some coincidence, I used that same ruse to talk to Henry Bell, he said he never sold anything of the sort. So I think they may have been the bones.'

Andrews sighed and scratched his beard. 'So we have one dead verger, and two possible connections to people – this Pierre Fontaine chap and Mr Bell the bookseller – who might be trading human bones. Which is illegal, I might add.'

'Yes, well, that's the French for you. But Maurice Sauvage did point out that the Catholics over there do still put a lot of faith in relics. And a saint like Swithun who has been lost for centuries, well, his bones might raise a pretty penny, or franc, on the black market, don't you think?'

'But what connected the murdered Anthony Preston to them?' Andrews asked.

'That's what you'll have to try to get out of Nancy, but, as you so rightly pointed out, when she said she had no reason, it really did sound like she knew someone else did. And that reason was the bones.'

Andrews closed the folder and let out a deep breath. 'There's a lot of leaps to make there, Miss Fawcett, but I think I follow. Somehow, perhaps as far back as 1910, St Swithun was miraculously found. The discovery was written about in a records book that was then kept safe for nigh on fifteen years, until it was stolen and used to locate the new resting place of St Swithun, for the nefarious reason of selling his bones on the black market on the Continent. Various people – possibly Anthony Preston among them – found out and either he partook in the trade, earning himself a blow to the head for his trouble by a double-crossing partner—'

'Not Nancy then,' Cressida interrupted with a voice full of relief.

'Jury's out, could possibly be Nancy, she still has the fact that she was found with the murder weapon and the body not exactly going for her.'

'Oh, shucks.'

'Or, he was silenced as he had found out their game and was going to report them. Hence why he wrote that letter. Or he might have known who wrote that letter. That's if that letter does indeed relate to selling the bones.'

'I think that's about the long and short of it, yes, Andrews,' Cressida concluded. 'And, for what it's worth, I don't think Nancy was in on it. I think the murderer, the person who most probably also has the bones of St Swithun, if they're not on their way to France already, is still at large. And if they've killed once to keep their secret, then heavens knows, they could kill again.'

'So, you think we have a murderer on the loose in Winchester?' Andrews asked, leaning back in his chair and fixing Cressida with his steely gaze.

Her simple reply was, 'I do, Andrews. Yes.'

21

Cressida was released without charge, on the assurance that she would contribute towards the Metropolitan Police's Benefice Fund to the tune of five pounds, and that she promised not to steal another policeman's helmet ever again.

The air outside the police station had become bitingly cold and she pulled her warm cashmere coat around her and clutched Ruby tight to her chest. A weight in her coat pocket reminded her that she still had Anthony's keys on her, and as she thought, the policeman – Duncan was it? – on the front desk, had assumed they were hers. She patted her pocket and took her bearings.

The daylight had almost faded and the lamps along the old paved and cobbled streets of Winchester were being lit by the lamplighter with his long rod and hook. Cressida shivered as she remembered Nancy's words from this morning before any of this had happened. *The Silent Friar... he's as tall as a lamplighter...*

She watched a little more, transfixed as the man in the long, warm coat, steadily went from lamp to lamp, lighting the gas flame in each one. Then she shook herself out and walked briskly down the steps of the Guildhall and back towards her aunt's house, wondering what admonishments she might face from Aunt Mary if she'd caught wind of her niece's scandalous arrest. Alfred, she assumed, was well established now at the Wykeham Arms, a pint of ale in hand and making friends and affable conversation at the bar.

She sighed. Alfred... she hadn't anticipated him joining her and Dotty on this trip out to the Hampshire countryside, or at least she hadn't until a few days ago when he'd suggested that he 'come along for the ride' too. Ever since their stay in Scotland in the summer, where he'd been lined up as a suitor for some pretty, young heiress, she'd realised that she had some feelings for him. And being that they were capital-F Feelings, she was confused by them. Despite her personal views on marriage, Cressida had been brought up in such a polite society that she realised she couldn't justify a relationship with Alfred outside of the holy bounds of matrimony. She'd flirted with chaps, of course, and indeed she had been temporarily linked to the late Lord Canterbury, who had been good enough to try to win her affection by giving her Ruby. She was the first to admit that she might get carried away with her high kicks and high jinks when she'd had a martini or two, but she wasn't one of those girls who threw her reputation to the wind for a good time. Not often, anyway. But the thing was, she knew deep in her heart that she didn't want just a dalliance, or a tryst, with Alfred. She couldn't bear something merely casual or, worse, fleeting.

'I just don't know how I feel, Rubes,' she confided in her precious pooch. 'On the one hand, he's the most perfect man; but on the other, I've never felt like I've needed or wanted one.'

Ruby snorted in a sort of reply.

'Still, I suppose nothing needs to be decided right at this minute.' Cressida sighed again and walked on, though she had to admit that as she passed the now darkened shop windows and braced herself against the odd squall of leaves that billowed down the covered arch walkways of the ancient city, she found herself more than once or twice thinking of the deep brown eyes, jauntily held pipe and all-round handsomeness of a certain Lord Delafield.

Walking through the maze of old streets, Cressida took the road that would take her closest to the cathedral. From there, she could walk across the small park, through the chestnut trees, back to Cloister Close. She could hear her shoes on the cobbles and the gentle murmur from inns and alehouses as she made her way back, and although the sky was now dark, the city's gas lamps blazed with a comforting light. It was only as the road petered out and became a pathway by the edge of the cathedral green, near the old graveyard, that she felt less confident being out, alone, in the dark. She had been investigating, and she might have ruffled some feathers. Perhaps walking around the city by herself wasn't a sensible idea? Especially if, as she believed, there really was a murderer at large.

Cressida shivered and walked on, leaving the light of the city lanes behind her and plunging herself into the darkness of the green. Light from the houses on Cloister Close beckoned her on, and the cathedral itself was still glowing gently from the lit candles and gas lamps within it. Cloister Close was picture-postcard perfect, with Aunt Mary's house being the jewel among the Georgian and Queen Anne-style buildings. But as Cressida neared it, she remembered the keys that she'd found in the pocket of the verger's robes. She put her hand into her pocket and closed her fingers around them. What had the dean said? *The cathedral owns five and seven Symonds Street...*

She quickly diverted away from the welcoming glow of Priory House and walked in the other direction along the lane, noticing how centuries-old brick walls seemed to hem her in on each side. The narrow, cobbled lane turned sharply and she could well imagine these shadowy corners concealing all sorts of spectral figures. She bent down and picked up Ruby, both for her own comfort and in case the small dog got lost in the gloom.

After a few more yards, the high brick wall on one side ended and gave way to pretty front gardens outside what looked like Tudor almshouses. Cressida peered through the gloaming and saw the house numbers in smart brass numbers on painted doors in their gabled porches. A small gate opened to a path that led from the cobbled road towards numbers five and seven and Cressida, as quietly as possible, opened it and walked towards them.

Although she didn't know which house had belonged to the verger, she could see a light glowing in the front window of number seven, and the curtains were drawn against the darkness outside.

'Number five it is then, Rubes,' she whispered into her pup's ear and approached the door as quietly as possible, not wanting to disturb whoever was in number seven. The dean himself, perhaps, having moved over from the Deanery?

Cressida placed Ruby on the doorstep as she delved a hand into her pocket. She winced as she heard the hard metal of the keys jangle and paused in the darkened porch of number five, waiting to see if anyone had heard her. There was nothing except the hoot of an owl, so Cressida continued and used the glow coming from number seven's windows to see which key might be the most likely contender. Once selected, she fitted it neatly into its slot and carefully, quietly, opened the door to the small, terraced house.

It was pitch-black inside and Cressida feared that turning on a light would alert any passers-by to her presence. She cursed the fact that she didn't have her torch on her, though, as she stood in the darkness of the narrow hallway with the door now closed behind her, any warm glow from the city's street lights gone. She stood still and waited for her heartbeat to calm down and her eyes to acclimatise as best they could. And, gradually, she became aware of what was around her.

The house was modest, and old, with low ceilings and painted panelled walls that were glossy under her fingertips as she reached out to touch them. There was room for a narrow hallway table, however, and she thanked the gods of nosy parkers that, after a quick search, she found a small torch in one of the drawers.

As she switched it on, she took in more of her surroundings. Straight in front of her a staircase led up to the first floor and there was a door to her left, no doubt the mirror image of number seven next door. Beyond the stairs, the passageway led down to a small kitchen and what looked like a dining room at the back of the house.

She flashed the light up the stairs, but, all in all, it looked too dark and foreboding for her initial snoop, so she chose the door to her left and went into the bijou front room. The beam of the torch showed that it was sparsely furnished, with just two armchairs set either side of the fireplace and a sideboard fitted up against the opposite wall.

An old chest sat under the window and Cressida went over to see if it would open. But it was locked and neither of the other keys on the ring fitted it. She swept her torch beam over the room one more time and took in a few other details. The ticking carriage clock on the mantel was the only ornament, save a crucifix hanging on the alcove wall. A couple of watercolour paintings of rural scenes hung on the walls, but that was it.

Ruby had obviously got bored of this room and had toddled off to the next room along the passageway, which Cressida soon found to be a dining room, with a square oak gateleg table in it, surrounded by four oak wheel-back chairs. Again, there were some paintings on the wall and a bookcase full of linen-bound books, but what was most interesting was that open on the dining table was a large piece of paper: fine, thin paper like that a draughtsman used. Cressida peered closer. It was a floor plan, made up of solid black blocks and thinner lines connecting them.

Cressida cast the torch beam over them and focused on the cursive script. *A plan of the crypt of Winchester Cathedral.* Cressida pored over it, and as she did so, she wondered: Had Anthony been studying it before he was murdered in that very same crypt?

A gust of wind blew down the chimney and Ruby snorted and shivered as little dogs do. Cressida bit her lip. It must mean something that Anthony was killed in the crypt while a map of it lay open on his dining table. Evidently it was an important clue, but, even though she was desperate to take it and study it better, she knew she was already pushing Andrews to the limit with her investigation. If he found out she'd let herself into the dead man's house and stolen something that might be a vital clue, well, she might be in line for more than just a five-pound donation to the Metropolitan Police's Benefice Fund.

She looked at it again, trying to take it in. Passing her fingers over it, she followed the steps down to the depths and saw the narrow staircase that led from the northern transept. From there, she saw the horseshoe shape of the crypt where, at the apex, they'd found Anthony's body in front of the altar. She pointed her torch beam at the map and studied it closely.

It couldn't be... could it?

She looked back at the staircase entrance, where a line marked the doorway, and then again at the space behind the altar, where they'd found Nancy kneeling over the body. Cressida gasped, her interior designer's eye for detail once again leading her to spot something anyone else might have missed. The staircase doorway lines, and the lines behind the altar, looked exactly the same.

Could there be a doorway there too?

22

Cressida knew that taking the map would mean having to own up to Andrews, before she was ready, that she had the keys to this house. No, the map should stay here, and it would then be evidence for the police too. Surely they would soon make their way into Anthony's home to investigate. With that decided, she searched through the rest of the house, all the while contemplating the possibility of there being another entrance to the crypt.

There was no way of knowing how old that plan was. Perhaps an old entrance had been bricked up decades ago? She was thinking back to what she'd seen of the crypt's walls in the few minutes she'd been down there that morning, but nothing stood out to her. Though, to be fair, it was understandable that all she could recall was the terrible scene of the dead man and Nancy next to him. She hadn't taken the time to study the stonework behind them.

She crept upstairs, but there was nothing untoward in either of the bedrooms. One had a basin with rudimentary shaving equipment by the side of it. Only one of the rooms had a bed and it was neatly made, with a counterpane folded down around the mattress and the pillow sitting neatly on top of the sheet that was folded over the top of the quilt. Another cross hung above the bed, and there were more watercolours on the wall, but there was nothing else that seemed out of the ordinary for a bachelor clergyman.

With her torch beam leading the way, Cressida headed back downstairs and into the kitchen, which was pristine, if a little dated, and she wondered if the cathedral had updated these houses since the turn of the last century. An old iron stove filled the chimney piece, and the lack of heat from it was noticeable. With the verger dead, of course, there would have been no one to stoke it this afternoon and keep it going. The cast iron ticked occasionally as it cooled. Cressida's torch revealed a sideboard and some shelves, all clean and neatly filled with cups, saucers, a small jug and some side plates.

Cressida stepped back towards the hallway door, then noticed a calendar hanging on the wall. It was flipped over to show the current month and, along with notes regarding which services he needed to take, appointments with parishioners and various clerical meetings, there was a name noted three times a week, every Monday, Wednesday and Friday morning; Nancy Biddle.

Nancy was telling the truth, this is how you met, Cressida thought to herself, flashing her torch around the austere kitchen one more time. *Falling in love over the feather duster…*

With not much more to see in Anthony's cottage, Cressida decided she really must be getting back. She found Ruby patiently waiting on the doormat where she'd last seen her, and as quietly as possible, she let herself out of the house and locked the door again.

As she walked down the pathway, she glanced back to the pair of cottages. Number seven still had a light glowing and, through a chink in the curtain, Cressida could see a familiar figure. Geoffrey Sitwell, the dean, was standing there holding a book in his hands, reading it in front of the fire.

Cressida feared that he might look up and see her, so she walked backwards, disappearing into the darkness of the early evening beyond the cottages' front gate.

Cressida had much on her mind as she walked down the cobbled lane back towards Cloister Close. She could see the welcoming light coming from Aunt Mary's house, and this immediately cheered her up; she did so love her aunt and her inviting, happy home. Not to mention that there was a simply delectable amount of charming fabric samples to flip through, and her mind needed a break from this boggling case. But before she could make a beeline for the blue-painted front door, something caught her eye out in the small park between Cloister Close and the cathedral.

It was a dark figure, a cloaked one at that. Cressida turned and let her eyes adjust to the gloom of the park. She stood stock-still as she saw, picked out by the light of the full moon and the gentle gas lamp glow of the cathedral's windows, a figure that looked altogether like the Silent Friar.

He moved across the grass towards the graveyard and, Nancy had been right, he loomed tall and seemed to float. Cressida could feel her heart pounding and wondered if the Silent Friar could hear it, or sense she was there, watching him – it – cross the graveyard.

An owl hooted high up in the tree and Cressida startled. The Silent Friar stopped and she was sure she could see the cowled hood turn as if to look right at her. No face showed in the dark cavity of hood, nothing.

She held Ruby firm and stood her ground. If he was just a spectre, he would have no fight with the realm of the living. If he were a man after all, as Aunt Mary suspected, then she would fare better facing him head on than turning to flee.

She never had the chance to find out which, as, a second

later, the figure turned back and continued its way through the graveyard. Finally, it paused by what Cressida could just about make out was one of the buttresses. Then, with a strange flash of light, the figure was no more.

Cressida had just got her heartbeat back to a more normal rhythm when a hand clapped her on the shoulder.

She screamed.

23

'What ho, old thing,' the familiarity of the voice calmed Cressida down instantly.

Still, she pressed a hand to her heart to try to slow its beats again. Ruby snuffled and struggled, all these shocks to her mistress obviously not giving her the first-class carrying experience she was used to. She strutted a few yards away, her snubby nose and curly tail both in the air, then sat herself down and stared into the void.

'Alfred, you scared the life out of me.'

'Sorry, Cressy, didn't realise you were so jumpy. Where have you been, by the way? I popped back into see the old skin and blister at your aunt's house and she said you'd been gone for hours.'

'I got myself arrested, Alfred,' Cressida said matter-of-factly, and gave a wry smile as the shock registered on Alfred's face.

'You did what?' Alfred replied and, with a gentle hand on Cressida's back, walked them both towards the soft glow of light in front of the cathedral. 'I need to hear all about this, pronto.'

'I had to find a way to get into the cells and hear what Nancy Biddle had to say for herself. And it seems poor

Andrews has had a telling-off from the powers that be at HQ and shouldn't really be letting me, or any of us, help him so much. So I stole Kirby's helmet, threw it into the road and gave myself up for arrest.'

Alfred's face creased up in laughter. 'Oh Cressy, old thing. That is superb. Reminds me of Harry Bairstow, though he got sent to the beak and given a hefty fine. Still, he was under the influence of some of Alessandro's finest martinis at the time and had been stark naked, so...'

'I can assure you I was fully dressed! And refreshed only by Aunt Mary's tea.' Cressida laughed, relieved that Alfred saw the light-hearted side of most things. 'And thank heavens I was; those cells are as cold as a cocktail shaker. Still, it's that poor dray-horse I feel sorry for, he had to do some nifty dressage as the helmet rolled towards him. But I did get myself into the police station and Andrews relented enough to let me listen in on Nancy's interview.'

'Gosh, didn't she mind you being there?'

'Oh, she didn't know. It involved some Victorian pipework and a rather warm radiator. I'll explain more another time, but the important thing is that Nancy is sticking to her story and claims she entered the crypt just a moment before us. She found her lover prostrate on the altar steps, picked up the murder weapon and then we came upon her.'

'Like the Lady of Shallot,' Alfred said, uncharacteristically poetic all of a sudden, then clamped his teeth down on his pipe. 'And are there any witnesses to corroborate her story? Who saw her enter the crypt just before you did? In fact, did you see her?'

'Only before we entered the cathedral. I saw her running through the graveyard, but I didn't see her enter it...' Cressida paused, thinking of the ghostly figure she'd just seen walking through the very same spot. She clocked the thought, then continued, 'But she said she didn't hold out much hope of anyone spotting her as she says no one ever notices a servant, which I'm inclined to agree with. I must say, scintillating though Jane Austen's grave was, I would have thought I would have noticed her, but, to my shame, I didn't.'

Alfred nodded, then he took his pipe out of his mouth. 'Well, she makes a fair point. Do you remember the thief we had at the Mutton Pie Club? Several cufflinks and some nice tiepins taken from the cloakroom. Caused a right hoo-ha, with various Right Hons and Lord So-and-Sos accusing each other, whereas it was the new footman all the time. None of us suspected him as no one ever noticed he was there. Shameful really.'

'Well, there you go then.' Cressida shrugged. 'But let's hope she's wrong and someone in the cathedral did see her. If we can prove that she was barely down there long enough to say hello, let alone get into a quarrel and kill him, then we're closer to saving her from the noose.'

'Right.' Alfred pulled his coat closer around him and rubbed his hands together to warm them as they both stood there, pondering those words.

There was something else preying on Cressida's mind, though – the little adventure she'd just had in the verger's house. She was desperate to tell Alfred, but hadn't she promised him earlier that she'd only go adventuring with him by her side? He was all for her hot-headed madness, just so long as he was there for the ride... and she hated the thought of disappointing him. No, he could cope without knowing about the map of the crypt just yet. She'd tell him about it later, if it were necessary. But if Alfred did want in on one of her schemes, she had just the plan.

'Tell you what, Alfred, the reason you scared me just now was that I was sure I saw the Silent Friar crossing the graveyard moments ago. And it reminded me of seeing Nancy taking the same route this morning. I wonder if all this "servants aren't noticed" talk – not that I disagree with it, of course – is just cover and that's how she got into the crypt unnoticed, not having to walk down the nave or transepts and all that. I think there might be a door behind one of those buttresses.'

And maybe another one somewhere that leads down to the crypt itself, she thought, though she kept that last bit to herself.

Alfred crossed his arms. 'And don't tell me, you think it'll be a sensible idea to go and have a look for that now, do you?'

'No time like the present, Alf,' Cressida said, raising an eyebrow.

Alfred shook his head. 'Looks like Ruby is already on her way there.' He pointed to where the small dog was nose to the ground, sniffing her way around the side of the cathedral, her little pig-like tail wobbling as she went.

Cressida, living up to her reputation of being rather a hothead at times, followed her little dog, with Alfred, protestations unanswered, following on behind. She reached out a hand to help feel her way as the light dimmed considerably once they were out of the warming glow of the cathedral's west front.

The wind whipped around the side of the cathedral, and Cressida was reminded not only of the story about the cathedral being near collapse at the end of the last century, but also of other falling masonry, and indeed alabaster busts, that she'd come across recently. She pulled her coat closer around her and carried on. Ruby's mushroom-coloured body bobbed along in front of her, the dog's pale coat reflecting the ice-glow of the moon that had now appeared just over the treeline.

Cressida could hear Alfred's footsteps behind her, and it was the only sound now he'd stopped protesting about it being rather late and dark. He knew better than to try to stop Cressida when she had set her mind to something. *One of his best characteristics*, she thought, catching herself smiling just momentarily, before the reality of traipsing through a cold and windy, not to mention dark as the graves themselves, churchyard set back in.

'Found anything yet up ahead?' Alfred called from behind her just as Ruby, still out in front, disappeared from view.

'We might have done, hang on a tick.' Cressida raised a hand to halt Alfred in his progress before he walked into the back of her. She looked to see where Ruby had gone and wasn't surprised to see her pup sitting, globe-like eyes twinkling in the moonlight, at the base of an old wooden door. 'Oh, splendid job, Ruby. You are clever.'

'Ah, a door,' Alfred remarked as he appeared at Cressida's shoulder. 'Are we going in?'

Cressida nodded and reached out for the door handle. It was one of the iron rings, like that of the vestry, and it was cold in her hand as she held it. Very gently, she turned it until she heard a click, and then she paused.

'Alfred, I don't mind if you want to head back. Letting oneself into a cathedral after dark could be frowned upon by certain members of our society.'

'We're not exactly breaking in, old thing. I don't think the magistrates would look too harshly upon us. And anyway...'

'What?'

'You've already been arrested once today. Chances of another run-in with the law are slim. Or so one would hope. Policemen are like lightning; they rarely strike twice.'

Cressida grinned at him. Alfred had a knack of saying just the right thing when she needed to hear it. And with that, she pulled the door open.

24

Their footsteps echoed as they walked across the flagstoned north transept of the cathedral. The old wooden door had brought them into a sort of makeshift scullery, where Cressida presumed the clergy could make themselves a cup of tea and the cleaner could wash out buckets and mops. An oil lamp had been left burning in the room and Cressida had used it to get her bearings out in the corridor beyond. She and Alfred, with Ruby still scuttling along at heel, had made their way out of the scullery and along the corridor, finally emerging into the north transept, where the door to the crypt was.

'Shall we?' whispered Alfred.

'I'll go first,' Cressida said to Alfred's furrowed brow. 'I know the layout better than you, I assume.'

'I suppose so,' huffed Alfred. 'Take that lamp, though. By jiggers, it looks dark down there.' As they descended, he added, 'And wet.'

Cressida was the first one to splash her way into a puddle and was about to pick up Ruby to save her paws from the damp, but the small dog hurried on ahead.

'Fine, Rubes, but don't blame me when your tootsies get chilly.'

'So where did you find the body?' Alfred asked.

'Just along here. The crypt's a horseshoe shape, with a makeshift altar for the Canterbury candles at the very end. I think the central part of it is cordoned off as storage.'

'Storage? What for?'

Cressida smiled at him, their faces looking rather macabre in the cast shadows of the glimmering lamplight. 'Oh, you know, bodies.'

Alfred shook his head at her. 'Honestly, Cressy.'

They splashed on, their footsteps sounding terribly loud in the silence of the crypt. Cressida wished once again she'd had the foresight to bring a pair of her aunt's galoshes with her as she felt the dampness of the crypt's flooding seeping in through the leather of her shoes. She felt guilty, too, for not warning Alfred that his perfectly good pair of brogues might not have been the best shoes for the job either. Still, he hadn't complained, and she had to admit that she admired him even more for it.

'Here it is,' she whispered as they reached the spot, shaking one foot after another in the vain attempt to dry them off.

'Not much to see now,' Alfred said, looking around. One candlestick was on the altar, the other, Cressida assumed, was at the police station as evidence.

'The body was here,' Cressida pointed to the floor, where Ruby was snuffling around. 'And Nancy was just there, kneeling over him.' Cressida felt a shiver across her shoulders as she recounted the scene. 'It really was a shock, Alfred, to see the poor man like that.'

Alfred moved closer and rested a hand on Cressida's arm. 'It must have been—'

He was interrupted by a splashing from Ruby. She had hold

of something in her mouth and was thrashing it around, as much as a small dog could.

'What have you found there, Rubes?' Cressida asked, leaving Alfred's side, having given him the lamp to hold, and quickly taking the few steps between her and her dog. 'What is it? Let it go.'

A long red thread was hanging from Ruby's mouth. At the end of the thread, swinging like a plumb line, and glinting in the light of the oil lamp, was a small golden key.

'By Jove, what has Ruby found now?' Alfred said, bringing the lamp closer.

'A key,' said Cressida, studying it after taking it from the jaws of her tiny hound. 'And a small one at that. Not for a door, I think.' She felt her cheeks flush as she remembered that she'd just let herself in uninvited to Anthony's home. She hoped the dim light of the crypt meant Alfred couldn't see.

'A safety deposit box?' Alfred suggested.

'Possibly, but your average clergyman doesn't tend to have much in the way of a need for a safety deposit box. Still, it could be a box of some sort. A casket maybe?' Cressida thought back to the many mentions of bones, relics and reliquaries. 'Yes, maybe a casket.'

She stood looking at it a while longer and huffed out a breath.

'What is it, Cressy?' Alfred asked.

'I don't know. There's just something else about this key... something pulling like a thread in my mind... Oh, of course!' Cressida all but slapped her forehead. 'A thread. This thread!'

'What on earth do you mean, old thing?'

'This red thread. I found a similar one in the pocket of the verger's spare cassock. I didn't think anything of it at the time as the torn page from the records book seemed so much more interesting. But this thread is identical. So, this key must have belonged to Anthony.'

'Well, there you go. Mission accomplished and clue found,' Alfred said, looking about him as if the darkened crypt of one of the country's oldest cathedrals wasn't exactly the place he'd like to be in right now.

'A clue, yes, perhaps. But what does it tell us?'

'That you're trespassing after hours.'

Cressida almost dropped the key in shock. The voice had come from the far end of the crypt, nearest the door. The light back there was practically non-existent and was made all the more difficult to see into due to the light of their oil lamp.

'I say, who's there?' Alfred asked, his hand over his brow as he tried to peer into the darkness.

A dark, robed figure appeared by degrees, as if gliding over the silvery water of the crypt's floor. Tall, and straight-backed, it took Cressida a while to recognise the precentor coming towards them.

'Is it after hours? I hadn't noticed,' fibbed Cressida, pocketing the key as subtly as she could.

'It is indeed, Miss Fawcett. The cathedral is a house of God, and although it is a place for those who wish to pray at any hour of the day, to those merely wishing to gawp at crime scenes, it is now closed.'

'Of course. Our apologies.' Cressida clicked her fingers for Ruby, and Alfred came to heel too. 'We'll be off. Sorry.'

'Yes, apologies, old chap,' Alfred added, and followed Cressida out of the crypt.

The door to the scullery was now locked, so Cressida turned the oil lamp off and placed it on one of the stone steps nearest the door. Then she and Alfred, with Ruby leaving little wet paw prints after them, walked the length of the nave towards the west door. All the while, Cressida kept her hand on the small key in her pocket.

A clue indeed.

For she had a hunch that this key would fit into a casket. And she'd bet her Bugatti on the fact that the casket contained St Swithun's bones... And, more importantly, it might even lead her to the very unspectral face of Anthony's murderer.

25

Alfred left Cressida at the door of Priory House, and although a part of her was sad to see him walk off into the dark lane and back towards the Wykeham Arms, she was also immensely relieved to walk into her aunt's warm and welcoming hallway. However, if there was any evidence needed that society would crumble come any sort of revolution, the hallway was it. Even her ever-practical aunt, who usually had a backup plan for most outcomes and occasions, was suffering from the lack of a domestic servant in the house. Nancy's absence was notable from the pile of coats on the stairs, and the hats and gloves flung in all directions. The marble bust that had been home to Maurice's hat, now wore what looked like Dotty's scarf and Cressida's own driving goggles.

'For a muse, you don't look much amused,' Cressida muttered as she unbuttoned her coat. Her mind was fixed on the key she'd just found, and the possibility of a secret door behind the altar, which she may have discovered if the precentor had not disturbed them.

'There you are!' cried Dotty, who came down the stairs as Cressida was eyeing up the heap of coats and wondering where best to fling hers. 'Where have you been? Have you eaten? It's past eight o'clock! And why are your feet so wet? And Ruby...' Dotty bent down and scooped up Ruby, who settled into her arms.

'Well, I got arrested, then—'

'Pardon?' Dotty exclaimed. 'And why do I worry that being arrested is only the *first* thing on your list?'

'Let me get these damp shoes off and warm up by the fire and I'll tell you all about it. Assuming there is a fire without Nancy here to lay one?'

'Well, that's a story in itself, Cressy. Your aunt and I have been scratching our heads about how to do it, only knowing that logs are part of the equation, as is a match, though after our twentieth strike, we rather thought we were doing it wrong. Then your aunt remembered there was something called kindling that should have gone in first, so we tried again, and hey presto.' Dotty showed Cressida the roaring fire in the parlour's grate, and Cressida smiled at it and the proud grin on Dotty's face.

'It's magnificent, chum. The chief scout himself couldn't be prouder.'

Cressida sat herself down by the flames and set about recounting to Dotty what had happened that afternoon, from her arrest and the interview she had overheard with Nancy, to the adventure in the crypt. She decided to leave out the part about her letting herself into the verger's house, not because she wouldn't appreciate Dotty's angle on things, but she thought it rather unfair to tell Dotty when she hadn't told Alfred. Also, there was a small voice in the back of her mind that reminded her that, although her closest friends were very understanding about her investigations, they might take a rummier view of breaking and entering. So, she finished her tale instead by fishing the key on the red thread out of her pocket, and she passed it to Dot to look at.

'And so here it is. Our most recent clue, but, as Alfred said, it doesn't tell us much on its own. Though I'm fairly sure there's a casket, perhaps one full of bones, that this will fit.'

Cressida said the last bit with a certain relish, and Dotty blanched at the mention of bones. Still, she rallied and made a suggestion of her own.

'Can we make a list of all the clues and suspects, do you think? I know you're awfully good at keeping everything in your head, but I like to see it written down on paper. Helps me focus.'

Cressida grinned at her friend. It wasn't so long ago that Dotty had been wary of Cressida investigating murders; but now she was reading detective novels and getting stuck in.

With renewed energy, Cressida pulled herself up from her seat by the fireside and found some writing paper in her aunt's desk, plus a stubby pencil that looked like it had been rescued from down the side of the sofa many years ago.

'Here you go, Dot, and what a good idea. I'll start... there was the fact we found Anthony dead, with Nancy, my aunt's maid, standing over him with a candlestick.'

'Which looked bad for her—'

'Worse for him.'

'Naturally,' Dotty rolled her eyes. 'But it looked like an open-and-shut case, with Nancy in the frame for murder.'

'But I didn't believe she had a motive, and neither did Aunt M. She was so upset.' Cressida remembered the tears she'd overheard in the police station too. 'So upset.'

'And claimed she was innocent, which is what we really have to work with,' Dotty said as she scribbled down some thoughts. 'You said you overheard her say—'

'Not just overheard, she said it to us, to me and Aunt M, as if we'd be the only ones who'd understand. She said he was murdered by someone because of the bones. And more than that; selling the bones.'

'Right.' Dotty let her tongue slip out of the corner of her mouth as she wrote it all down.

'Then I found that torn-out page from one of the cathedral's record books, and a thin red thread, in Anthony's spare robe's pocket.' She hated not telling Dotty about the keys to the verger's house, but, luckily, Dotty was busy scrawling a large connecting line from what she'd written to the next sentence.

'Which you think links it to the key you just found in the crypt, where Anthony was murdered?'

'Yes, which, to my mind, means Anthony once had that key in his pocket too. So, it was his key. Or at least he had it for the time being. And it connects that key to what was written on that torn page of the record book.'

'Which was all about how St Swithun's bones had actually been unearthed after hundreds of years during the excavations of 1910. Therefore linking the key to the bones, hence why you think it's a key for a casket.' Dotty completed the thought process.

'Exactly, chum. Now let's not forget the letter I found in that poetry anthology, a book that had once belonged to Clara Sitwell – the late Clara Sitwell at that. That letter asked someone to stop doing what they had set out to do, that thing being ungodly and immoral, and not to mention, illegal. So, it's not a leap to think it relates to the selling of bones too.'

'Which all backs up Nancy's claim that Anthony was murdered because of this racket, not due to some lovers' tiff between the two of them,' Dotty finished off.

Cressida was desperate to tell her about the plan of the crypt she'd found in Anthony's house, especially while they were on this roll, but instead she suggested they look at the people they'd met. 'So, on to the suspects. First we have Nancy. Prime suspect in many ways, but also someone who we think has no motive. In fact, the very opposite as she now has no prospects, whereas marrying a nice clergyman would have made her life so much easier.'

'There's the dean himself,' posed Dotty.

'He does have a dead wife, and Alfred and I overheard Mrs Ainsworth saying something about "maybe he killed her" when we walked past her, but it could have been about something wholly unconnected. Plus, of course, Mr Sitwell was with me and Aunt M for a good hour before we discovered the body. And Anthony had clearly only just died, his blood was still seeping... well, I won't get graphic. But it puts the dean in the clear. He couldn't have done it. I'm his alibi!'

'Right, good point. So, then you saw the archivist, a Mr Flint,' Dotty marked his name down.

'Yes, as he'd been seen having an argument with Anthony quite recently. But he told me what the argument was about – a padlock, of all things! But it was that lack of a decent lock that had allowed the archive to be broken into and the 1910 record to be stolen – the book I think that torn page came from.'

'Which is now in police custody. Along with the letter and the poetry anthology.' Dotty dotted some letters and made some more connecting lines.

'Quite. Our Mr Flint wasn't particularly helpful, and he did argue with Anthony. He really seemed to love the archive. Aunt Mary said that the late Mrs Sitwell had helped him organise it all, and that she had been devastated when it was ransacked, which was only a few days before her death.'

'Poor thing. Drowned too. Ghastly,' noted Dotty.

'But Mr Flint told me that the bookseller, Mr Bell, had also been seen having a heated conversation with Anthony, and I must say he was a far more sinister figure than Mr Flint, when Alfred and I went to see him.'

'Why so? I seem to remember him, from our past visits here, as being rather a jovial chap.'

'I think anyone is when they see you walk into a bookshop,

chum. But he wasn't very forthcoming with us. He lied about the origin of the poetry book—'

'Allegedly. As discussed, it might have gone to auction, having come from Clara's collection,' pointed out Dotty.

'True, but it's unlikely poor, grieving Mr Sitwell would go all the way to Billingshurst to auction off his wife's old books. And then, of course, Maurice saw the shady Pierre Fontaine leaving his shop, having bought something that I know for a fact that Bell doesn't sell, namely books for mere decorative purposes.'

'I'll add that French chap to the list of suspects too. From what Maurice was saying, he's a bit sinister.'

'Speaking of sinister, there's Michael, the precentor. He just sort of looms, though Aunt M says he's married with two small boys. He's soon to move into the Deanery, she seemed to think he's quite the family man.'

'So if he had a motive for anything, it would be bumping off the dean, so he could move into the Deanery,' Dotty scratched her head. 'But it doesn't really give him one for killing the verger.'

Cressida furrowed her brow. Something had clicked then, but she didn't know what. She turned back to Dotty. 'So, is that all of it now? The precentor, Flint, Bell; none of them have alibis, as far as we know, though their motives are scant at best. This Fontaine chap seems to be the most obvious, if it is about selling relics—'

'And Nancy is still the one who was seen brandishing the murder weapon at the crime scene,' Dotty reminded her.

'Yes.' Cressida turned the small gold key over in her hand. 'If only I could find the casket this fits into.'

'Until then, will you give it to Andrews?' Dotty asked.

'Maybe. I suppose I should. But I'm worried that this afternoon's grace might have been a swansong for us. Someone high up, a Sir Mountjoy or something, has rather put the boot in and told Andrews that I shouldn't be helping him.'

'Kingsley Mountjoy?' Dotty looked up from her note-taking in surprise.

'Yes, that's the chap. Know him?'

'Rather. He's my uncle. By marriage, of course. To Mama's sister, Aunt Fiona. How rummy though that he doesn't want you investigating.'

'I would say it runs in the family, Dot, but you've got quite into it all this time.' Cressida raised an eyebrow at her friend.

'I only didn't want you investigating when alabaster busts were being hurled at you, or coshes aimed at your head. There's a difference to facing down a murderer on a speeding train or by the edge of a cliff, to here in Winchester. I feel safer here with the local constabulary out in force and your aunt's beautiful house to stay in. Tell you what' – she leaned forward over her pad of paper – 'I could ask Mama to have a word with Uncle Kingsley. She'd do anything for you after you found her diamonds.'

Cressida smiled. 'Would you, Dot? That would be simply marvellous.'

'Of course. Though, at the first gun that gets waved at you, I'm calling it all off.' Dotty smiled at her friend and threw a small cushion at her, then promptly sat more upright and pushed her glasses back up her nose.

At the very moment that Cressida had aimed the cushion back at her friend, Aunt Mary walked in.

'Oh, Cressida dear, really? What have you been doing? And where are your manners. Poor Dorothy here has almost single-handedly started that fire for us, and I don't know what I would have done without her.'

'Sorry, Aunt Mary.' Cressida stood up and gave her aunt a peck on the cheek. 'And sorry I've been out since teatime. Any luck with The Protocol?'

'No. Oh dear. I do miss Nancy. She'd only been here a short time and she'd already made herself indispensable. Better than Elspeth, who was three times as old and three times as slow at everything. Nancy, in a matter of a week or so, had sorted out my unused clothes and whisked them away, tallied up exactly which dishes I rarely use and placed some of your uncles' old suits in bags ready to be donated to charities. And there was a day that I walked into the kitchen and there on the table was all the silver, beautifully polished and catalogued. Said she was getting ahead before entertaining season, which was so thoughtful of her. I can see why Clara spoke so highly of her... most of the time, anyway.'

'Most of the time?' Cressida asked, sensing there was something more to that.

'Oh, only that if there was ever someone who was constantly active and determined to just get things done, it was Clara. Hard to keep up with, even for a maid as full of vim as Nancy. Poor Clara. Always had something to do, somewhere to be. She'll hate being dead.'

The rest of the evening passed pleasantly with the three women – four, if Ruby was counted – taking a light supper in the dining room, pre-prepared by Cook so that it was easy for the ladies to serve themselves. Aunt Mary apologised each time a potato had to be taken from a dish for the lack of a servant, until Cressida told her that it really wasn't a problem and in fact some of the very smart houses in London had done away with evening staff too. Dotty raised an eyebrow at this fib, but it pleased Aunt Mary, so she let it go with just a small kick under the table aimed at her lying friend's shin.

They then returned to the parlour, where the fire had burnt down to the embers, though it was easier to revive it than to start one afresh in the drawing room. Cressida was finally able to sit her aunt down and look through the samples that Maurice had bought. By the fire, she and Aunt Mary scrutinised the paisley prints, floral chintzes and lushly shimmering silks and Aunt Mary begrudgingly agreed that many of them – in fact almost all of them – would be a better match for her elegant parlour than the "really quite jazzy" wall coverings she'd seen at Lady Silverton's new modern place down in Sandbanks.

'We had a wonderful walk along the sands and took that chain ferry over to the other side of the bay where Peter Langton – you remember him, the one with the florid face and three boats – well, he laid on a champagne lunch for us. Luckily I'd packed sandwiches as he'd quite forgotten the lunch part. Also Mousey Silverton, you remember her – married to the chap with one leg and a penchant for watercolours – well, she wanted to go sea bird spotting, and luckily I'd brought my binoculars, though it turned out she mistook the sign at one of the beaches for meaning something quite different and got chased back to the main road by a man in the altogether. Naturists, you see, not naturalists. Anyway, she recovered from it all on this rather lovely, very modern chaise, you see, and that's when I first realised I liked the idea of the Nouveau style. Though I promised Mouse I wouldn't use any pattern with a, well you know, on it, lest it give her a funny turn.'

Cressida had listened in stunned awe as this story was told. No wonder her aunt had survived widowhood so well since Uncle Roly had died; she had a way of teaming her eminent practicality with her innate sense of fun. A role model indeed for a well-connected, well-off, single woman.

After they'd looked through a few more samples, Aunt Mary finally agreed that perhaps the orchid pattern was a no-go. Cressida tidied the samples away and Dotty told them all about the most recent detective novel she'd been reading. She had just got to the bit where a perpetrator had used lemon juice as a form of invisible ink, when a sharp knocking at the door startled them all.

Once again, a few moments passed before Aunt Mary rose from her seat with a 'bother it' and went to answer the door herself.

'Who can it be at this hour?' asked Dotty, peering at the carriage clock on the mantel that had just struck ten o'clock.

Cressida shrugged and strained her ears. She could hear Aunt Mary's voice but couldn't make out the person at the door. She got up and walked towards the window, pulling back the curtain to see who it was.

'Anyone we know?' Dotty asked, knowing exactly what Cressida was up to.

'Hard to see. But no, I don't think so. Oh, he's off.' She moved away from the curtain and let it close as Aunt Mary walked back into the room, her face pale and her countenance sombre.

'What is it, Aunt M?' Cressida asked, crossing the room swiftly to stand next to her, her hand on her arm.

'Terrible news.' Aunt Mary took a deep breath and ran her fingers over the string of pearls at her neck. 'I can't sugar-coat this, I'm afraid. I'll just out and say it. There's been another murder.'

Dotty gasped and Cressida closed her eyes and shook her head. 'Oh dear. Oh no.'

'It gets worse,' continued Aunt Mary. 'It happened just up the road here. Some sort of fight at the Wykeham Arms. Knives drawn.'

'Where Alfred is... is he...?' Cressida said, her eyes darting to where Dotty was sitting, speechless.

Aunt Mary steeled herself and carried on. 'A man was stabbed and died at the scene.'

'Who was it?' Cressida pushed, her heart thumping, and

was fearful when her aunt shook her hand off her arm and moved closer to the fire.

'I don't know who it was. As in, I don't recognise the name. Only that he died, there on the cobbles, just a few yards down that lane.' She shuddered.

'Do they know who killed him? And why?' Cressida had felt her shoulders unclench. Whoever the poor man had been, at least it hadn't been Alfred.

Aunt Mary looked at Cressida oddly, then sighed. 'No, not why. But as to who, yes, I'm afraid they do.'

'And?' Cressida asked, suddenly feeling like she didn't want to know the answer.

And she was right not to want to know, as Aunt Mary gripped the mantel shelf and answered her, her voice trembling.

'He's been arrested and taken to the station. *He* being our Alfred, Lord Delafield.'

26

'Alfred!' Dotty exclaimed, and Cressida too felt the need to hold onto something, lest her legs collapse beneath her.

Alfred...

Cressida clung onto the mantelpiece, her fingers gripping the sill. The only thing that could persuade her to let go – she wasn't sure at all that she could trust her knees not to buckle beneath her – was the sight of Dotty, pale and frozen to the spot on her chair. She needed her best friend, and Cressida had to be strong for her.

'Oh Dot.' She stumbled across the room and wrapped Dotty up in a hug.

'It can't be him, it can't be!' Dotty sobbed into Cressida's shoulder.

Aunt Mary, white as a sheet too after the terrible news, suggested she go and make some reviving tea and left the two friends together in their shock. It took all the time for her to work out how to light the stove and find the kettle and the tea, not to mention the milk and the tea service, for Cressida and Dotty to let go of each other.

'Oh Cressy, how could anyone think Alfred is a murderer?'

Dotty's voice was barely a whisper, as she finally wiped her eyes and rubbed the teary smears off her glasses.

'Of course he isn't; it doesn't make sense, Dot.' Cressida pulled her sleeve down over the heel of her hand and wiped at her eyes and under her nose. But her shock was subsiding, and her mind was whirring. 'We know Alfred would never do such a thing. I doubt he even owns a knife. His hands are always full of that pipe of his, and he's not likely to have gouged someone to death with it. We need more information. I'm going to go to the station now. Andrews must explain himself to me. Arresting Alfred, indeed! He should know better!'

Cressida had worked herself into quite a head of steam, and had got up to pace around the room when Aunt Mary pushed the door open with her hip and came in holding a tray carrying items that vaguely resembled a tea service.

'I'm afraid I haven't had much luck finding the correct cups and saucers and whatnot,' she said, indicating the lid-less teapot that sat steaming surrounded by a collection comprising one coronation mug, a small finger bowl and a stout pewter tankard. 'So, these will have to do.'

'Thank you, but I won't have any, Aunt Mary,' Cressida said, heading for the door. 'I have to go to the police station immediately and see what all this nonsense is about arresting Alfred.' She stooped to pick up Ruby and handed her to Dotty, yet all Dotty could do was stare into the fire, much to a confused Ruby.

'Cressida dear, at this time of night?' Aunt Mary protested. 'They won't let you see him. And it's late, and with everything that's been going on, well, it isn't safe.'

'This is no time for hand-wringing, Aunt Mary, you of all people should understand that. I have to go. I'm not exactly about to turn in for the night and sleep soundly now, anyway, am I?'

'No, dear. But you must be careful, there are obviously

some very dangerous criminals out there on the streets.' Aunt Mary poured some weak-looking liquid from the lid-less pot into the tankard, added what looked like cream and handed it to a less-than-enthusiastic Dotty.

'I know the way. I'll be quick as anything.'

Aunt Mary frowned at her niece, then stood up and embraced her. 'God bless you, Cressida Fawcett, you are as impetuous as I was at your age. There's a flashlight and some galoshes in the back hall. Take a warmer coat, for heaven's sake, and be careful.'

Cressida hugged her aunt, briefly but tightly, and although she couldn't think of the words to say it, she was grateful for her kindness. She also didn't need to be told twice, and in a few moments, with torch in hand and galoshes on, she was out of the door and back into the cold, crisp night air of Winchester's streets.

Ding, ding, ding... Cressida rang the bell on the reception desk of the police station. Whether it was due to the constant nature of police work, or the fracas that Alfred had obviously been caught up in earlier, the main door to the Guildhall was open and Cressida had managed to get through to the police department. She rang the reception desk bell again, desperate to catch someone's attention.

'Allo, allo, what's this? Can I help you, miss?' A rotund policeman in a smart, if rather taut, uniform appeared from the passageway behind the desk.

Cressida took her finger off the bell. 'Oh, good evening officer, my name's—'

'Miss Fawcett,' Andrews came into view behind the desk sergeant, the most serious look on his face that Cressida had ever seen. 'What are you doing here?'

'Is it true that you've arrested Alfred?' Cressida was blunt and to the point.

Andrews took a deep breath and exhaled before nodding.

'Why, Andrews? What on earth for? You know as well as I do that he would never kill anyone. Who is it anyway, who has died?'

The desk sergeant looked to Andrews. 'Shall I escort this young lady out, sir?'

'No, Duncan. I'll look after her.' Andrews moved from behind the reception desk and placed a hand on her shoulder, guiding her towards some old wooden chairs in the waiting area. 'Come along, Miss Fawcett. Sit yourself down.'

'I can't, Andrews. How can I sit down when my... my friend is wrongly accused like this?' Cressida felt an ache at the back of her throat as she stuttered over describing Alfred. With the first wave of shock and adrenaline over, she knew she was close to tears.

'Please, Miss Fawcett... Cressida. Sit down.' The DCI's hand was firm on her shoulder and Cressida found herself sinking down onto one of the leather seats.

'Andrews, this is all so ridiculous. Why have you arrested Alfred?'

Andrews sat himself down too and placed his hands squarely on his knees in front of him. He looked tired. 'Let me tell you what we know. It might not be easy to hear, but I promise I'll leave nothing out.'

'Thank you, Andrews,' Cressida said, though she found that her voice was no more than a murmur.

'A fight broke out outside the Wykeham Arms just before closing time. It seems a sailor was up from the coast and he had been hitting the local cider hard. He became quite a nuisance, spotted Lord Delafield across the bar and identified him as a member of the upper classes, though I don't believe he used those words. It seems he picked a fight with Lord Delafield, who suggested they take it outside, and Lord Delafield turned the fist fight into something more deadly. Witnesses say he drew a knife and lunged at the sailor, killing him with one blow. The land-lord sent a runner to us and we arrived to find Lord Delafield sparko on the ground too.'

'Sparko? Out for the count? Does he need a doctor?' Cressida asked, pulling her sleeves down over her hands again and wiping away the first of the anticipated tears.

'I don't think there's a medicine out there that can help him. If there were, the pedlars of such a thing would be coining it in.'

'I don't understand, Andrews?'

'He's drunk, Miss Fawcett. As a lord, you might say. It'll take a night in the cells just to sober him up.'

'Oh, Alfred.' Cressida shook her head, then rested it in her hands. Her mind was racing. She still couldn't believe Alfred would get into a fight, let alone pull a knife on an unarmed man. And to do so while so drunk? 'Andrews, can I see him? Can I talk to him, please?'

'Not tonight I'm afraid, Miss Fawcett. You know I'm already sailing close to the wind allowing you to help me with our investigations.' His voice was soft, but Cressida could sense the determination behind it. 'If I'm seen to be letting you in to conflab with a murder suspect, then the boss will give us hell.'

Cressida nodded, crushed and grief-stricken hearing Alfred described as a "murder suspect". She wiped some more tears away.

'Can I ask you something then, Andrews, before I go?'

'Of course, Miss Fawcett, what is it?'

'Who was the witness? Who said Alfred killed the sailor?'

Andrews looked at Cressida, his brow furrowed. After a moment, he replied.

'That's just the thing, Miss Fawcett. Everyone at the Wykeham Arms said it. They all saw him draw that knife.'

27

Cressida had possibly the worst night's sleep – or not sleep – she'd ever had. After running back to Priory House from the police station, with Andrews' words burning in her mind, she had collapsed into bed and sobbed.

That's just the thing, Miss Fawcett. Everyone at the Wykeham Arms said it. They all saw him draw that knife.

It couldn't be true, she had told herself as she lay in bed, drifting between a fretful sleep and sobs. Alfred would never carry a knife, let alone attack an unarmed man. And as for getting riled by jibes from a man unfortunate enough to be born into worse circumstances than his own... well, that wasn't Alfred's style at all. *Noblesse oblige*, that was his motto. Privilege entails responsibility... and more than that; kindness. Alfred would have shaken his hand and bought him another cider. Not suggested a fight. It was one of the things she... yes, she could admit it now, she *loved* about him.

Cressida had tossed and turned so much in the night that Ruby had taken sanctuary under the bed rather than her usual spot beside her. And it was in the first grey light of dawn that she emerged, with Cressida's silk eye mask hooked over an ear, to greet her mistress, who was already standing by the sash window in her pyjamas.

Cressida felt the soft nose of her pup against her ankle and bent down to pick her up, nuzzling her velvety coat as she stared out across the park towards the west front of the cathedral. She usually adored the morning light; she loved the way it dappled over the ceiling in her Chelsea pied-à-terre, reflecting off the River Thames; and usually she admired this autumnal soft light, which caressed the colours in the bedroom in which she stood. But all of that was far from her mind now.

Despite thoughts of Alfred's predicament dominating her reflections and nightmares throughout the night, one other thing had occupied her mind, and it was this that she pondered now. She was sure that she had glimpsed a robed figure, running ahead of her as she'd bolted back to Aunt Mary's after her worrisome talk with Andrews. She'd been too upset to be scared, or to even give it much thought at the time, but now she wondered who it was. The Silent Friar? A clergyman in a hurry?

Or maybe, just maybe, it was the person who had really stabbed the sailor, who had set up Alfred, who had... Her thoughts ran away with her again, and once more she recalled Andrews' words.

They all saw him draw that knife.

She shook her head. She hadn't seen it herself and she would never believe it. But perhaps it would be worthwhile asking around the inn this morning. Someone might have a different story. Someone might be able to stand up for Alfred and get him off this awful charge.

A gust of wind blew through the branches of the great horse chestnuts in the park. A stray bough curled itself onto what looked like a... noose... but the branch swayed again and the ghastly lookalike was gone. Cressida shivered. The downside to her ample experience in solving murder cases was that she knew exactly what happened to murderers.

She was already determined that Nancy would not face the hangman. So, she sure as billy-o couldn't let it happen to Alfred, either.

She had to find evidence that neither of them was guilty. And she had to do it before it was too late.

Washed and dressed, Cressida took Ruby with her on the hunt for breakfast, and was surprised to see Dotty sitting, pale and sullen, at the kitchen table. It was barely past dawn, and Dotty had never been an early riser. No doubt she'd had as rough a night as Cressida had.

As Cressida pulled out a chair, Dotty looked up at her and her face crumpled into tears again.

'Oh Dot.' Cressida left the chair where it was and hugged her friend. After a little while, she pulled back and told her the plan to visit the Wykeham Arms. 'You can come with me, Dot. Dare I say it, seeing the accused's distraught sister might pull some heartstrings. I'm sure someone there will help us. Alfred said the landlord was a jolly sort of chap and most affable. Surely he won't want to see one of his guests – an innocent man at that – be accused of something he didn't do.'

'If you think it'll help?' Dotty whispered, tired from her sobs.

Cressida shrugged. 'I hope so. It's something though, isn't it. We can't just sit here like proverbial lemons and do nothing. You know the old Fawcett family motto—'

'Fortune favours the brave,' Dotty answered.

Cressida shrugged again. 'Yes. Something like that anyway, but more spicy towards the French. Anyway, being brave is the gist of it, and we must be for Alfred's sake.'

Dotty nodded and got up from the table. She was still in her pyjamas, so while she washed and dressed, Cressida found some bread and cheese for her and Ruby's breakfast. The stove had been left to go out, so there was no hot kettle of water for tea, but Cressida didn't mind. She was feeling more positive now, having realised that the landlord of the Wykeham Arms could possibly help. He might be able to shed some light on what had happened, and perhaps before the morning was out, she would get Alfred out of jail.

Unfortunately for Cressida, and Dotty, not to mention Alfred himself, the landlord of the Wykeham Arms was of no help whatsoever.

'Morning, ladies,' he said as he unlocked the door to the pub, after Cressida's hammering on it with her fist had probably woken the whole street. She'd been keen to get inside the inn, not just in her eagerness to speak to the landlord, but also to get Dotty off the cobbled street – the cobbles themselves still being slick with blood from where the sailor had been murdered last night.

The landlord, though amenable once they'd been introduced, had the countenance of a man who was now saddled with more than he'd bargained for, and he told them as much as he brewed a coffee pot in the small bar kitchen.

'I'm not saying I'm not sorry for your situation, or even more so for that poor man who died last night. But, between us, it's me that I'm more vexed for. Police and murders do not bring a good atmosphere to a hostelry, and what with the 'flu a few years ago that did the rounds after the war, and that too and all, well, it's been hard getting staff and punters alike around here. Last thing I need is a reputation for being somewhere unwholesome and dangerous. And your friend can bear that in mind as he thinks about what he's done.'

The landlord's words started a fresh bout of tears in Dotty, which made Cressida frown. She placed Ruby, who had come along for moral support too, on one of the bar stools and clasped her friend's hand while she replied to him, despite his back now being turned as he dealt with the coffee.

'That's just the thing, I'm convinced Alfred wouldn't have done it. He's simply not a violent man.'

The landlord shook his head as he brought the steaming pot out and put it on the bar. As he poured them coffees, he told them what he knew. 'Gentlemen can often – how can I put it delicately to you ladies? – they can often have two sides to their characters. There's the side you see in your fancy drawing rooms and parlours, out at balls and playing whist with your grannies, and then there's the side of them that comes to alehouses, spoils for a fight, gets in there with their fists. Feels something for a change.'

Cressida bit her lip and shook her head. Now she wished Dotty hadn't come and didn't have to hear this – untrue as it no doubt was – about her own brother. But despite her strongest belief that Alfred was innocent, there was something that the landlord said that rang true. Alfred was a member of a gentleman's dining society – the Mutton Pie Club. And hadn't one of the members, only this spring, been a murderer? Not just a member, but one of Alfred's own friends?

Cressida shook that thought out of her mind and took her cup, shifting her weight on the bar stool. Ruby was perched on the one next to her and Dotty on the next one along. They must have looked like the oddest set of drinkers this pub had ever seen.

She looked at the landlord again as he took down a pint glass from a shelf and polished it with the tea towel that had been hanging from his waist.

'You say all that, but did you actually see anything?' she asked, then took a sip of the rich, hot coffee.

His reply was a blow and she clattered her cup back onto its saucer as he spoke.

'Yes, miss, I did. I saw him draw that blade myself.'

28

Cressida let Dotty go, as she slipped off her bar stool and rushed to the lavatories. There was no more consoling she could do at the moment, though she was pleased that Ruby had pined to be let down and had trotted off after Dotty. Hopefully, a tearful face was now buried in rolls of furry puppy fat.

Once Cressida was alone with the landlord, she asked him for more details.

'What blade? Alfred never carried a knife. A pipe, yes, but a knife? No.'

'Well, he had one on him last night. Sat right on that stool there, the one his sister has just left,' the landlord said and pointed to where Dotty had just been sitting, then went back to wiping a glass with his tea towel.

Cressida looked at the stool and the place at the bar, then back to the landlord.

'But what happened exactly? What did the sailor say to him?'

'As I said, miss, these young men can be quite different characters out of the drawing room.'

'Pish posh. Alfred isn't like that at all.'

The landlord just raised an eyebrow, and looked as if he wouldn't be changing his mind any time soon.

Cressida tried again. 'So, what actually happened?'

'A young man came in, drinking heavily. He called your friend some unsavoury names and challenged him to a fight. They took it outside, luckily, though the bar was empty enough. Just a few of the regulars. Still, I wouldn't have wanted that blood in the carpet, bar full of punters or not.'

Cressida furrowed her brow at him. So far this matched what Andrews had told her, but it still didn't make much sense. Andrews had said Alfred was so drunk he could barely stand – so how could he have wielded a knife?

'Had my friend been drinking?' she asked.

'Oh yes. Heavily. Hit the whisky hard, and the beer. Could barely speak.'

'Yet he could speak enough to suggest taking their grievance outside and then have the wits enough to best him in a fight?'

'That's the advantage bringing a knife to a fist fight gives you,' the landlord said, putting another glass back on the shelf. He then exhaled. 'Look, miss, there's not much more I can tell you. Rich bloke, got annoyed, went too far, killed a man. End of.'

Cressida shook her head, despairing. The landlord's testimony was the very opposite of what she'd hoped to hear. And it felt very much like he'd said all he was going to say on the matter. But Dotty was still nowhere to be seen and Cressida wanted to ask him about Anthony Preston too, so she changed tack, hoping the landlord would be more helpful on that matter.

'It seems deaths are all around us at the moment. Did you know Mr Preston, the verger at the cathedral, at all?'

The glass the landlord was wiping cracked in his hand and he swore under his breath before disposing of it and answering Cressida. 'That young man who died in the crypt? Yes, I did. He came in here for an ale or two of an evening.'

'*Died?* Murdered more like,' Cressida ventured.

'And only yesterday too. Two deaths in one day in this small corner of the world. Very strange indeed. Makes you wonder if they're wholly unrelated.' The landlord wiped another glass with his tea towel and put it back up on the shelf behind the bar.

'But of course they are! Alfred wasn't even here yesterday morning... I mean, not that he had anything to do with last night either...' Cressida puffed out her cheeks in exasperation.

The landlord looked at her oddly. 'I know you don't like to think of your friend as being part of anything untoward, miss, but to us he's just another outsider.'

'Another outsider?' Cressida had taken control of herself again.

'Well, you see, the verger had been in here many a time. But, more recently, he had been meeting outsiders here. People I didn't recognise. I felt like he was touting for some kind of business.'

'In what way?' Cressida thought back to what Maurice had said about Pierre Fontaine. The rogue French antiques dealer was definitely high on her list of suspects for Anthony's murder.

The landlord stopped wiping glasses and leaned his elbows on the bar as Cressida moved in to listen. 'Mr Preston used to keep himself to himself. Nice lad, fresh round the gills—'

'I heard he was quite sensitive,' Cressida interjected, and the landlord nodded.

'Yes, sensitive. That's the word. So, he would have an ale, maybe a second. Sometimes he'd be joined by one of the other clergy, but nothing more than that. Then, the other day, he started meeting up with outsiders, French and the like.' He pointed over to a small round table in the corner of the bar. 'There, at that table. That's where they sat whispering to each other.'

'And you think he was doing business with them?' Cressida asked.

'Oh, I know he was,' the landlord replied, rousing Cressida.

'What sort of business was it?' Cressida gripped her coffee cup.

'Bones.'

The landlord's answer chilled Cressida to the core, sending a shiver across her shoulders. Nancy's words came back to her – *selling the bones* – and she thought about the page from the stolen record book mentioning St Swithun. And she remembered, too, how quickly the bookseller, Henry Bell, had leapt to the conclusion that she was talking about selling relics – and that he had had dealings with Pierre Fontaine recently. She must speak to Mr Bell again and see if he had any inkling of what Anthony was up to.

She looked up at the landlord, who had pulled back from leaning on the bar. 'So, you think he was selling relics. St Swithun, I take it?' Cressida asked, hushing her voice, as even suggesting the selling of the saint's bones felt wrong.

The landlord just nodded.

'But why? Why would a man of the Church do something like that?'

'Why does anyone? For the money.' The landlord looked at Cressida, then huffed out a laugh. 'Of course, I'm sure a lady like yourself never has to worry about the pounds, shillings and pence, but the rest of us' – he started wiping the bar with his tea towel as if to make a point – 'all have to find them from somewhere. And Mr Preston was to be wed.'

'To Nancy Biddle,' said Cressida, which elicited a nod from the landlord. She tried to ignore the aspersions he'd cast against her regarding her wealth, but she had to admit he was right. She never needed to worry about where her money came from, and the amount that was deposited in her own checking account at her father's bank was always regular and most generous. She promised herself she'd do more than just give five pounds to the policeman's benevolent fund or whatever when she next could.

The landlord spoke again, bringing her thoughts back to the case in hand. 'And weddings can be expensive, especially when you're only on a clergyman's wage.'

Cressida shrugged.

'Still,' the landlord continued. 'Nancy's a nice girl. If anyone is innocent around here of anything, it's her. She were in here with Anthony just the other day and they looked happy as Larry together, the pair of them. Mark my words, miss.' The landlord leaned on the bar again and Cressida listened in. 'Mark my words. Young Nancy's innocent. She loved that man. Someone else murdered the verger, but it wasn't her.'

'And if it wasn't her?' Cressida asked, as the landlord stood upright again.

'Then that Silent Friar has struck again,' he said mirthlessly.

'Or worse,' Cressida added. 'There's still a very real murderer on the loose.'

29

The landlord just raised his eyebrows at Cressida and carried on wiping glasses. She thought about the bones.

'St Swithun himself... when you think about it, this should be national news. A saint, one of our own English ones, rediscovered after centuries. No wonder the bones are valuable in the wrong hands. I wonder how they never got into the right ones?'

The landlord frowned. 'I wouldn't know, miss. But you're right, those bones would be valuable all right. Valuable enough to kill over, I'm sure.'

Cressida nodded thoughtfully. She wondered if the Frenchman, Pierre Fontaine, was still in town, and asked the landlord if he'd ever stayed at the inn.

'No, miss, I'd have noticed a Frenchie staying here. I suspect he'd be at the Cross Keys or the Chesil. If he's here at all. Trains to Southampton are regular, and if he wanted to go back over to the Continent, he wouldn't have to wait long for a connecting ship.'

Cressida felt deflated. She was running out of leads.

A movement caught her eye and she looked over to where

Dotty was emerging from the lavatory, her eyes red-rimmed and her nose a sort of cherry-red colour, but her back straighter and her hair neatly brushed in its usual bob. Ruby was trotting along at her feet, panting as she kept up.

Cressida popped off her stool and was just about to take Dotty's arm and suggest they leave, when the landlord spoke again.

'Of course, there is someone who might have had a problem with Mr Preston, God rest his soul in peace and all that.'

'Oh yes?'

'That tall fella.'

This didn't narrow things down much. Cressida raised an eyebrow expectantly while the landlord continued.

'Stalks about the place, head of music, I think, over at the cathedral. Moving into the Deanery once his wife has finished with the decorators – you know the one.'

'The precentor? What would he have against the verger?' As Cressida spoke, she remembered how nearby the precentor had been when they'd found the body, and how he'd been so quick to point the finger at Nancy.

'You'll have to ask him yourself, miss, but all I know is that whenever the two of them came in here, there was terse looks and cross words, if you get my gist.'

Cressida thanked him for his time and, with an arm linked with Dotty's and Ruby at their heels, she left the Wykeham Arms, her mind racing. Terse looks and cross words did not a murderer make, but it was another lead. And it seemed more and more likely that Nancy was right. It was something, and someone, connected to selling St Swithun's bones, who was responsible for Anthony's death, not her.

Proving Alfred's innocence was Cressida's priority, but for now she was at a loss as to how to help him, and it seemed likely that if she could get to the bottom of the murder in the crypt, she might find out the truth about what happened last night outside the pub, too. The precentor, with his connections to the cathedral and animosity towards Anthony, well, he would have to be questioned next.

She just hoped that she would get to the bones of the matter before it was too late, for both Nancy and her own dear Alfred.

Cressida and Dotty walked the short distance from the Wykeham Arms back to Priory House in glum silence. Ruby scuttled along next to them, stopping to sniff the kerb every now and again, or chase a skittering leaf. The sky was grey and heavy with autumn clouds and the wind whistled down the narrow street, whipping at their ankles as they walked. Cressida kicked a loose cobblestone, but it was held firmer in its fundament than she had thought and she yelped as her toe took most of the force.

'Oh darn it.' She hopped for a few paces, then felt her shoulders sink as the realisation of Alfred's predicament took centre stage in her mind again. If only Andrews would investigate it properly! Who were these witnesses, exactly? Where was the knife now?

She had another thought too and shared it with Dotty.

'Have you put in that telephone call to your Uncle Kingsley yet, Dot?'

Dotty looked aghast at her friend. 'Don't be vulgar, Cressy. Alfred's fate lies in the balance! I can't be thinking about pulling strings to let you go listening in on police interviews at a time like this.'

'Don't be ticked off, Dot.' Cressida halted their walk and looked earnestly at her friend. 'It's not for me. Your uncle is the head commissioner or whatever of the police force, isn't he? Saying yay or nay to me helping out Andrews isn't the point, it's the fact he should be able to at least get Alfred a fair hearing and as much legal help as he can.'

'Oh, yes.' Dotty was contrite. 'I see what you mean. Sorry, Cressy.'

Cressida squeezed her friend's arm as they walked on. 'No apologies needed, chum. It's a terrible situation. But we will prove him innocent, Dot, there's no two ways about it,' Cressida said confidently.

Confident wasn't how she felt, however, and the thought crossed her mind that both Alfred and Nancy had been caught red-handed. What were the chances, really, of them both being in the wrong place at the wrong time and accused of a vile murder they didn't do? But she had been convinced Nancy was innocent. And she *knew* Alfred was.

She just had to prove it.

Once back at Aunt Mary's house, Dotty had summoned her strength and as soon as they'd walked in the door, she'd put in a telephone call from Aunt Mary's receiver to her mother, both to tell her the distressing news about Alfred and suggest she contact Sir Kingsley Mountjoy as soon as possible.

While Dotty had been doing this, Cressida had sought out the warmth of the fire in the parlour and as she'd stood toasting her chilled hands her mind had whirred. She desperately needed to see Andrews again, and of course she needed to speak to Alfred this morning. But before that, she needed to piece together the clues, if she could call them that, in her mind. So as soon as Dotty came back into the room and sat herself down by the fire, Cressida spoke to her.

'Dot, can I run some ideas past you?'

'Is it about how to help Alfred?' Dotty looked up hopefully from the fire, pushing her glasses back up the bridge of her nose, then resting her hand onto Ruby's tummy. The small pug had been doing what she did best, which was offer comfort to Dotty, and had decided that today's salve to Dotty's wounded soul would be tummy tickles.

'Maybe. There was something that the landlord said about the two murders being connected.'

'But how can they be?' Dotty sat up straighter and Ruby jumped off her lap and nosed herself closer to the fire. 'There's nothing to link them, is there?'

'I don't think so. Apart from the fact that both were "caught red-handed", as they say, at the scene and with the murder weapon.'

'Well, there's been a mistake made about Alfred and that's all there is to it, I'm sure.'

'I quite agree, chum. And I'll convince Andrews to let me see him, he'll have to let me, especially once your Uncle Kingsley gets in touch and agrees that I'm a bona fide visitor and all that. But, in the meantime, what if the landlord is right and there is a connection that we're just not seeing yet? And the thing is, without speaking to Alfred or knowing more about what happened last night, well, we've run out of leads there. But we do have some more avenues we can go down with Nancy's case. And maybe, just maybe, we'll find that link and score a win for Alfred too.'

Dotty shifted in her chair. 'I see your point, Cressy,' she said, readying herself with a push of her glasses. 'Did you speak to the landlord about it while I was... well, while I was indisposed?'

'Yes. And he said he was sure that Anthony was selling relics to Continental types.'

'Catholicism is still the dominant religion in France, of course,' volunteered Dotty. 'So, it would make sense that they would have the market for high church types of things.'

'That's what Maurice said too. Let's assume, safely I hope, that this Pierre Fontaine was definitely the connection to selling bones on the Continent.'

'Yes, all right. Let's suppose that. You said he was seen leaving Mr Bell's lovely bookshop.'

'With a parcel of some kind too. Books, by his own admission, but—'

'But he could be lying,' Dotty said matter-of-factly.

'The landlord also said that he believed Nancy was innocent. Suggested Anthony was no doubt trading a stash of saintly bones to the highest bidder to make more money to pay for their wedding. Which ties in with what Nancy said when she was arrested and later interviewed; that she believed it was Anthony's involvement in the bones that got him killed and it was nothing to do with her. Oh, and interesting point to note, the landlord – I never did catch his name – confirmed they were a couple. He'd seen them in the pub, at the saloon bar. Said they were "happy as Larry".'

'Not very discreet, don't you think? For a couple who didn't want the cathedral community to know about them?'

'Yes, that thought occurred to me too. And he agreed that Anthony was a sensitive soul, almost delicate in nature.'

Dotty took in what Cressida was saying and then turned to look into the fire. After a little while, she turned back and said, 'Would Anthony be involved in selling saints' bones then? A sensitive soul like everyone says he was? A man who didn't like the sound of bells pealing and needed quiet contemplation time... a holy and devout man at that. Do you think he'd be the type to start trading illegally? It seems out of character, as well as being against his faith and against the law.'

Cressida couldn't help but agree with Dotty's opinion. 'There seem to be a few out-of-character things going on around here. Alfred for one, and Anthony Preston, as you say, for selling the bones, potentially. And even Clara Sitwell, going for a swim when she wasn't a good swimmer.'

'And a bookseller selling decorative books to a Frenchman but not to you,' added Dotty.

'Quite. Anyway, the thing I most took away from my chat with the landlord was that the precentor wasn't best pleased with Anthony about something. I think he should be next on my list to question about these bones and the selling thereof. Don't you agree, Dotty?'

'I do, Cressy.' Dotty rubbed her hands up and down her arms to fend off the chill. Then she looked back at her friend. 'And I know that if anyone can find out what's going on, and save Alfred from this miscarriage of justice, it's you, Cressy.'

Cressida felt her nose fizz and a tear creep into the corner of her eye. She hugged her friend and held on to that thought.

I will find out who the murderer – or murderers – are, she assured herself. *I just have to.*

30

Dotty had needed to make some more telephone calls, so Cressida was alone as she walked across the park to the cathedral, except, of course, for Ruby bumping along by her side. She thought of Alfred, who was no doubt feeling the chill of the bare window in his cell. A shiver coursed down her spine, and she wrapped her coat tighter around her and hurried on.

So many thoughts were going through her mind and none of them made sense – especially not Alfred's predicament. But the mystery of Anthony being killed for selling relics was also weighing on her mind. Would a man of the cloth – a sensitive, religious man – really risk eternal damnation by selling St Swithun's bones for money?

The west front of the cathedral loomed up in front of her and Cressida made a beeline for the door. Once inside, she strode down the northern aisle towards the transept in which the mighty organ had been installed. If the head of music was to be found anywhere, it would be there, surely? Cressida, with Ruby bounding along next to her, made short work of the length of the aisle, stepping over Jane Austen's grave as she approached the transept.

'I know you had your worries of the heart, Jane,' Cressida whispered to the long-dead author. 'But at least none of your suitors ever landed themselves in the nick.'

That the organ was in the same part of the cathedral that housed the door down to the crypt wasn't lost on Cressida. Once she was there, however, she was stumped. There was no sign of the precentor and the organ was locked up. The shutters were brought across the keyboard and the entry to the raised platform where the organist usually sat was chained off.

Cressida stuck her hands on her hips. 'Most frustrating, Rubes. And it's not like he doesn't usually just come out of nowhere at me and—'

'Can I help you, Miss Fawcett?' The precentor, as if on cue, loomed out of the shadows and approached her.

'Oh. Just who I was looking for.'

The precentor nodded his head and waited patiently for Cressida to start.

'I'm not sure if you've heard the terrible news about Winchester's most recent murder? I'm very sorry to say that my dear friend, Lord Delafield, is currently in the clink, wrongfully accused of the crime.'

'I am sorry to hear that, Miss Fawcett. And yes, I did hear of it. It doesn't sound like the sort of thing a young gentleman would do at all.'

'Yes!' Cressida agreed, perhaps a little too eagerly, but it was refreshing to finally meet someone around here who didn't seem to think Alfred was a murderer. 'He can't have done it, he's really not the type.'

'And let me guess, others around here are keen to pin the murder on him?' the precentor said, looking through his round-framed glasses and down his long nose at her. Still, his words were balm indeed and for the first time since she'd met him, Cressida started to warm to him.

'Yes, the landlord of the Wykeham Arms for one,' Cressida said, then exhaled out a long sigh.

'I wouldn't believe a word that comes out of that man's mouth. I assume he told you that I wasn't terribly friendly with Preston too? Perhaps he tried to suggest I had something to do with his murder?'

'Y-yes,' Cressida agreed hesitantly. 'How did you know that?'

'Well, for the simple fact that you're here, searching me out. And that I know what he's like.'

'Which is?'

'Have you seen the price of beer in his establishment?' The precentor crossed his arms as if to emphasise his point.

Cressida almost laughed, but kept a straight face. The precentor might have his large nose out of joint about beer prices, but he had been astute enough to guess why she was here.

'I'm not a beer drinker, I'm afraid. But why do you think he'd believe you might know more about Anthony's death?'

Michael unfolded his arms, looked up to the heavens with a sigh, then looked back at Cressida. 'Preston and I came up through Oxford together; we were both theologians at Corpus Christi, so we've known each other a long time. I veered towards the music, whereas he was always more involved with the spiritual side of the Church. Not that I'm not spiritual, but I find my solace in music and feel it brings me closer to God. Preston preferred a quiet church, somewhere more meditative. It's why he retreated down to the crypt, away from the bells and organ music.'

'Was he often in the crypt?' Cressida asked.

'Yes and, of course, with the Canterbury candlesticks on display, he needed to keep an eye on them.'

Cressida's eyes narrowed as she listened, a thought occurring to her. *You would know where to find him if you wanted to kill him... But why would you want to do that?*

'So your views on how your religion should be practised differed, but that's hardly motive...' Cressida looked up to see the precentor's shocked face. 'Sorry, forgive me for thinking out loud, I didn't mean to—'

'Accuse me to my face? I'd rather that than behind my back. And sadly, I think you'll find throughout history a difference in how one practises one's religion is *exactly* what motivates man to kill fellow man. However, in this case, it very much isn't.'

'So why would the landlord of the Wykeham Arms suggest I talk to you?'

The precentor drew himself up to his full height, which must have been well over six foot tall. He peered down at Cressida as if weighing her up. She wondered if this was what it felt like to be a mouse under the talon of an owl and did her best not to react to his gaunt, ghoulish figure. She reminded herself that this man was married and had children, which made her feel better.

Finally, the precentor spoke again.

'It's no secret that Anthony and I disagreed on many things. For instance, we had a heated argument about the organist. I asked him to play during cathedral visiting hours, give the pilgrims and worshippers, even the tourists, something uplifting to listen to while they were here, but Anthony told him to stop.'

'And that upset you?'

'Church hierarchies are complex things, but, that aside, I wasn't expecting Preston to be so angry at the poor organist. It wasn't like him.'

'Out of character?' Cressida thought back to her conversation with Dotty. Had Anthony been acting differently recently too?

'Yes. Quite out of character. But he'd been like that for a

little while. Ever since the robbery at the archive, now I think of it.'

Cressida nodded thoughtfully, and in her pause the precentor continued.

'And yes, we came to blows, metaphorically speaking. Not just about the organist, but Preston was too old-fashioned. He was keeping the cathedral back, stopping it from modernising. Yes, Vaughan Williams might not be to everyone's musical taste, but progress, Miss Fawcett, progress. Preston would have had us back in the eighteenth century, or worse, the sixteenth, and have done with all the stained glass, the saints, the carvings and the music. He was puritanical at heart, I fear.'

Cressida felt that now wasn't the time to mention that Ralph Vaughan Williams, the modernist composer, was one of her neighbours in Chelsea, and instead encouraged Michael to carry on. 'And the pub landlord knew of all this? How?'

'He came across us once when we were at loggerheads, saying things we perhaps did not mean in the heat of the moment. We are both... *were* both... spiritual men, but also passionate about out roles in this beautiful church. That Anthony was so against the music, the bells... it pained me, for as Abbot Suger said back in the twelfth century, "Man may rise to the contemplation of the divine through the senses." We need music. We need art.'

'Well, on that I certainly agree. As a lover of beautiful things too, I can't imagine craving a life of quiet and minimal decoration. I can see you're passionate about your department and the music here in the cathedral, and—'

'Passionate, yes. But I would never have taken mine and Anthony's arguments as far as... well, as far as someone obviously did. But...' the precentor tailed off.

'But what?' Cressida asked.

The precentor inhaled and took himself up to his full height again. He looked as if he was weighing up telling Cressida or not. Then he spoke.

'But there is someone who might have.'

At that moment, a peal of bells rang through the cathedral and the precentor, letting the cacophonous sound wash over him, raised his face to the heavens and closed his eyes.

Cressida had no time for appreciating the sound of the bells now, and hated being left on a cliffhanger, so she pressed him for the answer. 'Who? Who would kill Anthony over a disagreement?'

The precentor lowered his face and met her eyes again, then simply pointed up towards the bell tower.

31

'The head bell-ringer?' Cressida asked, recalling his name. 'Nigel Havering?'

The precentor nodded. 'The very same, yes. I can't say more, to do so would be very unchristian, but whatever feelings I held towards Anthony's lack of musical appreciation, Mr Havering felt it tenfold.'

'He organised that twelve-bell practice just to spite poor Anthony,' Cressida recalled. 'And then didn't even attend it himself.'

'Yesterday morning?' the precentor asked, and Cressida nodded. 'Strange,' he carried on, 'as I did see him here in the cathedral just before we were alerted to Anthony's demise.'

'Where did you see him?' Her interest was piqued.

'Just here by the organ, why?' The precentor looked cautiously at Cressida as if realising that he'd said something incriminating.

'So, both you and Nigel Havering were here, just outside the crypt, around the time that Anthony was killed?' asked Cressida.

The precentor exhaled, then drew himself up again to his

full height. 'I had nothing whatsoever to do with Anthony's death, Miss Fawcett.' He pierced her with his eagle-like eyes again before carrying on. 'Nigel and I agree on many things, but the man has a cruel streak. Ask Judith, she'll tell you.'

'Judith, from the bell-ringers? Aunt Mary's friend?'

'Yes, she is your aunt's friend, isn't she? Helping find her a new maid, I hear.'

'Yes. And speaking of maids, did you see Nancy Biddle enter the crypt? Just before the verger was murdered.' The precentor had just admitted to being right there by the door, surely he must have seen her.

The tall, gaunt man stared down at Cressida before he answered. 'No, I did not. But she was in there, so why does it matter if I saw her or not?'

Cressida thought back to the map, to the possibility of the secret tunnel.

Because if she used a secret passage to enter the crypt, any of you could have done so, too, Cressida thought to herself, though to the precentor she just shrugged and then bade him goodbye as he swept his robe around and strode off into the depths of the retro-choir.

Cressida pondered on what he'd just said. He'd very firmly pointed the finger at Mr Havering, who, by all accounts, might deserve to have a finger pointed at him. But the precentor had also admitted, whether he realised it or not, that he had no alibi for Anthony's murder. He had been near the entrance to the crypt, and although he'd seen Nigel Havering, he didn't say that they'd spoken or that Nigel had seen him.

Perhaps it was time for Nigel Havering to be questioned. And if he couldn't back up the precentor's alibi, then the man who had just pointed his finger at him would climb right up the list of suspects.

Cressida was left standing by the organ in the north transept, very close to the door of the crypt. As keen as she was to meet Nigel Havering and find out a little more about the 'cruel' head bell-ringer, she couldn't help but remember the plan of the crypt she'd found in Anthony's house. She wondered if Andrews was at this very moment having the door lock forced for him as he went about his investigations into the verger's death, or if he were channelling all his investigative skills into proving Alfred innocent instead. In any case, she had a head start on investigating the former... and she truly believed that these two murders, so quick one after the other, must be related. If she could just get to the bottom of who killed Anthony Preston, it might lead her to who had set up Alfred for whatever dastardly reason. She thought all of this as she stared at the old wooden door, daring herself to go down there again and see if there really was a secret second door. She looked down at the small dog, who had been obediently by her side the whole time she'd been quizzing the precentor.

'Ruby, if not now, when?'

She took a deep breath and then walked briskly across, closing the distance between the organ and the crypt in moments. She pushed open the old, rough, wooden door and peered down to the murky depths of the crypt. Morning light was doing its best to penetrate the narrow windows, but it took a while for her eyes to adjust to the gloom. She carefully picked her way down the stone steps and splashed into the first puddle. The noise echoed around her – *splash splosh splash*.

Cressida could feel the damp seeping into her leather shoes again, and tried as much as possible to stick to the flagstones that looked as if they had the shallowest puddles in them. Ruby looked to be doing the same, and hop, skipping and jumping, they both reached the makeshift altar, which was now devoid of candlesticks and golden altar cloth. It was just a table under those trappings and its spindly legs and the varnished wooden top looked out of place down here in the rough-hewn stone of the crypt. Out of place – out of character. The many things that seemed so out of character over the last day or two were fore-most in her mind as she searched the area behind the table.

She tried to recall the map of the crypt she'd seen and the etched line behind these stones. Barely any light reached the curved niche and Cressida thought back to Ayrton Castle, where she'd been this summer. It had been home not only to a murderer, but to secret tunnels that were concealed behind panelling with hidden catches and spring-loaded locks. She shook her head. Those ingenious little catches and springs would do nothing to move tonnes of solid stone.

Then she saw it.

Not solid stone at all, but an expertly painted panel that looked just like stone, especially in this half-light.

'Oh Rubes, jackpot I think,' Cressida whispered, as she ran her fingers around it. Now she'd got her eye in and, more impor-tantly, was feeling the changing textures between real stone and panel, she found a very discreet handle. 'Ouch,' she gasped as she broke her nail against the clasp. It wasn't budging for her; there must be a knack to it. She sucked on her finger and needled the chipped nail shorter with her teeth while she thought.

Nancy could have entered through this passageway. That would explain why nobody saw her go into the crypt.

But then, someone else could have used the hidden passageway to get to Anthony, too.

Someone who knew the cathedral's secrets all too well.

Someone who knew all about the bones. And who was prepared to murder to get their hands on them.

32

Cressida didn't like being beaten by something, but she'd tried all she could to get the secret passage open and couldn't do it. There was obviously a catch or a handle she'd missed, but in some ways, it didn't matter; her point had been proved. There was a secret – and possibly ancient – passage into the crypt.

She hurried out of the crypt, not wanting to be caught investigating down there, and slowed her pace to a more normal speed – one that pugs could more easily keep up with – as she approached the bell tower. She stopped when she reached it, and felt the unexpectedly strong force of a certain pup barrel into the back of her ankles.

'Ruby, I must say, you're a heavier hound than I realised. There are diets I could put you on, you know.'

Ruby snorted as Cressida wrapped her arms around herself and gazed up into the heights of the tower. Bell ropes were hanging down but had been neatly scooped up and clipped to hooks high up on the wall. No one was around. The recent peal that had left the precentor in paroxysms of delight must have been the end to a practice. Even if he had been leading it, Mr Havering was now nowhere to be seen.

Cressida could glean no more of use from the empty space, so she left the cathedral by the main door, wrapping her coat more warmly around her as the sharpness of the chill in the air caught her off guard. She reached down to pick up Ruby, as much to act as a muffler for her hands as to save the small dog from too much walking.

Once upright with Ruby firmly in her arms, Cressida took her bearings. Not just geographically – she knew where she was all right – but figuratively. Where had the last twenty-four hours got her? Two dead bodies, not forgetting mention of a recently departed third. Her aunt's maid, Nancy, arrested for the first murder; that of her fiancé, Anthony Preston, the cathedral's verger. Dear, dear Alfred arrested for the second murder; that of the nameless sailor who had drunkenly insulted him. And the other recent death was Mrs Sitwell, the dean's wife. An accident, apparently, but Cressida couldn't shake the fact that she had been so closely linked to the cathedral community. She had also been the owner of a book of poetry that contained a letter warning someone that they were about to do something immoral and illegal.

And then, of course, there were the mysterious bones of St Swithun. Hidden safely for hundreds of years until they were discovered just over a decade ago, hidden again and now... sold? Who had found them? Was it Anthony? Had he really been so uncharacteristically involved in selling them, despite his religious fervour? Or had he, as Cressida suspected, died protecting them?

Cressida sighed heavily. So many questions. But her most recent lead had been Mr Havering, the supposedly cruel head bell-ringer. Where would she find him now? Without knowing where to begin, she headed back to Priory House. It would be no bad thing to check in on Dotty and hope that she was bearing up under the horrible weight of worrying about her brother. And perhaps with her help, Cressida might be able to untangle this increasingly impossible case.

Moments later, Cressida was unbuttoning her cashmere coat and trying to find a place to leave it in the hall. She chose the newel post at the end of the banisters, as that at least was off the floor, and paused as she tuned in to voices in the parlour. There was a male voice, but not one she knew, and her aunt's. She knocked briefly on the door before letting herself in.

'Cressida dear, do come and sit down. Are you cold? You look pale as anything. Did you just take the one coat out with you this morning? It's perishingly cold. From now until at least mid-March, I never venture out without at least one thermal. Top or bottom, doesn't matter, but at least one.' Her aunt bustled around her and gestured for her to take a seat by the fire.

There was no sign of Dotty and when Cressida asked, Aunt Mary just raised her eyebrows, indicating that Dotty was upstairs.

'Before you go to her though, dear, I'd like you to meet Mr Havering.'

Cressida couldn't believe her luck. It was slightly awkward that she was meeting the person she had been looking for in her aunt's parlour, especially given the sort of questions she wanted to ask him, but it was an opportunity she couldn't miss. Especially when Aunt Mary left the room, muttering something about finding the silver for laying the table for lunch.

'Mr Have-a-ring,' Cressida started and then cursed herself for getting the pronunciation wrong. She was quickly corrected.

'Hay-vering. Like the horse food,' he enunciated, as if it had been said many a time before.

'Of course, I'm so sorry. And I'm Fawcett, like the American for tap. Not fork-it, like some people think.' She gave a nervous sort of laugh, hoping that the ice was at least broken, and she started with her first question. 'What brings you to Aunt Mary's?'

'Ah, well, I'm not sure if you heard about the tragic passing of Clara, the dean's late wife, but because of it we have a position available on our bell-ringing team. I've come cap in hand to ask if your aunt would like to join us.'

'Oh, marvellous,' Cressida said. 'I'm sure she'd love to. We met her friend Judith earlier and she's a bell-ringer – sorry, campanologist.'

Mr Havering's face changed from one of conviviality to utter distaste, a change so quick she hadn't seen one like it since Popsy Farr-Williams mistook a dry gin martini for a very dirty vodka one at her debutant ball. 'That woman,' he spat, which again had been like Popsy Farr-Williams with the brine-infused vodka, 'doesn't know her pulls from her peals. Plus, she'd climb those ropes if she thought they'd get her further up the social ladder. If I could replace her, too, I would.'

Cressida stopped thinking about martinis, as welcome as one would be right now, and appraised Mr Havering's furious expression. *He has a cruel streak*, wasn't that what the precentor had told her? And he was certainly showing it now. The phrase '*replace her, too*' caught in Cressida's mind... *Is this man capable of some very deadly replacing?*

'Oh, why don't you like Mrs Ainsworth? She seemed very passionate about her ringing. Isn't that, at heart, what any hobby should be about?'

'Judith, Clara... busybodying hobbyists are not what campanology needs. Professionalism! Dedication! That's what ringing is all about. Getting most out of the bells, not chinwagging with your friends and thinking it's all jolly holidays and nice noises, with a bit of fruit cake and a moan about the cost of school fees thrown in at the end.'

Cressida thought that was *exactly* what she expected it

would be about, and couldn't see her affable and, above all, practical aunt getting involved in it at all. But she was interested that Clara Sitwell had been.

'Was Clara a good ringer?' she asked, hopefully nonchalantly.

'Better than some, but she spent too long talking, God rest her soul. She was a member of the team for the social side, not the ringing.'

'The precentor said he admired your dedication to the bells.' Cressida tried flattery, it usually worked. She omitted the part where the precentor had dropped Nigel right in the soup for the possible murder of Anthony Preston.

'He did, did he? Well, sound man that. Unlike his wife. Thought he was wavering in his ambition, but that's good, good. Preston out of the way, maybe he'll come round to it all again.'

'His ambition? "Preston out of the way"? What do you mean?'

'Eh?' Havering had been lost in his own thoughts rather and had turned from her to look into the fire. He turned back. 'Oh, nothing, nothing.'

'Do you know anything about the death of Mr Preston, Mr Havering?' Cressida asked, rather pointedly, and hoped her aunt wasn't about to come back in with another of her badly assorted tea trays. But Havering's answer shocked her more than being served tea from a finger bowl.

'Preston's death? Well yes, I do as it happens...'

33

'You know something about Anthony's murder?' Cressida was all ears. 'What, exactly?'

Nigel Havering leaned back in the chair and Cressida felt uneasy about how comfortable he'd made himself in her aunt's house, and more so, in what had been her uncle's favourite chair. Roly Dashwood-Howard (Bart) had died several years ago and, although he'd left Aunt Mary comfortably off and living in this wonderful house, Cressida knew her aunt missed the conviviality of having a partner. It occurred to Cressida, as it never had before, that her aunt was one of the few women who hadn't suffered any loss of independence through marriage. Even her own mother, Mary's sister, Rosamund, had had to give up her life in London when she'd married Cressida's father, and although she'd always say she was happy, and that she adored their life together, it had been on his whim, not hers, that they'd travelled so much. When not in far-flung climes, they lived at Mydenhurst, their rambling Jacobean mansion in Sussex. Aunt Mary, however, had continued all of her hobbies and maintained all of her friendships here in Winchester, and she'd had the gently humorous Roly to share it all with. Cressida identified this as something to be unpacked at a later time, but for now she returned her mind to the case – and the man – at hand.

She narrowed her eyes at Mr Havering, for he was no Roly Dashwood-Howard (Bart), but hoped it just looked like she was interested in what he had to say. As indeed, she was.

He steepled his fingers in front of him as he spoke. 'Strange, don't you think, for a man so well liked to be murdered?'

'I hear that *you* didn't like him much.' Cressida knew this was bold, but Mr Havering irked her and her tolerance for niceties was wearing thin.

'Oh, that's quite true. I had no respect for the man at all. A traditionalist, stuck in the past. Hours he spent in that archive, obsessed with finding relics from the olden days.'

'Relics or *the* relics?' Cressida chose her words carefully, wondering if Mr Havering would catch on.

He certainly did, but it was Cressida who was now put on the spot. 'What do you know about them?'

'Only that there's a rumour that St Swithun's bones were unearthed during the floods of 1910, and that perhaps they've been found again recently, having been lost since the sixteenth century.' Cressida kept her truth to a minimum; there was no need to lie when one could do that. 'But I didn't know that Anthony was "obsessed" with finding them, as you say.'

'Yes.' It was Havering's turn to narrow his eyes. 'Well, he was. Obsessed. To the extent that he'd plead the need for silence as he researched and prayed for divine inspiration in finding them. No doubt it's what got him killed.'

Cressida's mind flashed back to the open plan of the crypt on Preston's dining-room table. Had he been searching for the reliquary in the crypt when he was murdered?

'You think his obsession with these relics was what got him killed? Not a lovers' tiff with Nancy, his fiancée?'

'Fiancée?' Nigel laughed. 'Was she? Well I never. Sly old

dog that Preston. Nice-looking young thing she is too, but a maidservant and a man of the cloth? The thought of it!'

This attitude annoyed Cressida. Why shouldn't Nancy Biddle and Anthony Preston find love, despite their stations in life? That it was laughable in the eyes of someone like Nigel Havering only bothered her more. But she didn't want to get distracted debating the British class system now; Havering had said he believed the verger's passion for the past, and for relics in particular, had got him killed.

'Back to the relics, Mr Havering. Do you think Anthony had found the bones of St Swithun?'

Mr Havering shot her a piercing look. His fingers were still steepled in front of him and the flickering light from the fire lit his face with a devilish glow.

'I think he did, yes. Though he hadn't told anyone yet.'

'How do you know then?' Cressida asked, leaning forward in her own chair.

'I saw him carrying a box, about so big' – he gestured the size of about a shoebox to her – 'furtively down to the crypt.'

'When?'

Havering raised an eyebrow at her and paused. Cressida could see he was relishing this part of the conversation, making him in her eyes just the same as the gossiping busybodies he claimed to loathe. Finally, he replied.

'Why, just yesterday morning. During bell-ringing practice.'

Just before he died... Cressida thought to herself. *If so, why hadn't she seen this box when they'd found the body?*

She kept this thought to herself; she didn't need to share her revelations with Nigel Havering. Instead, she pushed him on his own alibi.

'Bell-ringing practice. The one you organised, I believe, but didn't in fact attend?'

'How do you know that?' His disposition changed again. He

wasn't a man who liked to be challenged, it seemed. But Cressida didn't want to land Judith in it, so she doubled down.

'But it's true? You organised a practice of the twelve-bell peal especially at the time when you knew Anthony would want quiet contemplation, and then didn't even attend it yourself? Why was that?'

The fire either glowed redder or Nigel Havering's face blushed puce. He spluttered out a 'pfft' and 'well, you see', but it was obvious that he didn't like being called out on his petty and spiteful behaviour. But, of course, petty and spiteful behaviour was not murderous behaviour, and so Cressida relaxed her shoulders and smiled at him.

'I'm terribly sorry, Mr Havering, it was really not my business to ask that. How you run your bell-ringing practices is your own affair. I've heard the head campanologist at Westminster often likes to listen to the peal from outside the cathedral to hear the tones better.'

'Quite, quite. Advanced technique. Very modern.'

'That wasn't what you were doing though, was it?'

Havering shuffled in his chair. He was looking more and more uncomfortable as the conversation went on, and Cressida knew she better wind this up quickly before he clammed up altogether, or indeed Aunt Mary appeared with the coffee.

'Even though you weren't in the bell tower, you were still in the cathedral, were you not? You just said you saw Anthony carrying a mysterious box into the crypt.'

Havering nodded. 'If you must know, I wanted to hear how loud the bells were. I wanted to prove to Preston that he was being far too sensitive a sod and that really they weren't all that loud, even on a twelve pull.'

'Oh, they're loud all right. I was there, I heard them,' recalled Cressida, blowing a stray hair out of her eyeline with a puff.

'Well, be that as it may, that's what I was doing there.'

'We were touring the cathedral, Aunty Mary and the dean and I, and I didn't see you.'

'Oh I saw you, all right. I was, ahem, standing slightly concealed.' Havering looked down at his hands. Cressida got the gist, though. He'd been lurking, probably waiting to see poor Mr Preston run out of the crypt, his hands over his ears, pleading for quiet. The precentor had been right, Mr Havering really did have a cruel streak.

Was that all he'd been doing, though? Or did the cruel streak stretch to murder? He had no alibi, except admitting that he had come up with a petty plan to ruin Anthony's quiet contemplation. Despite nodding along to his words, Cressida couldn't discount him from her lists of suspects yet. He was potentially a witness too, and she needed all the information she could get.

'Just one more question, if I may, Mr Havering. From your vantage point, could you see if anyone entered the crypt or not?'

Havering paused and stared into the fire. Then he looked at Cressida. 'You mean after Preston?' He'd twigged instantly what she was asking. 'No, no I didn't. Not since Preston entered just before the practice started. No one else entered or left the crypt until you, your aunt and the dean did.'

'No one? No one at all?' Cressida confirmed.

The head bell-ringer nodded in the affirmative. 'No one.'

Cressida looked at him for a moment longer, then moved her gaze to the flickering flames of the fire. Nancy must have used the secret passage to enter the crypt. There was no other way. And she had seen her head towards the cathedral just before her tour had started.

I thought she was going towards the scullery door that Alfred and I found last night, she thought, tapping a finger on her knee as she thought. *But she must have gone further around the side of the cathedral to where the passage comes out. But why hide that from the police? Surely she should have told Andrews, showed him how easily a murderer could have got in and out without being detected?*

A spark flew from the fireplace and landed on the Persian rug in front of her. Cressida quickly smudged it out with the toe of her shoe before it could burn the fine silk of the carpet. As she did so, another thought came to her: the reason why Nancy hadn't told Andrews about the passageway, and it had nothing to do with people not noticing servants moving among them. She may not have murdered Anthony, but there was something Nancy wasn't telling them. A reason why she didn't want the police knowing about her secret passage.

She's hiding something.

Whether it was the something that had got her fiancé killed, Cressida had to find out.

34

The door to the parlour opened and Aunt Mary came in, carrying with her a tray loaded with various cup-like receptacles and pots of steaming coffee and tea. Dotty followed behind her, and Ruby pricked up her ears and marched over to her second-favourite human.

Poor Dotty looked paler than ever, her bobbed chestnut hair appearing limp rather than having its usual fresh-conker gloss. She said a polite hello to Mr Havering and then took herself off to sit on the chaise longue under the window, where she rather listlessly stared out at the wind whipping through the autumn leaves. Cressida's heart went out to her, and her stomach twisted as she thought of Alfred's plight.

She got up from her seat, excusing herself from Mr Havering, and joined her friend.

'Did you manage to speak to your uncle, Dot?' she asked softly.

'Hmm? Oh, yes. Well, Mama has, I think. They're doing what they can, but Mama says they have to be awfully careful not to be accused of nepotism. The nephew of the police commissioner can't simply get off scot-free, not without it going to trial.' Dotty wiped her eyes with her hanky. 'Oh Cressy, it's all such a mess. I wish we'd never come!'

'I'm so sorry, Dotty. I wish we could wind back the clocks too.'

'If your aunt's maid had never been arrested, then she would have finished making up the spare bedrooms and Alfred could have stayed here with us and none of this would have happened.'

Cressida paused. 'Say that again, chum?'

Dotty looked at her, then said it again. 'I said, if your aunt's maid had never been arrested then she would have made up the spare rooms—'

'And Alfred would have been here with us rather than in the Wykeham Arms,' Cressida said, thinking it over.

'Have you thought of something, Cressy?' Dotty asked hopefully, punctuating her sentences with sniffs and blows of her nose into her handkerchief.

'I thought I had... but no, it's gone. Something you just said, though.' She sighed. 'I don't know, Dot. It's all so confusing. What's more, Mr Havering over there' – she nodded to where the still red-faced man was accepting a utensil jar of coffee from her aunt – 'insists that he saw no one enter the crypt after Mr Preston and before Aunt Mary and I did, or indeed anyone exit it. So, Nancy was lying about being a servant who is never seen and all that. She really didn't enter the crypt during that time. Not by that door anyway.'

'There's another door?' Dotty asked, and Cressida nodded. She'd felt so bad not telling Dotty about her early-evening flit into the verger's house, but she'd kept her in the dark about it long enough. In discreet whispers, Cressida told her friend about letting herself into number five Symonds Street and how she'd found the map of the crypt in the murdered man's home. 'So, you see, I had to check to see if there was another way in. And, by jiggers, I think I found it.'

'You must tell Andrews,' Dotty urged. 'He'll be awfully cross that you haven't. Also, I know that look you just had when I mentioned Nancy and the spare bedrooms. You really do think Alfred's predicament might be linked to the poor verger, don't you?'

'Yes, I do.' Cressida nodded. 'There's something odd about them both being caught red-handed, and of course we know Alfred would do nothing of the sort, so why would he be set up like that? What is his arrest hiding? And for it to happen on the same day as Anthony's murder. I just don't see it as a coincidence.'

'You're right, Cressy – banishing all thoughts of "why would Alfred do it?" as we know he wouldn't, only leaves room for the thought "why would someone claim he did?" and that's a whole different angle on it.'

'Exactly. Let's go and see if Andrews will let us see him now. And I think we should head outside anyway. I don't know about you, but I'm not so fond of the company in here at present.'

'Rather,' Dotty agreed and whipped a small compact mirror out of her handbag and checked her face. 'I'm done with moping, it gets one nowhere. Let's see what we can do to help Alfred.'

A moment later, having turned down the offer of tea from a sugar bowl and an egg coddler respectively, Cressida and Dotty were walking through Winchester's bustling town centre, Ruby darting in and out from around their ankles. In order to present as composed an appearance to Andrews as possible, Cressida had suggested the long way round to the police station so that Dotty's cherry-red nose and red-rimmed eyes had a chance to calm down. Cressida also wanted to have a chance to think through all the things she now knew.

'Dotty, there's something I can't fathom,' Cressida said as they weaved their way through the shoppers and day-trippers towards the market square.

'What is it, Cressy? Apart from how anyone could think Alf could kill someone?'

'Well, it's why Nancy would lie about the secret passageway.'

'What do you mean?' Dotty asked, as she pulled a handkerchief out of her pocket and blew her nose again.

'I think she must have used that secret passage to get in.' They had stopped in front of an antiques shop window, better to bide their time and check their reflections in some of the mirrors on display. Cressida continued: 'But then, why lie about it?'

'Because admitting you know about a secret passage doesn't look good. It would make her seem even more suspicious,' Dotty rather sensibly replied. 'Anyway, just because *you* found one doesn't mean she did. Maybe she's right, she just slipped into the cathedral and the crypt without anyone noticing. Maybe Mr Havering is mistaken. He seems the sort of chap to not notice servants. He really might have not seen her, even though she walked right past him. In any case, the fact you've now unearthed that secret passage brings in so many more "what ifs" that I should imagine any case against Nancy would crumble in court. Especially if she has a decent barrister.'

'Were you reading those detective books again, Dot?' Cressida asked. 'That all sounds like something some fictional detective would say.'

'Yes. I must admit, I'm finding them a good distraction. I only hope we can get Alfred as good as barrister as the poor suspect had in the one I'm reading. He really wiped the floor with the prosecution.'

Cressida was about to comfort her friend and say all sorts of things about top barristers in London that she was sure she knew, when she noticed something in the shop window. 'Dot, look at that.' She pointed to a set of silver teaspoons displayed in their velvet-lined box. Then she cupped her hands over her eyes and leaned in against the window. 'I recognise them.'

'What do you mean, Cressy?' Dotty asked, bending down to pick up Ruby, then passing her to Cressida as she pulled away from the window.

'I recognise them. Well, not them per se, but what's on them. You'll never believe this, but they have the Dashwood-Howard crest on the end.'

35

The bell tinkled and it reminded Cressida of Maurice's disdain for such niceties. She wondered if she should tell him about poor Alfred, and made a note to put in a telephone call to the Liberty exchange when they were back at Aunt Mary's. But, for now, her bloodhound-like nose was drawn to the Dashwood-Howard teaspoons, and, with Ruby clamped under one arm, she reached into the shop window display and picked up the box.

'Can I help you, miss?' the shopkeeper asked from behind a desk, at the back of the dark and overly cluttered antiques shop. Large pieces of what Cressida's mother always called 'brown furniture' filled the floor space, and on top of the tables and on the shelves of the dressers were ceramics and glassware, from vases and cachepots to delicate cranberry-coloured port glasses and tea services. The desk at which the shopkeeper was sitting was at the far end of the shop, where the natural light from the window was replaced by several lamp stands with fringed shades, all no doubt for sale too.

'I'm just interested in these silver spoons, Mr...?' Cressida asked, hoping she sounded bright and breezy. She didn't want to, as Andrews would say, ruffle any more feathers.

'Pargeter,' the shopkeeper replied, as he pulled a pair of pince-nez spectacles from the pocket in his waistcoat and placed them on his nose. He took the box of spoons from Cressida and looked at them. 'Recent acquisition. Bought them from a man who had several other pieces with him.'

'Which were?' Cressida asked, looking around the cluttered shop.

The shopkeeper sighed, opened one of his desk drawers and pulled out a ledger.

Cressida's heart beat faster as she wondered if this might be the stolen record book. But no; it was full of a very different sort of script, with much more modern column headings and the like. It was just the shopkeeper's own private record of what he bought and sold.

He looked at it, licking a finger and turning a page until he came to some quite recent entries. 'Ah, here we are. Teaspoons, six, silver with engraved crest.' He nodded to the box. 'And tea service, Limoges circa 1890. That's on that dresser over there. A silver hairbrush, engraved CT, maker's mark Sheffield, 1897. And silver teapot, London maker's mark, 1790. I thought I might keep that one for myself. Very nice piece.'

'Who was it that sold them to you, Mr Pargeter?' Cressida asked, as Dotty perused the tea service that the shopkeeper had indicated on one of the dressers.

'A Frenchman, by the name of...' He ran his finger along one of the rows and found the entry. 'P. Fontaine.'

'Pierre Fontaine,' Cressida confirmed, whispering it to herself, but the shopkeeper heard.

'Yes, that's right. Pierre. Very bad English. Had to do most of the deal in my schoolboy French. Still, I got good prices for them.' Pargeter looked satisfied.

'These spoons. I believe they're stolen.' As Cressida said this, the countenance of the shopkeeper changed completely.

'Stolen? How dare you! I do not deal in stolen goods. I am a fine art and antiques dealer, not a fence for local thieves.'

'How do you know they're local then?' Cressida asked, and the shopkeeper blushed red. She carried on. 'These spoons have my late uncle's crest on them. They come from my aunt's house, just a few streets away from here. I wonder if, when I tell her to come and see for herself, she might recognise her tea service and silver teapot too.'

'It would explain her serving us tea in egg cups recently,' Dotty piped up from over by the dresser, gently putting one of the delicate china teacups down. 'I'm sure I've been served tea by your aunt in these before.'

Both Cressida and Dotty's eyes, and two more frog-like ones from Ruby, stared at the shopkeeper, who ahemmed and made a show of closing his accounts book and putting it back in his drawer.

'All I can say is that it's your aunt's business if she's selling off the family heirlooms. You might want to check to see if that's the case before accusing innocent shopkeepers of fencing stolen goods.'

'I will,' Cressida said, affirmatively. 'And when she says she hasn't, I'll be back here with the police. You have been warned. And as for Pierre Fontaine, well, he's a known rogue and not someone you should be buying from.' Cressida held Ruby firm, despite the dog's squirming. 'Come on, Dotty, let's leave this chap to stew in his own juice for a little while.'

'Yes, the police are expecting us,' Dotty said, quite innocently, but it made the shopkeeper blush a deeper shade of crimson. Cressida saw this and played on it.

'Yes, they are. And they'll be very interested in what we've found out.'

'Wait, stop!' The shopkeeper stood up from behind his desk

as they turned to leave. 'Please don't report me to the police. I bought those items in good faith. But yes, I have heard on the grapevine that some thieves have been operating locally. That's why I felt better buying from a Frenchman. It seemed less likely that he'd be the local thief.'

'Did he say what he was in town for? And why he had English silver on him?'

'No... though he did mention that he was on his way to Henry Bell, the bookseller. I got the impression that he knew him quite well. But I promise you, I didn't know those items were stolen. I can sell them back to your aunt at a very reasonable price. Cost, even.'

Cressida just glared at him. 'If we find out that that tea service and teapot are hers, along with these spoons, which I'll take now, thank you very much, you'll be packaging them and delivering them to Priory House at no charge at all.'

'Priory House, did you say?' The antiques dealer furrowed his brow. 'On Cloister Close?'

'Yes, why? Does that ring a bell?'

'Yes: those local thieves I've heard rumours about. One of the other dealers, John Healy over on Archery Lane, well, he said something about a house clearance from Priory House.'

'House clearance?' Cressida asked, more than intrigued.

'Yes, a house clearance. After a death.'

'I can assure you that my aunt is still very much alive.'

The shopkeeper shrugged, and with that, Cressida and Dotty left the antiques dealer in his cluttered shop, and with silver teaspoons and small pug held tightly, they walked towards the Guildhall, and towards Alfred in the cells.

36

'That gave me the chills.' Cressida gripped Dotty's arm as they upped their pace along the market-stall-lined street towards the Guildhall. 'What Mr Pargeter said about my aunt and a house clearance.'

'Yes, it was frightfully odd. A mistake though, of course. Gossip and whispers have a habit of changing completely as they're passed around from person to person. Not to mention wishful thinking on someone's part.'

'I hope no one wishes my aunt were dead!' Cressida stopped suddenly and Dotty gave a yelp as she was pulled back by her arm.

'Of course, no one wants your aunt dead, Cressy. That's not what I meant at all. Just that it might be wishful thinking on some dealer's part to want to get into Priory House for all the lovely antiques. So, a rumour that might have started out as "wouldn't it be nice if perhaps once Lady Dashwood-Howard is no longer with us, God rest her soul, we're the dealers put in charge of the house clearance" very quickly becomes "there's going to be a house clearance at Priory House".'

'Hmm.' Cressida slowly started walking again. 'I'm not

convinced, Dotty, but thank you. It eases the mind a little to know there might be some other explanation. And speaking of explanations, I've been thinking about the bits of evidence we've found in the verger's murder case.'

'Oh yes?' Dotty asked.

'It occurred to me when I saw Mr Pargeter run his finger over his accounts book. And I thought, if only we knew more about that page from the records book I found in Anthony's robe pocket. And the letter I found in the poetry book.'

'Perhaps also the handwritten dedication in the front of the anthology? Oh, hold on a tick, Cressy.' It was Dotty's turn to stop walking suddenly this time and, in a similar way, Cressida found herself being pulled backwards as Dotty fished around in her handbag.

Cressida had always thought Dotty's handbag was inordinately large, and knew it to usually contain various items, from handkerchiefs to boiled sweets. Once, there was even a bag of acorns in it, and Cressida had never got to the bottom of that one. Now, however, Dotty pulled out one of her detective fiction books.

'I knew I'd heard about it, or read about it, recently,' Dot said as she clamped her bag under her arm and flicked through the pages of the book. 'Here in this novel, the detective uses a handwriting specialist; someone who can match writing from the same person, and more than that, even work out the person's personality from their handwriting. Isn't that interesting?'

'The first bit, yes. The second, I'm sure is bunkum, but you're right, Dot. We should ask Andrews to get the writing analysed. See if we can match the letter hand to anyone else's around here. And we should check the writing in the cathedral archive books and see who wrote about St Swithun's bones resurfacing.'

'Spiffing idea, Cressy,' Dotty agreed, and they walked on through the market square towards the Guildhall. The pair of them, and Ruby, who had been happily toddling along in their wake, were brought up rather abruptly when Cressida recognised someone.

'Dot, don't look now, but isn't that Aunt Mary's friend, Judith Ainsworth? There, talking to... Oh my, definitely don't look now, but she's talking to Mr Bell, the bookseller.'

Dotty did her best impression of looking into a shop window, hand cupped to her brow, while subtly looking over. 'He's changed a little since I last saw him, but you're right, that's him and definitely Mrs Ainsworth, holding a book. Let's get closer and see what we can hear.'

'Dotty, head for that bench,' Cressida whispered, and they both walked as quietly as possible over the cobbles to a seat that was just behind where Mrs Ainsworth and Mr Bell were talking. Sitting down, they tried to catch what the pair were saying.

'... Are there any more like this... Isn't it a sign he...' The words came from Mrs Ainsworth but were too caught in the wind to be intelligible.

'... No I don't think... Why would he... Not for...' the bookseller replied, equally as disjointedly.

'... But her books... Soon after she...'

'... The man has every right... Grieve like that... Moving out...'

'... Ridiculous... Every last one gone... Not the done thing...'

Dotty sighed and leaned over to whisper at Cressida. 'It's very hard to make out what they're saying.'

'I know, the dratted breeze keeps taking their words away. But they're not agreeing, that's for sure. It seems Mrs Ainsworth is angry about something.'

'That book she's holding. It sounded to me like she was asking if there were more like it, but I don't think she really wanted the answer to be yes. Perhaps she—'

'Ssh, Dot, she's coming over.' Cressida hushed her friend as

Mrs Ainsworth noticed them and, having bid what looked like a terse farewell to the bookseller, started to walk towards them.

'Good day, Miss Fawcett, Lady Dorothy,' she said, then paused as she shoved the book she was holding into her pocket. 'Lady Dorothy, I heard about your brother. For what it's worth, I don't believe he'd have anything to do with it.'

'Thank you, Mrs Ainsworth,' Dotty humbly replied. 'For what it's worth, nor do I.'

'I see you know Mr Bell?' Cressida filled in the silence.

'That charlatan,' she almost spat out the words. 'Claims to know the provenance of all his books. Well, I'm sure he does, but he lies about them too.'

This sounded awfully familiar to Cressida, and she was intrigued. 'Go on?' she prompted.

Mrs Ainsworth didn't need much prompting. She patted her pocket. 'He said this book was from a dealer he'd come across in Kent, but I recognise it as one of Clara Sitwell's. You see, she and I were great friends, and I miss her terribly. So, I got the notion into my head to visit Bell and see if he had any copies of the books that she and I used to enjoy. She often lent me her volumes on poetry, and I was always a great admirer of Tennyson. I was sure Bell would have some of his collected works and I thought I'd treat myself to a volume in Clara's memory. Well, to go there and find just the volume I was after was one thing, but to then recognise it as Clara's *actual* copy was quite another!'

'How do you know it's hers?' asked Dotty.

Judith Ainsworth pulled the book out of her jacket pocket and opened it. Cressida had expected to see something similar to the dedication in the poetry anthology, so was surprised when she saw something else entirely.

'This jam stain here.' Mrs Ainsworth pointed to a dark purple mark across the first stanza of 'The Lady of Shallot'. 'Clara dropped her scone when we were reading it to each other. I remember it clear as day. She had just read the lines, "Willows whiten, aspens shiver; the sunbeam showers break and quiver," when the scone she was holding broke in two and half fell onto the page.'

'And Mr Bell denied it was hers?' Cressida pushed on.

'He did indeed. Said it was from Kent and denied that any of his books had come from the Deanery. Until I showed him the jam stain and told him that story. Then suddenly he changed his tune and admitted it and said why shouldn't the dean get rid of his late wife's books.'

'I wonder why he felt the need to lie about it?' Cressida asked.

'This is precisely what I asked,' Mrs Ainsworth continued. 'He said he was respecting the dean's privacy. His right to divest himself of his wife's books without the whole cathedral knowing about it.'

'I can see his point, I suppose,' Cressida admitted begrudgingly. 'I hear the dean has moved to a much smaller house on Symonds Street now, so perhaps he doesn't have room for them?'

'Room for them?' Mrs Ainsworth was taken aback. 'A whole house for a single man? No, there's something else happening here, you mark my words. Why would you get rid of your wife's books so quickly after her death?'

'Grief, I suppose, can make people do all sorts of things,' suggested Dotty.

'*Grief?* He should be honouring those books, not getting rid of them. There's something rummy going on there, I can feel it in my bones.'

Bones... thought Cressida as Mrs Ainsworth bid them goodbye. *Bones are at the heart of all of this. I just wish I knew why...*

37

'Gosh,' said Dotty. 'What do you make of that, Cressy?'

Cressida puffed out her cheeks and let out a long exhale. 'I'm not sure, Dot. But I can't imagine the dean has been anything other than above board as he deals with his late wife's estate.'

'But selling her books off?' Dotty blanched, as if this was the icing on the cake after all the shocks she'd had over the last few hours.

'He's a book lover himself though,' Cressida countered. 'When I left Mr Preston's house, I saw the dean in the window of the house next door, reading a book by the lamplight. I don't think he'd be the sort to cart off a barrow of them to Mr Bell to sell, anonymously at that. Perhaps someone else took the books and sold them, without him knowing. He seems like such a nice chap too, and he clearly loved his wife very much.'

'Like Nancy loved Anthony,' Dotty said rather morosely as they got up from the bench and headed towards the police station. 'And he still ended up dead.'

. . .

As they approached the Guildhall, the realisation that dear Alfred was locked up behind those walls hit Cressida harder than ever. She remembered the draughts that had whistled through the barred windows, no glass to impede the elements from their mission to get inside. She shivered and took the steps up to the arched doorway of the building as quickly as she could. Once inside, she strode straight up to the police desk and rang the bell.

'Yes, miss?' the sergeant on duty asked, appearing from a door behind the desk.

'Hello. Constable Duncan, is it? Chief Inspector Andrews, please. And quick as you can, thank you!' Cressida entreated and was pleased that the policeman took her seriously, nodding his head and disappearing into the bowels of the police station before re-emerging and beckoning for them both to follow him. Moments later, Cressida and Dotty were in the interview room, and soon DCI Andrews and Sergeant Kirby entered and took seats opposite them.

'Good day, Lady Dorothy, Miss Fawcett,' Andrews said, though his demeanour suggested to Cressida that perhaps it wasn't a good day after all.

'How's Alfred bearing up, Andrews?' Cressida asked, gripping Dotty's hand in the one that wasn't holding Ruby, and was relieved when Andrews answered positively.

'He's a little confused still, which is to be understood, but he's in quite good cheer. He's eating well.' Andrews huffed out a little laugh, then became more sombre again. 'I don't think the enormity of his situation has sunk in, though. The seriousness of it, if you will.'

'Oh dear,' Dotty whispered and looked paler than ever.

'I see,' Cressida said, with more authority. 'Alfred is a perfectly sensible fellow, I'm sure he understands. Though I should imagine his lack of concern comes from him knowing that he is innocent.'

Andrews merely raised an eyebrow. 'And we've had word from Sir Kingsley Mountjoy,' he said, which made Dotty look up hopefully. 'He's aware of the situation, from the family side. And he rather cryptically withdrew his opposition to you working with us. So, how can we help today, Miss Fawcett?'

'Well, that is good news. And you *can* help us, yes. I have a request, Andrews,' Cressida was straight down to business, placing Ruby on the floor so she could lean on the table and look Andrews square in the eye. 'It was Dotty's idea, actually. We wondered if you could get some handwriting experts to look at the letter that I found in the poetry book. We rather assume it might be Clara Sitwell's writing. In any case, we feel that one of these handwriting chaps might be able to find out. And the torn page from that archive record too. You never know, analysing the handwriting might tell us about the state of mind of the writer—'

'We're one step ahead of you there, Miss Fawcett,' Andrews said, and indicated to Kirby, who reached down and pulled out a large evidence bag. From within it, he retrieved not only the torn page but what looked like one of the archive records.

'You found where the page is from?' she asked eagerly, leaning forward.

'We did,' replied Andrews. Kirby carefully flipped through the pages and showed Cressida where her page would fit, then he pointed out another torn edge behind it. 'And look, there's another page missing.'

'So is this the stolen record book? Well, that's a start, isn't it, Andrews? And what's written in it? Is it all about St Swithun and his bones?'

Cressida reached for the book, only to have it pulled away from her.

'Andrews? May I?' she asked.

'It's a fingerprint thing, I'm afraid, Miss Fawcett, I can't let you touch it.'

'Why on earth not? I'll wear gloves. Sir Kingsley has autho-
rised us to work with you after all.' Cressida reached for the
stolen record book again.

'I'm sorry, Miss Fawcett,' Andrews said, looking awkwardly
at Dotty as he put the book back in the evidence bag.

'I don't understand. Fingerprints? Does this mean you
found it somewhere... well, somewhere odd?'

There was a pause while Andrews braced himself and
Cressida looked befuddled. She reached for Dotty's arm again.

'Andrews? Where was it?'

'The book was found during a police search after the arrest
of Alfred, Lord Delafield—' Andrews said, again glancing at
Dotty as he spoke.

'Yes, yes. But where?' Cressida needed Andrews to just spit
it out. But when he did, she paled with shock.

'A police search of the Wykeham Arms, Miss Fawcett. That
record book, the one that matched the torn sheet you found in
the verger's cassock, was found in Lord Delafield's bedroom.'

Dotty almost fainted in her chair. Cressida's mind was
buzzing, but more than that, her stomach was churning. Kirby
was dispatched to find them both some hot, sweet, strongly
brewed tea, and while he was gone, Andrews explained more
about the search to them. But none of it helped either of them
feel any better.

'The landlord showed us into Lord Delafield's room, and we
didn't have to look too hard to find some damning evidence.'

'*Some*? You mean there's more than just that archive book?'

'Yes, Miss Fawcett. And you're right, the record does
contain more information about the finding of the bones of St
Swithun back in 1910. A Mr Walker, the diver, retrieved them
from the trench under the cathedral and presented them to the
dean of the time, who identified the reliquary from one of the
medieval paintings. The notes get a bit scrambled about where
they had been hidden, and I'm afraid the other torn-out page,

which we didn't find with the record book, may contain the vital information. Anyway, I digress. While we were searching Lord Delafield's room, I'm afraid to say that we also found a long black cassock, like that worn by the clergy around here—'

'The Silent Friar,' Cressida whispered to herself. Hadn't she seen that very same apparition just after Alfred had been arrested? So it couldn't have been him, not that he would have been up to any such nonsense, dressing up as a ghost. And hadn't she seen the apparition, or whatever it really was, on the side streets between the cathedral, her aunt's house and the Wykeham Arms? She narrowed her eyes in thought.

'I'm sorry, miss?' Andrews asked her. 'The silent who?'

'Oh, nothing. Just some superstitious nonsense from round here.'

'I see. Well, the cassock was found, and then the archive record book, minus a page or two. I do admit, it's all very odd and not at all what we were expecting.'

'They must have been put there, Andrews, by someone else. What's the word...'

'Planted,' said Dotty authoritatively. 'I know that from my novels.'

'Quite, yes. Planted. Or, if not, then perhaps Alfred found them, and wanted to keep them safe and didn't have a chance to tell any of us before he was caught up in that fight. That makes more sense, surely?' She had to admit, as sure as she was of Alfred's innocence, the current evidence was all very confusing.

'It does, indeed. And once we have a proper discussion with Lord Delafield, when his head is fully compos mentis, we can establish if that's the case. But, for now, you can see that this evidence puts us in an awkward spot, what with the death of the cathedral's verger being so tied up with the archive record book, as you yourself keep saying, Miss Fawcett.'

Cressida harrumphed. 'Ridiculous notion, Andrews. And anyway, Alfred was still in London when Anthony was killed, most likely boarding the train with you, Dotty.' She looked to her friend, who was leaning over to stroke Ruby's soft velvety fur. 'Dotty?' Cressida nudged her and Dotty sat up straight again, and wiped a tear from the corner of her eye.

'Sorry, yes, it took us a while to find the platform because the stationmaster was busy helping a circus troupe get their escaped monkey back into a cage and we had the most perfect view of a family of cockatoos making merry up in the roof space. It took us quite some time to find and board the Winchester train, and we were certainly there, fending off capuchins, at the time Cressy said she was stumbling across poor Anthony.'

'That's as it may be, you understand that all of this – not to mention the witnesses who placed him at the scene of the sailor's death, knife in hand and "doing the deed" as it were – means we simply have to keep Lord Delafield in custody.' Andrews at least sounded apologetic, if not a little deflated. Cressida hoped that it meant that the DCI couldn't possibly imagine Alfred committing the crime, either.

'He had nothing to do with that fight outside the pub and I think we, all of us sitting here around this table, know that,' Cressida said bluntly.

'Be that as it may,' Andrews conceded, 'the fact that Sir Kingsley Mountjoy is his uncle is actually the worst possible outcome for Lord Delafield. We can't be seen to be favouring him or giving him any preferential treatment.'

'But you'll let common sense prevail, surely, Andrews?' Cressida hadn't intended her voice to sound quite so much like she was begging, but it did.

'If he's innocent, then all will be well. But if he's not...'

'He is,' Cressida and Dotty said in unison. But Cressida knew that she had to prove it, even to a policeman as well known to them, and as 'on side' as Andrews. She had to solve Anthony's murder and find out what was really happening around here. Because she did agree with Andrews in that

Alfred's situation had something to do with Anthony's death. Whether it were planted, or had been found, the cassock and book proved it. So, as she had already suspected, solving the first murder would no doubt lead to an explanation for the second.

One thing was for sure. If she didn't find out who did kill Anthony, and the sailor in last night's brawl, then Alfred might end up in the dock for at least one of the murders. And it was clear that someone very dangerous, and very clever, was still out there on the cobbled streets of Winchester, perhaps right now planning their next murder.

She had to catch them, and fast.

38

The atmosphere in the gloomy interview room of the Victorian police station hung heavily, with both Cressida and Dotty frustrated and anxious and Andrews and Kirby trying their best to keep everything above board and done by the book.

'I just refuse to believe any of it,' Cressida said, finally uncrossing her arms and sipping her tea. The sweet, dark liquid hit the spot and she began to think more clearly. 'I mean to say, I don't doubt that you found those items in Alfred's room, but I'm certain he is being set up.'

Dotty stayed silent, staring at her teacup as Andrews answered. Ruby, not liking being ignored, started whining, and Cressida leaned down and picked her up.

'The landlord said he was the only other one with a key and that no one had been near the guest bedrooms since Lord Delafield was arrested.'

Cressida frowned. 'Still, Alfred a murderer? It doesn't make sense. Just because Nancy might not be...' Cressida tailed off, thinking of the secret passage she'd found into the crypt.

Andrew's response, however, surprised her. 'Well, on that we do agree. While you've been following your little investigative threads, we've been doing proper police work, and I have to say, your first instinct was probably correct.'

'You mean Nancy is innocent?'

'Well, she's no longer under arrest. We let her go when the pathologist assured us that the blow to Anthony's head simply couldn't have come from a woman as short as Nancy, even if she were standing on the steps of the altar. And when we took her away, we discovered that although her hand was covered in his blood, it was no more than if she'd picked up the candlestick. Plus, she was still wearing her white pinny under her coat, which was open at the time she was taken away from the scene, and there was no blood spray on it at all. Whereas the altar cloth had blood drops on it, as you'd expect for something a few feet away from such a brutal murder.'

Dotty wrinkled her nose. 'I'm not sure I'm altogether happy Uncle Kingsley gave his thumbs up to us helping out if this is the sort of information we're now privy to.'

'I am. And I'm glad I was right.' Cressida leaned forward, careful not to squash Ruby, and placed her teacup down on its saucer. 'So, Nancy couldn't have been standing closer than four feet or so away, and therefore she couldn't have killed him.'

'Exactly. Hence why she's now been released.'

'Well, your aunt will be relieved,' Dotty said matter-of-factly. 'No more Protocol living.'

Cressida was pleased, and more so that her intuition had been correct. As she was sure it was for Alfred's charges too. And although she didn't relish the grisly details, she was appreciative of Andrews sharing them with her and thought he deserved to know the latest in her own investigation.

'You know, it is good to find all that out, as I was almost starting to doubt myself. And Aunt Mary will be delighted, since she has always been convinced that Nancy was a good egg.'

'Were you really doubting yourself, Cressy?' Dotty turned to look at her.

DCI Andrews and Kirby cocked their heads too as she replied.

'Yes. That secret passage, you see.'

'Secret passage?' Andrews blurted out. 'What secret passage?'

'The one I found this morning. Leading from behind the altar, or at least the stone steps where the makeshift one for the Canterbury candlesticks had been positioned, to who knows where, but I assume out behind the back buttresses of the cathedral's east end. It explains why no one saw Nancy enter, not your witnesses or Mr Havering, the head bell-ringer, who I spoke to this morning and insisted that he'd seen no one entering since he'd seen Anthony going down to the crypt.'

'Miss Biddle never mentioned a secret passage. She insisted she'd made her way down to the crypt by the normal entrance. She gave us that excuse that no one ever notices the servants.'

'Which I do believe, by the way,' Cressida chipped in, 'but in this case I think she might have actually used the passageway, but she didn't want to let you know as she thought it would make her look very suspicious. It made her seem suspicious to me too, I must admit. Until the pathologist's report came back, it wasn't looking good for her. I wouldn't blame her for not muddying the waters with a secret passage to boot.'

'Well, it certainly does explain how someone else might have got into the crypt without anyone noticing.' Andrews twisted the pencil he was holding as he thought.

'And, once again, I'd bet my Bugatti that it's someone who knows the cathedral inside out. Someone from this very community.'

The four of them sat in silence for a moment or two as these words sank in. Then Cressida asked Andrews the question she and Dotty had really come all of this way for. She asked if they could see Alfred.

To her relief, Andrews nodded. 'Kirby, take Miss Fawcett and Lady Dorothy to the cells and give them five minutes.' He reached out a hand to Dotty. 'I am sorry, Lady Dorothy. You know I'm only following procedure and we have to look into the cassock and stolen record book before I can let Lord Delafield go.'

'I understand,' Dotty said, accepting Andrews' hand.

Cressida smiled at him and he gave her the briefest nod in return. Then Cressida, one arm holding Ruby and the other linked with that of her friend, prepared herself for another trip to the cells.

'What ho, old thing! And sis too, splendid,' Alfred said, standing up from the cold, hard bench in his cell to welcome Cressida and Dotty in, as if he were hosting them for tea at the Ritz. There was no bounce to his voice though, and Cressida could feel the chill air billowing in from the unglazed window.

'Oh Alfred,' Cressida said, holding back tears the best she could. Dotty had immediately rushed forward and embraced her brother and Cressida realised that what he didn't need was two weeping willows coming to see him. She blinked back what she could and wiggled her nose to stop it from fizzing. She put Ruby down on the floor, grateful for the chance to subtly wipe a tear from her eye as she stood upright again.

'Come now, Dot,' reassured Alfred. 'I'm sure this is all some big misunderstanding. I'll be out of here by teatime, no doubt about that.'

'I'm not so sure, Alfred,' Cressida warned him. 'Have you heard what they found in your room at the inn?'

Alfred looked at her quizzically and she filled him in. As he listened, he gradually sat himself down and lowered his head into his hands. Dotty rubbed his shoulders as she sat next to him. Ruby even tapped his foot with one of her paws.

Suddenly he brightened. 'Well, dash it all, a cassock and a book from an archive. Having those in one's room – not that they are mine, of course – it's not exactly a hangable offence, is it?' He looked up at Cressida.

'Well, no. But they also have the knife you supposedly stabbed that sailor with, and it's covered in his blood and there were witnesses, apparently.'

Alfred deflated a little again. 'Ah. I see. Well, no, I don't see. I can't remember any of it,' he said, rubbing his fingers through his hair.

'What do you mean?' Cressida sat down next to him and tried very hard not to place a comforting hand on his knee. Now was not the time to explore *those* feelings. Especially not with Dotty, tears freely running down her cheeks, sitting the other side of him.

'Just that. I can't really remember much after leaving you, when we found that key.'

'We'd been in the crypt and Michael – the precentor – all but chased us out,' she reminded him. 'You gallantly walked me back to Aunt Mary's and then went to the inn. Andrews said a sailor was having too much to drink at the bar and started calling you names, and you took umbrage and suggested you take it outside.'

Alfred shrugged. 'I remember walking back to the inn, though after that... nothing really until I was on the ground outside with a few men holding me down. Then there were police whistles and shouting, then I woke up this morning in here and Andrews told me I was under arrest for some chap's murder. I swear, Cressy, I don't know how any of this happened.'

'I believe you, Alfred, I really do,' Cressida agreed. 'But I'm worried that drinking so much means you can't remember anything. And you'll need to remember *something*, otherwise the beak might think you're some sort of berserker, a violent whirlwind of a man with no sense of responsibility!'

'Calm down, old thing, I doubt it'll get to that. And also, that's the odd thing. I don't remember *anything*. Not even drinking.'

'The landlord at the pub said you hit the whisky hard, after drinking beers too.' Cressida looked at him oddly. 'Don't you have any memories of that at all?'

Alfred shook his head. 'A pint perhaps. But no, I don't.'

'The Mutton Pie Club has got you too used to drinking, perhaps, Alf,' Dot suggested. 'And you didn't realise your limits?'

'But I don't even remember ordering a whisky. The night I ended up on the boat train to Paris with Corky Butterford and Ferdie Von Westphalen and woke up in Calais with a thumper of a headache and a bill for twenty croissants, well, I don't remember the boat bit but I sure as anything remember thinking it would be an awfully fun idea to see how much rum I could get into me.' He shook his head, then thought better of that motion and just held his palm to his forehead instead.

'There's something else you should know, Alfred. They've released Nancy. The evidence didn't point to her killing Preston in the end. But the thing is, what with the cassock and the cathedral's record book found in your room, well...' Cressida let her sentence drift off.

'They think I've got something to do with the verger's murder?' Alfred said, with remarkable clarity.

'I know it's barmy, Alfred, since you weren't even here, but they have to look into how those things got into your room,' Cressida nodded. 'But, Alfred, we'll work out a way to clear your name, I promise.'

'I hope so, old thing. Mighty chilly in here.' Alfred shuddered as he looked up at the barred window. 'And if I can't prove I didn't kill that man, and I can't remember what actually happened, then I'm in the soup, aren't I? In fact, not just in any old soup, but soup that is boiling away nicely and ready to be served.'

39

Cressida and Dotty walked glumly away from the police station. As they approached the cathedral green, Dotty's pace slowed and Cressida turned around to see to her friend.

'Dot, you really don't look well.' She looked around and could see Ruby following her nose towards Aunt Mary's house, diverting here or there when something interesting crossed her path. 'Let's go home and warm up by the fire. Regroup, as it were. Papa always said a tactical retreat should never be seen as a failure.'

'I do feel rather tired,' agreed Dotty with a nod. 'And crying always leaves one with a headache, don't you find?'

'Yes, crying is the absolute worst, Dot. Just be grateful that, unlike me, your eyes aren't swollen and your nose isn't blocked, that's how I look for at least two days after a good blub.' She hugged her and they walked back towards Priory House.

The first thing Cressida noticed when they walked through the door was that the hallway was once again pristine. The hall table looked polished and the stairs were clear of assorted coats, gloves and hats. The bust of the Roman muse no longer sported a scarf and the newel post was free from outerwear.

'Nancy must be back,' Cressida said, taking her coat off and, as if by magic, Nancy herself appeared.

'Let me take that, miss, and yours, my lady,' she said, bobbing a curtsy to Dotty.

'Thank you, Nancy,' Cressida said, handing over everything except Ruby. 'And how are you?'

'All well, miss, all well.' She curtsied again and disappeared with their coats.

A hello was shouted from the parlour and Cressida and Dotty followed the voice to find Aunt Mary sitting by a roaring fire, a proper cup of tea in her hand.

'Cressida, Dotty,' she greeted her guests. 'Now, tell me, you two, how is Alfred?' She leaned over and patted the seat of the chair next to her. 'Come and sit and tell me everything. Is he all right? Has he eaten?'

'Bearing up, all things considered.'

'Very rum affair, all of it,' agreed Aunt Mary. 'But you were away quite some time. And why have you got a box of my teaspoons sticking out of your handbag?'

Cressida had quite forgotten the visit to the antiques dealer, but quickly handed over the box. 'They are yours, aren't they? Forgive me for even asking, Aunty M, but you didn't pawn them, did you?'

'Heavens no! Where did you find them?'

'In an antiques shop in town. There was a tea service there that I think I recognised as yours too and perhaps a silver teapot. The owner, a Mr Pargeter, said he'd bought them all from that Frenchman who Maurice recognised, along with a silver-backed hairbrush. Though it was initialled CT, so I didn't think it was yours.'

Aunt Mary, who had closed the box lid on the teaspoons, looked up at Cressida and said, 'Thornton.'

'I'm sorry?'

'Thornton. That was Clara's maiden name. She lost a silver-backed hairbrush just before she died. I remember her telling me all about it.'

'Was she burgled at the Deanery? The robbery at the archive... someone could have been targeting local houses too?' Dotty asked, from her place by the fire. Ruby, who had taken little coaxing to jump onto her lap, snuffled in agreement.

'Not that I know of. And, as far as I know, I've not suffered a break-in here either. I don't know how they'd have got hold of these teaspoons.'

Cressida took this all on board. A picture was starting to form in her mind as she pulled all the different threads together. Then she excused herself and left them both in the parlour. In the cool of the hallway, she could think.

A secret passage... a secret lover... so many actions out of character for all involved. Stolen teaspoons and thieved archives. The selling of silver and of holy saint's bones, for small change or small fortunes...

She looked up the stairs and, without another thought, headed up to the servants' quarters on the top floor.

40

Cressida climbed the stairs to the very top of the beautiful old house, where, up in the eaves, there were rooms for servants. And, Cressida noticed as she passed an open door, here was the linen cupboard.

'If only the spare bed had been made up,' she whispered to Ruby, who had made it clear that despite loving her mistress's best friend and her comfortable lap, she had not wanted to miss out on the action.

Ruby snorted in agreement and Cressida picked her up, then covered the distance down the corridor towards the room at the end that she assumed must be Nancy's.

She knocked softly and then when a faint 'come in' was heard, she opened it.

'Oh, hello there, miss,' Nancy said, turning around to face Cressida, having been unfolding some clothes on the bed. 'Give me a few minutes to freshen up, miss, and I'll be down to serve lunch.'

'Good heavens, Nancy, don't even think of it. I haven't come up here to chivvy you into more duties. Of course you must freshen up. I know what those cells are like.' Cressida shivered at the memory.

'How so, miss?' Nancy asked.

'I've been to visit my friend Alfred, Lord Delafield. He's in the same cells you were. Accused of killing someone too.'

Nancy's face changed from being mildly inquisitive, nay, even amused, to being deathly sombre, with narrowed eyes, and a pair of arms now crossed firmly across her chest. 'Not Tony?'

'No, no...' *Not yet*, Cressida thought, but she didn't think Nancy needed to know that he had items that linked him to Anthony's murder found in his room. It was all poppycock anyway. She looked Nancy straight in the eye. 'Another poor soul.'

'If you don't mind, miss, I've had an awful day or so. I'd like some time to freshen up now, miss, if that's all right with you?'

'Of course, of course. I'm sorry, Nancy. I just wanted to... well, this might seem presumptuous, but I just wanted to ask if, when you entered the crypt—'

'Please, miss, the memories are still so...' She crunched up her face and balled her fists. 'So ghastly for me.'

'I'm sorry, Nancy. I'm just trying to find out who murdered Anthony. See justice done. Now you're released, I don't believe the police have any leads, but I might do. And one of them involves a secret passage—'

'No, no, don't say it. Please forget you found it, if you have.' Nancy was holding onto the end of the metal bedstead and Cressida could see the whole frame shaking. 'Don't tell anyone you know about it, miss, please.'

'Why, Nancy? I'm afraid I've already told the police.' Cressida took a step towards the young maid, but she waved her away and Cressida stopped. 'Nancy, is there someone threatening you? Someone who told you not to say you'd seen them?'

'Miss, please,' Nancy urged, and with one more glance

around the small attic room, Cressida bowed her head and retreated, closing the door behind her.

Ruby had been a paragon of doggy delight and had settled quietly in Cressida's arms while she'd spoken to Nancy. Now, however, she struggled to be let down and then, with a wag of her tail, she nosed her way into the linen cupboard, where Cressida found her snortling around the lower shelves. 'Cupboard' was a bit of an understatement, it being the size of a small box room. At the rear of it, under a window and in between the shelves, was a sturdy wicker hamper and Cressida sat herself down on it. She needed a few minutes to think.

Something was bothering her, and it wasn't just Nancy's determination not to speak of the secret passage into the crypt. Cressida was sure she was hiding something, or at least knew more about Anthony's killer than she was letting on. But it was something else that was tugging at her mind.

Cressida looked around the shelves, and didn't even flinch when the spring-hinged door closed on her with a creak, then a click. The room smelt fresh: clean linen and lavender water. The shelves were piled high with blankets, eiderdowns, sheets and towels. Her aunt, despite not knowing where this cupboard was in her own house, definitely had enough in it. Then Cressida cocked her head to one side. She got up and moved along one of the shelves, where she saw folded trousers and neatly pressed shirts.

'Uncle Roly's old clothes,' she whispered to Ruby, who had started to quietly pine at the closed door. Cressida touched the soft fabric of the well-worn shirts, then noticed that his old Hussar's uniform was hanging neatly from the back of the door. The same uniform as the one in the framed photograph of Uncle Roly looking so handsome on horseback that was in the parlour. Aunt Mary liked to have things to remember him by and had obviously kept these old shirts...

'Oh.' Cressida realised what her eye for details had subconsciously taken in while she'd been talking to Nancy in her room. 'Ruby,' she hissed in a whisper. 'That's what was so odd about that whole interlude, well, apart from Nancy.'

Ruby sat herself down on her little mushroomy derriere and blinked at her mistress.

Cressida took a deep breath, then whispered to her dog again. 'The room was fresh and clean, like this cupboard, but unlike this cupboard, or even this house, there was no sign of her supposed fiancé. There were no pictures of Anthony.'

Cressida thought it through. Nancy might not have many pennies spare for a photographic portrait, but Anthony would have done. It's exactly the sort of thing a lovestruck man would do; spend money on things like studio photographs of his sweetheart and in turn give her one of him. She thought back to last night and her clandestine search of his house. There had been no photographs in there either, not even one by his bed or a framed one on the mantelpiece.

Cressida sat still as she heard footsteps outside the cupboard. Nancy was getting back to work. A look passed between small pug and hot-headed mistress and before either of them could change their mind, Cressida opened the cupboard door and slipped back down the corridor to Nancy's room. She gently opened the bedroom door and found herself looking at the room again. Sloping eaves made it hard to hang much in the way of art, but there were cheery chintz curtains at the window, and a floral counterpane on the bed. There was a mirror on top of a chest of drawers and a small side table next to the iron bedstead.

Cressida cast her gaze about the room. Simple, pleasant... but devoid of anything personal. There was no sign of Anthony being in this girl's life at all. No book by the bedside with a signed dedication, no photographs, no postcards resting against the mirror.

The mirror... Cressida walked up to it and gave it a good once-over. It was oval, made of mahogany or possibly rosewood, with a nice little inlay of marquetry around the frame. Beneath it were three drawers within the stand and Cressida cautiously pulled out the middle one. It stuck slightly, and Cressida had to add some welly to her pull, but finally the drawer came out and the reason for the stiffness was revealed. Inside it, cramming the drawer full to the brim, were newspaper articles and cut-out pictures from what must have been monthly parish magazines and cathedral newsletters. Cressida picked up the top few, which had got caught down behind the drawer and needed a tug to be freed.

It was the most extraordinary thing: all of the snippets, the pictures and the news features were about Anthony Preston. The articles were of no real consequence, sometimes just his name added to a list of attendees at a cathedral meeting, or a note of thanks mentioned in print for his thoughtful sermon during an Armistice Day service. There were some photographs, again, from parochial or church magazines: Anthony and Michael, the precentor, standing by the west door, then another of Anthony and the dean playing chess against some of the boys of Winchester College.

'How strange,' Cressida whispered to Ruby. 'I know they were being discreet, but I would have thought that might entail a photograph under the pillow.' She looked over to the bed, then shook her head. 'Or a framed picture of them both in the privacy of her own bedroom, or his house.' She placed the clippings from the magazines and newsletters back into the drawer, struggling as Nancy obviously had, too, to close it properly. She continued her train of thought inside her head.

Why would she have so many trivial bits of news about him? When she could have asked him, and talked to him about all of this while they were together, clandestine or not. This seemed more... obsessive. Like someone who would collect pictures of movie stars or club singers...

Cressida was about to turn and leave when she noticed a piece of paper sticking out of one of the smaller drawers underneath the dressing-table mirror.

What was it? A small piece of purple suede, but also a corner of paper. A paper ruled with red lines. One she recognised as being very similar to the page she'd found from the stolen record book.

'Cressy!' The call reverberated up the stairs. 'Cressy, where are you?'

Cressida's heart skipped several beats, and she moved back towards the door before the footsteps that were coming up the stairs could get any louder. She pulled the maid's bedroom door closed and stepped quickly along the landing, Ruby at her heels. She stood outside the open linen cupboard, where her aunt found her.

'Ah, there you are, dear. Oh, and is that my linen cupboard? Good heavens! Anyway, Nancy the dear girl has served lunch. I think it best we show our faces, as it's so good of her to crack straight back on.'

'I quite agree, Aunt Mary,' Cressida demurred. Though her mind was still caught on the scrap of paper – and more, the small piece of purple suede leather.

41

'Thank you, Nancy, and it is good to have you home,' Aunt Mary said, looking more content now that she was seated at her dining table with someone spooning peas onto her plate for her.

'Thank you, ma'am,' Nancy said, 'it's a relief, to be sure, but I'm heartbroken about my Tony.' She sniffed, and wiped her nose on her cuff, sending some peas flying.

The three ladies waited until she had finished serving the chicken and had left the room before talking amongst themselves again.

Cressida kept wondering about the piece of paper she'd spied in Nancy's room; and why the scrap of purple suede seemed so familiar. Then, as she ate her chicken and listened to Dotty explaining how her parents were organising a barrister to defend Alfred, it came to her, helped by the fact that Aunt Mary had allowed some of her library to spill out into the dining room. Books. She'd seen that suede before at Henry Bell's bookshop.

Nancy came into the room and cleared the plates. After thank-yous had been given, the young maid looked at her mistress and spoke.

'If you don't mind, ma'am, I have some errands to run. I'll finish clearing and be out for a little while, by your leave.'

'Of course, child, do as you need.' Aunt Mary granted her permission and Cressida smiled. With Nancy out of the house, she could sneak upstairs and retrieve that piece of paper.

And a few minutes later, that's just what she did.

Dotty had settled herself back into the parlour with a book, but Ruby, with her head cocked on one side, implored her mistress to take her with her. So, the two of them headed up to the very top of the house once again. Cressida was careful not to make too much noise – Nancy might not be in the house, but it wouldn't do at all to be caught snooping around the servants' quarters twice in one day. She carefully opened the door and was once again in the maid's bedroom.

She took the few steps over to the dressing-table mirror swiftly, and pulled open the drawer with the piece of paper sticking out of it. Unlike the middle one, which was jammed full of articles about Anthony, this one opened easily.

'Hmm, Ruby, what have we here?' she murmured to her dog, putting Ruby down as she pulled out the folded paper. Her hunch had been right; to her untrained eye, it looked very similar to the one that she'd found in Mr Preston's pocket. 'Didn't Andrews say that that there was another page missing from the stolen record book? This must be it!'

She opened it up and read the cursive writing. It described a meeting of the Winchester Cathedral clergy during the shoring up of the foundations, the provenance of the 'Swithun Case', and that a certain Mr Cardew would be responsible for taking it higher up the... The writing left the page and nothing but ink splotches formed the back of it.

Cressida pocketed the piece of paper. And there was something else she clocked too; in this same drawer, there was a note.

Cressida unfolded it and read it. It didn't say much at all, just a list of various household items: letter tray, toast rack, platter, hairbrush...

Hairbrush? Cressida wondered to herself as she pocketed this list. She had to get this to Andrews, and pronto.

Cressida raced back down the stairs. Aunt Mary's telephone was in a small study room to the back of the house with views over the gardens. Cressida poked her head into the parlour, letting Ruby waddle in through the open door to go and sit with Dotty again, who Cressida was relieved to see had nodded off in front of the fire.

Aunt Mary was nowhere to be seen, so Cressida let herself into the study and picked up the receiver.

The operator put her through to Liberty of London's Haberdashery and Upholstery Fabrics department and the familiar and reassuring voice of Maurice came on the line.

'Good afternoon, Miss Fawcett. Any decisions yet on the silks?'

'No such luck I'm afraid, Maurice, and even worse than that, things have got a bit spicy here since you left yesterday.' She went on to tell him about Alfred's arrest, choking back the emotion as she described the pieces of evidence found in his bedroom at the inn. 'So, you see, Maurice, he's in a bit of a bind, there's no two ways about it.'

'And you say he couldn't remember anything? Nothing at all?'

'Drunk apparently, but it didn't sound like him.'

'Sounds more like a sleeping draught to me.'

'You think he was drugged?' Cressida frowned down the line. 'I suppose that does make sense.'

'There's been a spate of robberies recently where the victim was drugged before they had pocket watches lifted from their person. A good Samaritan gone bad as it were, as the thief helps the drunken lord to the hansom cab – he gets home all right, but his pockets are lighter.'

'A jade's trick if there ever was one.' Cressida could feel something forming in her mind, but as interesting as Maurice's insight was, it wasn't the reason for her call. She changed the subject, hoping Maurice wasn't pressed for time with a line of people at his cutting table waiting for fabrics. 'Maurice, you know that Pierre Fontaine you told me about?'

'Unfortunately, yes.'

'Well, I think he was selling stolen goods locally. Goods stolen from houses nearby. The local antiques dealers would have been suspicious if someone local had come in to sell them, but a local person could have worked with the Frenchman as he was more oblique. Easier for the dealers to pretend that due diligence had been done.'

'Someone local, like who?'

'Well,' the thought came to Cressida as she spoke to him. 'Like a maid.'

Cressida ended the call to Maurice, her mind abuzz. There was something about the sleeping draught and the thievery... an escalation perhaps, from pocket watches to... what? Bones? Murder?

Cressida pushed open the door to the parlour. Dotty was still fast asleep by the fire, and to Cressida's surprise, Aunt Mary was slumped on the sofa too. Cressida crossed the room to them, shaking them both by turn and trying to rouse them. But they were sound asleep.

Dead, as it were, to the world.

42

Cressida placed the fireguard over the grate and stepped softly around her dozing aunt and Dotty. A nice nap was the most natural thing after lunch. And they'd both been put through so much recently, she didn't want to wake them. Better they sleep and save their energy. She, however, wanted to find DCI Andrews. She had a theory forming and knew he would be the best person to talk to about it, but before then, she had to head back out into the chill and ask a few more – probably awkward – questions of some of her suspects.

Cook was still in the kitchen and Cressida asked her if she wouldn't mind looking after Ruby and giving her some scraps while she popped out. Cook yawned, covering her mouth with her arm as she did so, but nodded and Cressida left Ruby looking longingly at the cut of beef Cook was preparing.

Outside the front door, coat, hat and gloves on, Cressida turned down Cloister Close towards St Swithun Street. She was headed for the Wykeham Arms, where she was going to demand to see Alfred's room. He had been drugged, he must have been. And she might find evidence of that among his belongings or on the nightstand.

The hostelry came into view as she turned the corner and she realised that the afternoon light was already fading. The lamps in the pub were lit, giving it a warm and welcoming glow. She headed for the door and pushed it open. Several pairs of eyes turned towards her as she entered, and pint glasses were left suspended in the air. A moment or two was all it took for the drinking punters to resume normal behaviour, but by this time Cressida had been clocked by the landlord.

'Good afternoon, Miss Fawcett,' he said cordially.

'Good afternoon. I have a favour to ask, if I may.' She had come prepared this time and knew what to ask for. 'As his sister is indisposed,' she chose that word carefully, 'and I'm the only other person in Winchester who knows Lord Delafield, the police have asked me to pop into his room and see if I can find him a change of clothes. He'll be up before the beak soon and it doesn't do to look a scruff. He might have spent a night in the cells, and more by the time he appears in the court, but there's no need for him to look like it.'

'I don't think a fresh shirt and a fancy tie will help him much, what with the evidence they found, but fill your boots. Here's the key.'

The landlord passed over the key to guest room two and directed Cressida up the back stairs. She found her way up the narrow staircase to the landing above and up here the chatter of the pub below her was muffled by the ancient beams, Turkish floor runners and many pictures hanging on the wall.

Room two overlooked the road towards the front of the property and as Cressida entered, she noticed that the first lamps were being lit outside in the street. She turned on the lamp by the side of the bed so she too could see better in the gloaming and set about her search.

She muttered as she looked around, seeing the hook on the back of the door where the cassock must have been found by the police. 'How could anyone have believed Alfred would be disguising himself as a ghost?' It was ridiculous, she thought to herself as she saw his valise open on the unused bed. Inside it were the usual manly things, a shaving kit and some spare clothes. She closed the bag. Despite making this up as her excuse, she did actually want to rescue Alfred's belongings – especially if there was a thief about.

As the catch snapped shut, she noticed a side pocket to the bag. A piece of paper was sticking out. It was in Alfred's hand-writing; a list of places with annotations next to them. Cressida whispered them to herself. 'New Forest – quiz C on love for ponies, might be better on foot. Supper at Chesil – good food. Beaulieu – if Monty Montagu around, could have full tour of Palace House. Seaside – romantic walk on beach?'

She read them through again, sitting herself down on the bed as she did so. A tear pricked the side of her eye, and she dabbed it away with her sleeve. All this... for her. She'd not dared hope that he might feel the same way about her as she did him. The tears came more freely as she folded the paper up and pressed it to her chest, before putting it in her pocket.

She had to prove Alfred was innocent. His life, and perhaps the happiness of the rest of hers, depended on it.

Wiping away her tears, Cressida picked up Alfred's bag and went back down to the main saloon of the pub. The landlord was nowhere to be seen, and the locals were quietly drinking their ales. She clocked the dean sitting on his own at a small table, nursing a pint. She hadn't anticipated seeing him, but perhaps this was her opportunity to confirm something Judith Ainsworth had said.

As she greeted the dean, he gestured for her to join him.

'Moving in?' he asked, pointing to the valise.

She shook her head. 'Mr Sitwell, can I ask you something?'

'Of course.' He looked at her inquisitively. 'Your aunt says you have a nose for solving mysteries. I hear you've been busy trying to figure out what happened to poor Anthony. How can I help?'

'I found one of your late wife's books in Bell's bookshop yesterday. And Judith Ainsworth said she did too. She was rather upset that you seemed to be selling off Clara's books so soon after she died. She said she felt something rummy was going on.'

The dean looked taken aback. 'Clara's books? I'd never sell those. Which ones?'

'An *Anthology of Modern Poetry*, that was the one I found. It had a dedication to Clara in the front, and I think Mrs Ainsworth found a copy of Tennyson's poems.'

'Clara loved Tennyson, "the mirror crack'd from side to side" and all that.' The dean gazed sadly into his pint of beer. 'But I didn't sell them. I would never sell anything that was Clara's, although...' He stopped talking and turned his head away from Cressida. She thought she could see a glistening in his eye, but he blinked a couple of times and then turned back to face her. 'The thing is, I've been cursing the fact that I can't remember what things we used to have in the Deanery. I spent so long in the cathedral and working on my ministry that although the items in our house always seemed so familiar, I realise now that I'm unpacking, that there just don't seem to be as many things as I thought we had. But, now you say it, the Tennyson and the poems, of course I remember we had those. The Tennyson of Clara's was a first edition, I believe, given to her by her godmother.'

'So how did they find their way into Mr Bell's shop?'

The dean shook his head. 'I don't know. I don't know at all.'

'And her hairbrush.' Cressida remembered the silver-backed brush in the antiques shop. 'You didn't sell that either I assume?'

'No. Hairbrush, you say? A silver one, with her initials on it?'

'Yes!' Cressida said, perhaps rather too eagerly in the

circumstances. 'With her maiden name though, as the second initial. CT for Clara Thornton.'

'Yes, that's right. Gosh, you really have been investigating. Now that was something *she* noticed. Just before she died. She always kept it on the dressing table, but then one day it was gone. She told me not to make a fuss and that she'd ask Nancy if she'd seen it. Nancy was always very good at cleaning the silver. But before I could find out any more about it, Clara had...' He looked out of the window again. Cressida understood. He didn't need to say anymore.

However, as certain thoughts moved into place in her mind, like a quilt taking shape with all the right patches fitting together, Cressida knew she had to ask him a very difficult question. 'Mr Sitwell, I know this is an awful thing to ask, but can you tell me more about Clara's death? I understand she wasn't a confident swimmer, and of course, when she died, the river was long past being warm enough for swimming.'

The dean pushed his pint of beer to the side and gripped his hands together, almost as if he were praying. His words came out slowly and with quite some effort. 'There was never any suggestion that she was swimming. Where did you get that notion?'

Cressida could see the pain etched on the dean's face and hated the fact that she was having to bring up this terrible subject. 'Aunt Mary, she just said that Clara had never been a strong swimmer, so I assumed she...' She let her words tail off as she realised the mistake she'd made.

The dean was shaking his head as he spoke again. 'She was found in the Itchen, floating like Ophelia among the rushes. Just by the college, which is barely any distance from the cathedral and the Deanery.' He closed his eyes at the memory. 'She had not been swimming, Miss Fawcett. She was fully clothed, coat and boots and everything. She had fallen in and drowned.'

'Who found her?' Cressida asked, remembering Nancy's

words to the dean as she knelt over the verger's dead body. *Oh Mr Sitwell, it reminded me so terribly of your poor wife...*

'Nancy did. She'd been with her all morning but said Clara had gone out for a walk with a friend. She was very distressed when she found her, down by the college bridge.'

'As distressed as she was when she found the verger?'

'Yes, quite so,' the dean agreed.

'And who was the friend? Who was with Clara when she fell in?'

'I believe it was the precentor's wife.'

He has a wife and two young boys... Cressida's aunt's words rang through her head. And another thought occurred to her too; the precentor and his wife were now living in the Deanery. The picture-perfect and hugely spacious house once occupied by the man sitting in front of her – and his dead wife.

Cressida inhaled, letting her thoughts sit tight in her mind. Then she girded herself for action. She thanked Mr Sitwell for his time and promised to return the poetry anthology as soon as it was released from police evidence. She looked around, but there was no sight of the landlord behind the bar. With Alfred's bag in her hand, she turned to walk out the door. And that's when she noticed something.

Something that changed – or perhaps confirmed – everything.

Above the door of the pub, there was a sign. A licensing sign, telling all who could read who was licensed to sell beers, wines and intoxicating spirits on this premises. And the name on the sign was Robert.

Robert Biddle.

43

Cressida pushed open the door and briskly walked through the streets of Winchester.

'How could I have been so foolish!' she chastised herself. 'Poor Anthony only ever wanted the relics safe; it was everyone else who wanted to sell them,' she muttered as she turned the corner of the cobbled street. Alfred's valise was heavy in her hand, and she moved it from one side of her body to the other as she tried to pull her coat around her to keep off the chill.

Of course Alfred had been set up. And she walked a little faster, hopeful that she could finally start putting all the pieces of this mystery together – and save him from the noose.

'But Pierre Fontaine...a connection from the Continent, perhaps? And that parcel he was holding... it's the key... or do I have the key?' She continued muttering to herself as she retraced the journey from the Wykeham Arms to her aunt's house. She turned the corner from St Swithun Street into Symonds Street and hurried as she walked in the shadows.

Almshouses replaced the high wall alongside her and Cressida saw some lights on as she walked on by. Number seven was dark, but was she mistaken or was there a glow coming from behind the glazing on the door of number five? The verger's old house, which should be empty...

Instinctively, Cressida pushed open the gate at the end of the garden and quietly closed it behind her. She walked up the path to where it split between the two houses and put the valise down. Delving into her pocket, she found the keys she'd been hiding. Only Dotty knew she had them.

Dotty... Cressida wondered if she was still asleep in front of the fire. She needed to get back to Priory House double quick, but she also needed that map of the crypt. And if that was a light on inside, it meant someone else might be beating her to it.

Quickly and quietly, she found herself sliding the key into the lock. She turned it and the door opened. Without making a sound, she let herself in and, grateful for her previous visit, knew the layout without having to make a noise searching for the torch in the hall table's drawers.

She stepped cautiously along the hallway, noticing that the light she could see through the glazed front door must have come from the dining room. She crept up to the door, glad of the dark shadows of the narrow hallway that concealed her as she peered into the room. The map was still on the table; she could see it thanks to a portable oil lantern on the mantelpiece.

Someone had let themselves in, prepared to look around in the dark...

Someone who is still here.

She inched further into the room. It wasn't a large dining room at all, and the table was almost within reach if she dared stretch her arm out into the light. No... she'd need to be closer to reach the map. She edged in, every inch giving her a slightly better look at who might be in the room – and the owner of the lantern. Gradually, the room gave up its secrets and she grew bolder. There was no one there.

She grasped the edge of the map and began rolling it up, better to carry it to Priory House, where she so desperately needed to be now. Despite the map being made of thin, tissue-like paper, the noise of it being rolled up crackled like fire against the silence of the house. Cressida cursed under her breath. Then the lantern flame flickered in its glass dome.

Someone was behind her, she could sense it. She turned around, holding the table behind her to steady her nerves.

Out of the shadows of the hallway loomed a figure clad in a hooded cloak. *Tall as a lamplighter...*

The flame flickered again, making the figure in front of her seem almost ethereal and blurred as to where the cloak shape ended and the endless gloom of the hallway began.

'Who are you?' The quiver in Cressida's voice matched that of the tremble in her legs.

She leaned back on the table as the figure grew larger, coming towards her through the doorway.

Could this be the Silent Friar? The ghostly spectre itself?

As if in answer to her question, the cloak shifted and a very real, and very human hand was revealed from the folds.

And in it, a very real, and very sharp knife.

44

'Who are you?' Cressida asked again, her eyes not leaving the glint of metal. She gulped, as the table pushed into the back of her legs, and she edged along it, but the cloaked figure bore down on her.

'Give me the map,' the figure growled. A male voice, which matched the height and hands of the cloaked ghoul.

'Tell me who you are,' Cressida asked again, her hand reaching out behind her and feeling the rolled paper of the map. There was no answer, but in one motion, Cressida managed to grab the map and swipe at the figure.

Whoever this is, she thought to herself as the figure lurched backwards, *it's no spectre...*

All it took was that moment of distraction for Cressida to duck out of the door next to the figure, whose voluminous cloak billowed around them, hindering their reactions.

'Where've you gone?' Cressida heard the disgruntled voice say as she darted down the hallway and out of the front door. She dashed down the pathway, hurdling over Alfred's valise that she didn't dare pick up, lest doing so slowed her down. She could hear footsteps thundering down the floorboards behind her, and she guessed that the Silent Friar, for what else could she call him, was still in the house while she grappled with the latch on the gate. Not daring to look behind her, Cressida tore off along the cobbles, desperate to get to her aunt and Dotty.

A scuffle and some swear words behind her – due to a non-hurdled valise, perhaps – didn't stop her in her tracks and she carried on down the lane until she could see the turning into Cloister Close and the porch light of Priory House.

A horrible thought had occurred to her as she'd been running. The drugging of Alfred, of those victims in London who had lost their pocket watches while they slept... why of course Dotty and Aunt Mary had been drugged!

They weren't sleeping after a good lunch... even Cook was yawning!

Cressida cursed herself as she took the steps up to the front door two at a time. And her thoughts moved on from Maurice's words of warning about sleeping draughts; whoever had killed Anthony had done so to steal the casket of bones off him. The casket that he had been seen entering the crypt with. And why did she even know about these bones in the first place?

Because Nancy Biddle, her aunt's maid, had mentioned them.

Cressida reached for the large brass doorknob and then said something very unladylike under her breath as the knob failed to move.

'Locked out, dash it all!' Cressida pressed her shoulder against the door, but that was pointless. The large, old door was firmly locked. Leaning against the door, she caught her breath and braced herself to look down the lane from where she'd just come. There was no sign now of the Silent Friar, or whoever it was, looming out of the darkened corners of the high-walled road. Thank heavens. The crashing sound she'd heard, and the very this-worldly cursing, may have come from the fact that her assailant hadn't figured on Alfred's valise being left slap-bang in the middle of the garden path. The thought that those dramatic robes, put on to disguise and to scare, had probably become ensnared in Alfred's valise's handles almost made her smile. But there was no time for that. She had to get into the house.

Cressida looked over to the window. She'd stood there herself only the night before, peeking through the curtains to see who had come calling so late at night. That the curtains weren't closed now against the early-evening autumn darkness just showed how long Dotty and Aunt M had been sparko. Leaning over the metal railing, Cressida peered in and could see Dotty, still asleep by the fire, and her aunt's ankles and shoes hanging over the edge of the chintz sofa. Then, suddenly, just as Cressida was thinking she needed to go and fetch Andrews to help her break into her aunt's house, a little mushroomy face with two shining black eyes appeared at the windowsill.

'Ruby!' Cressida almost laughed in relief at the sight of her. The small dog disappeared, then jumped up again and Cressida noticed that near where her paws grappled with the windowsill was the catch for the large sash. And it was open.

'Oh Ruby, you clever little dog.' She blew a kiss to the small pup through the window. Folding up the map into a more manageable size, she slid it into her trouser pockets, before leaning over the railings and pushing up the window.

She was in.

45

Cressida slid off the windowsill and into the parlour. She swept up Ruby into a hug and kissed her mercilessly, with little opposition from the pug herself.

'Oh, you clever, clever houndlette,' she said, finally putting Ruby down and then kneeling in front of Dotty, who was slumped in the armchair. 'Dot, Dot! Wake up,' she said, then shook her friend.

Dotty didn't move. Was Cressida too late? Had they been overdosed and left for dead?

'Dotty, please, please, wake up!'

'Hmmm, what's happening? What are you doing, Cressy?' she asked blearily.

'Oh Dot, thank heavens you're all right.' Cressida leaned in and hugged her friend.

She quickly checked on Aunt Mary and was just rousing her when a noise from the kitchen disturbed her. Cressida looked down at Ruby, who panted for a second or two, then trotted off in the direction of the kitchen. About thirty seconds later, she came back at a much faster pace to her mistress's side and snort-snuffled at her.

'What is it?' Cressida spared Ruby a quick look while still trying to wake her aunt, who was lying on the sofa fast asleep. At least she was breathing, Cressida had checked. Ruby barked, or at least her version of barking, and Cressida turned to look at her again. Then she noticed the movement in the hallway – a shadow that passed quickly across the door frame, a shadow darker even than the gloom of the unlit hall.

Cressida heard the door unlock and the large doorknob turn. There was no way she could catch up with the intruder in time to stop them, but she did rush back to the open window in time to see another cloaked figure disappearing down the steps and fleeing through the park in the direction of the cathedral.

'That wasn't the same person,' Cressida murmured, then hit her head on the raised sash window as a hand on her shoulder made her jump.

'Sorry, Cressy,' yawned Dotty. 'But what on earth is happening?'

Cressida rubbed her head and sat down on the windowsill. She still had some thinking to do, and although time was pressing, for a moment or two she felt safe, here in Priory House, with her best friend, her dog and her still gently snoring aunt.

'Dotty, I'm so sorry I left you,' Cressida started. 'I-I thought you were just sleeping, heaven knows you deserve a bit of peace, but you weren't sleeping, you were drugged!'

'What do you mean, drugged? Is that why I was so tired? I thought it was the stress of worrying about Alfred.'

'No. I mean, look at Aunt M over there.' Cressida pointed to her aunt, still snoring, though with a throw that had been left over the back of the sofa covering her to keep off any chill. Even in a drugged sleep, she seemed prepared for everything. 'That's not a quick afternoon nap, is it?'

Dotty nodded. 'I see. Gosh. So, where did you go?' Dotty asked, gently moving Cressida off the windowsill so she could close the sash and keep out the chill.

Cressida stood up and wrapped her arms around her. She still had her coat on, but even so, she moved across the room and stood in front of the fire to think.

'I went to the Wykeham Arms. I think that place is at the heart of all of this. You see, Maurice warned me that thieves these days were drugging their victims, and it chimed with the fact that Alfred was so obviously drugged last night. There's no way he would get so blotto that he'd forget everything. The only way that happens is when someone is drugged.'

'Oh yes, like when Minnie Carruthers had that accident at school and Matron got hold of Major Carter's morphine from the war and when Minnie woke up, she'd no memory of the accident. Or the day before it. In fact, I think she lost October entirely.'

'Exactly. So, I thought Alfred must have been drugged and the source of it lay in the pub. And I can tell you I found out something very interesting while I was there. Did you know that the landlord of the Wykeham Arms is a certain Robert Biddle.'

'Nancy's... father?' Dotty guessed.

'I think so. Or uncle or close relation or something. And that Geoffrey Sitwell, the dean, had most definitely not been selling his late wife's books, whether to Mr Bell or to an auction.'

'How did they come to be at Mr Bell's bookshop then?'

'He couldn't tell me. Though he thought that perhaps they'd been stolen.' Cressida found the poker and prodded some life back into the fire while she was thinking. 'Dot, something else just happened too. I saw lights on in Anthony's house, and since I wanted the map of the crypt anyway, I went in. And, you won't believe this, but I was attacked by a tall man in a long black cloak...'

'Attacked?' Dotty grabbed her friend by the arm. 'Why didn't you mention this first? Honestly...' She rolled her eyes, though held onto her friend's arm as she did so. 'And you wonder why I worry about you getting involved with all these murders.'

Cressida smiled at her friend. 'Well, you've been a great help, chum. Top brass. But that man in a cloak, as I'm sure it was a man, is still very much out there. He chased me out of the house, and although I lost him when I came here, there was another cloaked figure here in this house, clanking around, while I tried to rouse you.'

'Really?' Dotty stepped back in surprise. 'Here, while we were sleeping?'

'Yes. But you weren't just sleeping though, were you, Dot.'

'Drugged,' Dotty whispered. 'Gives one the shivers to think about it. I wonder how?'

'I'm fine, so it can't have been over lunch.'

'Nancy left us a tray of tea before she went out,' Dotty recalled. 'You were upstairs, so your aunt and I poured ourselves a cup... Oh Cressy, that reminds me. I forgot to tell you something. I'm not sure it's of interest or not, but it seems like it might be.'

'What is it?' Cressida looked inquisitively at her friend.

'Like I say, it's probably nothing, but your aunt mentioned something about Judith living at the Deanery now. Judith Ainsworth.'

'Meaning Judith is Michael the precentor's wife?' Cressida's mouth gaped open in a really very unladylike way. 'Judith was great friends with Clara Sitwell.'

'Who used to live there too, before she died,' whispered Dotty.

'She did indeed, Dot, she did indeed. And you're right, that is very interesting. How did we not know that!' Cressida shook her head.

'Does it change anything?' Dotty asked.

'Yes, I think it does. I think it changes quite a lot.' Cressida stared into the fire, willing the flames to help ignite her own thoughts.

Nancy had drugged her aunt and Dotty... but Judith now lived at the Deanery...

'Dot, I think something is about to happen in the crypt. Will you come with me?'

'Of course, Cressy, but...' Dotty hesitated, 'shouldn't we telephone Andrews? You know how awfully cross he gets when you – well, we – charge onwards without telling him.'

Cressida, who had started pacing as her mind had raced, stopped. With an exaggerated exhale, she nodded. 'Yes, all right. That's not a bad idea, Dot. If what I think is about to happen is actually about to happen, we might need him there.'

Cressida left the parlour and a moment later was down the hall, Aunt Mary's telephone receiver in her hand.

'Operator? The police station please. Yes, I'll hold. Quick as you can though, please...' Cressida's patience was tested as various lines were connected until finally the familiar voice of DCI Andrews came on the receiver. 'Andrews? Good, yes, it's me Miss Fawcett. Andrews, look here, I think something's about to happen in the cathedral crypt... Yes, Andrews, I think lives do depend on it. Some very close to my heart, you see... Yes, well, I'll explain it all later. Please, Andrews, do trust me on this. And hurry. Bring Kirby and make sure his pencil is sharp, there's much to jot down... Yes, I know I'm being bossy, but Dotty and I will see you there. And hurry, Andrews! Faster than a falling soufflé! We need to catch a killer!'

46

With Aunt Mary groggy but awake, and made as comfortable as possible, and Cook tended to in the kitchen, Cressida hurriedly helped Dotty on with her coat and they closed the large door of Priory House behind them. Ruby was having none of this being left behind lark again and marched as swiftly as her little pug legs could carry her as they crossed the park to the cathedral's west doors.

'So why the crypt, Cressy? Why are we meeting Andrews there?' Dotty asked, just about keeping up, both in step and in train of thought.

'Because the crypt is the link to everything. Somewhere in that cathedral were the bones of St Swithun, and until 1910 they were properly hidden – lost even – but once they were found, they were hidden again, this time to keep them safe. Do you remember Andrews telling us that there were two pages missing from the cathedral record book that they found, planted I'm sure, in Alfred's room? I'd found the first page in the pocket of Anthony's spare cassock, and I found the second page in Nancy's bedroom this afternoon.'

'You're sure it was? The second page, I mean. From that same record book?' Dotty asked, losing her breath a little due to the quickness of their pace.

'Yes, I think so. It spoke about the same subject and made more sense of what we knew already. Finding those relics in 1910 was of such ecclesiastical importance, they were kept secret until the church knew what to do with them. But Anthony, I think, made it his mission to find out where they were, hence having this map of the crypt in his home. All he had needed was to find the right record book in the archive, the one that covered the time when the bones were found, and where the dean and the verger, back in 1910, had hidden them.'

They had reached the cathedral and Cressida pushed open the ancient, heavy wooden door. Inside the nave, the two young women, and even younger pug, could hear their footsteps echo as they made their way towards the crypt.

'What do you think we might find? Dotty asked in a whisper.

'Hopefully DCI Andrews and Sergeant Kirby.'

'Yes, but beyond the police, why are we here?' Dotty asked again.

'I think Anthony Preston had found the relics before he was killed. I think he'd studied the map, been in the archive and discovered where they were.'

'And then he started selling them? That doesn't seem like the sort of thing he'd do, does it? Very out of character,' Dotty said as they reached the door at the top of the staircase that led down to the crypt. Cressida placed her hand up against it.

'Far too out of character. So much so that I don't think he was selling them at all. But they are the reason he was killed. And I think they might still be here.'

The door swung open, and Cressida switched on the torch she'd grabbed at the last minute from the hall table at Priory

House. Her aunt's forward planning had obviously been rubbing off on her.

The three of them descended, with Ruby jumping down each step a little less elegantly than the other two. The torch beam illuminated the crypt, arch by arch, puddle by reflective puddle. A noise, far off, in the nave of the cathedral, made Cressida and Dotty jump, but Cressida shook it off and instead of being frightened off mission, she retrieved the map from her trouser pocket.

'Anthony must have had this map open on his kitchen table for a reason,' she said, passing Dotty the torch so she could open it out and have a look. 'I only spotted the secret passage entrance, but perhaps he'd kept it and hadn't given it back to the archive as he was adding his own rubric to it.'

'How do you know it's from the cathedral archive?' Dotty held the torch as steadily as she could as she spoke.

'Watermark up in the top corner, look.' Cressida pointed it out and Dotty followed it with the torch beam.

'I see,' Dotty nodded. Then she had another thought. 'Well maybe, after the break-in, he didn't trust the security of the archive,' Dotty suggested, and Cressida nodded.

'Perhaps.'

'Who do you think did break into the archive, Cressy?' Dotty whispered, then shuddered again as a drip splashed down near them, its sound magnified by the vaulted ceiling above.

'I have a suspicion, but it's not quite clear yet.'

'Do you think all the things that have been stolen, like your aunt's spoons, were taken by the same person who now wants the bones?' Dotty asked, and Cressida looked up from the map.

'I don't think so, Dot. They seem trivial in comparison, don't you think? Selling silver spoons for a few shillings isn't anything like organising a Frenchman to come over and fence relics across the Continent.'

A rustling behind them diverted their attention.

From the direction of the stone steps loomed a cloaked figure, the glint of a knife flashing from behind the folds of its cloak. Cressida gulped and Dotty grabbed her arm. Ruby snarled and yapped, though, as the figure approached, those yaps turned to whimpers and the small pup hid behind Cressida's ankles.

'Who are you?' Cressida called out to the cloaked figure, who was bearing down on them.

Then, another noise, this time from behind them and Cressida dared to glance towards it. The secret passage door was slowly opening and from behind it crawled out another cloaked figure, its face disguised under a cowled hood.

'C-Cressy...' Dotty gripped her arm tighter.

'Both of you, show yourselves,' Cressida demanded, as she and Dotty edged backwards through the crypt.

'There's nowhere you can run to now,' the first figure said, and Cressida recognised the voice but couldn't quite place it. Her heartbeat, already rising faster than the mercury at midsummer, only beat more quickly as, from behind the first figure, a third, smaller, cloaked figure, emerged from the darkness. Dotty was weaving the torch beam between them, and squeezed Cressida's arm tighter as the second figure who'd crawled out of the passage also flashed the blade of a knife in the torchlight.

'You shouldn't have meddled,' the first figure said, advancing towards Cressida.

'We had to find out the truth... and Alfred, we had to...' Cressida faltered as the figure bore down on them. She squeezed Dotty equally as tightly, both of them gripping onto one another.

'Dot, I'm sorry,' Cressida whispered, as she heard Dotty say a quiet prayer.

Was this the end? Had her hot-headed investigating really landed her – and darling Dotty – in the soup this time?

Cressida held her breath as Dotty's torch light dimmed, flickered, then went out.

The crypt was in darkness.

47

Without the benefit of sight, one's other senses take over. Or so Cressida thought as she heard what could only have been described as a blood-curdling scream. To her hugest relief, she knew it hadn't come from Dotty, neither had the splashing foot-steps, which sounded like they'd come from the direction of the secret passage. Then there was tussling and grappling, cloth being ripped and curses uttered.

Were the cloaked figures fighting? Amongst themselves?

Cressida wasted no more time and wrenched Dotty away from where they'd been standing. Her knowledge of the crypt was better than Dotty's, and improved by the fact she'd just been studying the floorplan. She pulled them both into the central storage bays, roped off and full of unused chairs, stacked up on top of each other, and trestle tables leaning up against tombs. A soft nuzzle at her ankle told her that Ruby was with them, much to her relief.

What must have been only minutes later, but had felt like aeons as they'd crouched hidden, three strong lantern lights flooded the crypt with light. And following them came more torch beams and the clattering of boots on stone steps, as

Andrews, Kirby and several of the local constables poured down into the crypt.

'Thank heavens,' Cressida said, then looked up to the mass of stone above her. 'Really, thank you. Come on, Dot, time to show ourselves. The cavalry is here.'

Dotty opened one eye from her position crouched next to a pillar. Then she visibly relaxed as she saw Cressida's hand outstretched towards her and the comforting words that were echoing around the pillars of the crypt; 'I'm arresting you in the name of the law...'

'Andrews?' Cressida called out, emerging with Dotty to quite the scene. At least ten or so local policemen had accompanied DCI Andrews, and Kirby, who stood shorter than usual due to still not having a replacement helmet. Several of the local bobbies were cuffing the three figures, one of whom was having it done while on the floor.

As Cressida walked towards them, Andrews looked up and Cressida saw what she thought was a look of relief, tinged with frustration. And, suffice to say, it was one she knew well.

'What ho, Andrews,' she said, once up closer. Dotty was brushing herself down and sweeping cobwebs from her skirt, while Ruby had gone off exploring. 'Thanks awfully for coming to the rescue.'

'When one is summoned using a falling soufflé as a guide, well...' Andrews gave Cressida a rare smile. Then he looked serious again. 'Are you all right, though? And Lady Dorothy?'

'Yes, quite well, aren't we, Dot?' Cressida answered.

'Yes. Well, slightly confused, but all right, yes. Cressy, what's going on? Who are these ghoulish figures?' Dotty asked, and Andrews took his cue. He leaned down and pulled back the hood of the figure lying on the floor, the one bested in the fight.

'Mr Biddle, the landlord of the Wykeham Arms,' said Cressida ruefully. 'Looking for the bones?'

Biddle looked up at Cressida and snarled. 'Why didn't you just stop nosing around, eh?'

His voice she recognised. He'd been the figure who'd attacked her in Anthony's house.

'Did you enjoy your trip?' she asked innocently enough.

'Eh?' Biddle looked at her, and even Andrews and Dotty shared a glance.

'Trip. Over Alfred's bag on the pathway. Andrews, I wouldn't be surprised if you find a scuffed knee or a hurt elbow under that ridiculous cloak. This was the same cloaked figure who threatened me with a knife at Anthony's house.'

'I'll add that to the charge sheet,' Andrews replied. 'But why? And what were you doing at the murdered verger's house?' He looked exasperated.

'Ah, well, this.' Cressida pulled out the map. 'It's rather important. It's a map of the crypt and it showed me that there was a secret passage.'

'The reason you thought Nancy could get in with no one noticing her, and meet her fiancé, Anthony... and...' A look dawned on his face. 'How someone else could get in and out as well, just before her.'

'Exactly.' Cressida had noticed that a few more figures had arrived and were standing at the top of the steps into the crypt. Cloaked in dark robes, but not ghoulish, she recognised their faces as being Mr Sitwell, who had perhaps decided the cathedral was a better place than the Wykeham Arms if one was to be maudlin, and Mr Flint, who had no doubt heard the commotion from his archive. She thought they'd be interested in what she had to say, and as they walked over, Andrews took it upon himself to unveil the other hooded figures. The first one, who had arrived behind the original attacker, and was the smaller of the three, squirmed as the hood was pulled back from her face.

'Nancy,' Cressida said, as her aunt's maid was made to drop a pillowcase to the floor. It clanked with a metallic twang as it hit the ground, and a silver sugar bowl rolled out and did a turn or two of the flagstones before coming to a stop.

'Nancy was the murderer after all?' the dean said, coming to stand next to Andrews.

'No, sir,' Andrews replied. 'Not according to the pathologist and the expert on blood spatter.'

'I think that's your murderer.' Cressida pointed to the third figure, the one who had crawled through the secret passage, elbows covered in dust, and who was now having the hood pulled off their head.

The torch beams that had been haphazardly lighting the vaulted arches and pillars all centred on the third figure. And when the hood was pulled back there was a gasp.

The dean blanched. He was the first to speak.

'How could you, Michael, how could you?'

48

'Michael? The precentor?' Dotty sounded incredulous.

'Why not?' Cressida said. 'He knew the cathedral well enough. This map, and others like it, would have been kept in the same archive drawers as the sheet music. But more than that, it's only Michael, and his wife Judith, who have the motive necessary to kill Anthony.'

'You were sure Nancy didn't because she was so upset about finding her fiancé dead,' Dotty reminded her.

'And I wasn't wrong. I think Nancy did love Anthony. But, sadly for Nancy, I don't think Anthony returned the feelings. Or had any idea Nancy felt that way at all.'

'He would have done...' Nancy started, but Robert Biddle shushed her.

Cressida continued telling the police her theory, and looked at the maid as she did so. 'Nancy, you were sweet on him, and collected every picture and mention of his name that you could. But there was no reciprocation of it in his own house.'

'So why say he was her fiancé? And Mr Biddle backed it up,' Dotty pointed out.

'But did you notice that it was *only* Mr Biddle that backed it up. Saying he'd seen them in the pub together, when, according to Nancy's version, they'd been very discreet and would never have been seen in public looking "happy as Larry". But a father likes to embellish about his daughter, I think. That is what you are, aren't you, Robert? Her father.'

The man in cuffs grunted.

Andrews filled in more of the story. 'While she was in custody, Mr Biddle here was the only person to visit Nancy. He stayed for a good while, until we had to pull him out as it all started to sound a bit conspiratorial.'

Cressida fixed Andrews with a glare. 'So, you knew he was her father? And didn't tell me?'

Andrews had the decency to look at his shoes for a moment. 'It was before Sir Kingsley had given us permission to include you, Miss Fawcett, and then, yes, apologies, it seemed old news by the time he had. I rather thought your own sleuthing would have found that out at any rate.'

'Hmm,' Cressida narrowed her eyes at her favourite police-man, but wanted to carry on while she had their attention. 'Anyway, it seems to me that Nancy claimed Anthony was her fiancé to strengthen the case for her innocence, not disguise any guilt. She didn't know that the pathologist would prove she didn't do it and she thought her strongest defence was to claim their love for each other. And she *was* truly upset. The man she was sweet on, utterly captivated by and all that, was dead, in front of her.'

'But why had he written her a little note to summon her if he wasn't her fiancé?' Dotty asked.

'I don't know...' Nancy sniffed. 'I was so excited to receive it I didn't expect it at all. But it made it more believable that he and I were going steady.'

Andrews scratched his beard. 'Are you getting all this, Kirby?'

The sergeant nodded as he scribbled in his notebook.

'You can add lying under oath to the charge sheet.' He frowned. 'Making up fiancés left, right and centre.'

Cressida nodded at Andrews, but looked at Nancy again. 'But someone did send you that note. Someone who knew how sweet you were on Anthony, who knew you'd run straight into his arms at the slightest prompt.'

'Who knew?' Dotty asked, finally putting the useless torch away in her coat pocket.

'Clara Sitwell, I should imagine. And after her death, her dear friend – Judith Ainsworth. Clara and Judith shared many confidences,' Cressida thought about the books. 'A true friendship until... Oh dear. Oh yes. That all makes sense now.'

'What?' Andrews and Dotty both asked in unison.

But Cressida didn't look at them. Instead she released herself from Dotty's arm and walked over to the dean. She placed a hand on his sleeve.

'Geoffrey. What I'm about to say will be hard to hear, but I think you have a right to know. Poor Clara.' She bit her lip, then took a deep a breath. 'It all started with the petty thieving, I suppose. Nancy, you were at fault there.'

'Don't say anything, child,' her father growled. 'Stay quiet.'

'I can't, Pa, not anymore,' Nancy sobbed. 'It's all got so out of hand!'

'Started as petty thieving, didn't it? Fencing things through the pub until the local antiques dealers got wind of it and you had to stop. Books, silverware...'

'Ah, is that how Clara's books got into Mr Bell's bookshop?' Dotty asked, and Cressida nodded.

'Which is why he lied about where he'd got them – he couldn't say he'd been accepting stolen goods. But a first edition of a Tennyson book is worth something, so he kept a keen eye on the thieves and what they were up to.'

'It's very sad to think that one's maid is thieving from you, very sad indeed,' said the dean, 'but I think I could have taken the news quite well, Miss Fawcett.' He nodded at her hand that was still resting on his arm.

'Oh, yes, I'm sorry, Geoffrey. My fault for taking so long, but then it has been a particularly tricky case this one, with all sorts of different aspects to it. And I'm afraid worse news is yet to come for you, some very upsetting news indeed.'

'Nancy stole Clara's hairbrush, do you think? The silver one?' Geoffrey asked. 'A terrible loss, but...'

'Yes, but it's more than that, Mr Sitwell. Clara died before any of this had happened.' Cressida gestured to the three cuffed, hooded, figures. 'But she had to die before it could happen.'

'What are you saying?' The dean rubbed his forehead with his hand and looked perplexed.

'I'm afraid your wife's death was no accident. Clara was murdered.'

49

'Murdered? My Clara? She fell... Judith said so...' Geoffrey stammered.

'Judith Ainsworth. Wife of this man here?' Cressida pointed to the handcuffed precentor. 'This man who had no real alibi for the time of Anthony's murder, and appeared on the scene pretty quickly after we'd found the body, his elbows as dusty as they are now. This man who has now moved into your old home, the lovely Deanery, a house much admired by his wife. His wife, who said she'd do anything to afford the school fees for the lauded Winchester College, here in the city.'

'She killed Clara?' The dean was taken aback still, reeling from the news. 'For school fees? I don't understand?'

'Me neither, I'm afraid, Miss Fawcett,' Andrews crossed his arms. 'How did you get to that? There was no suspicion of Mrs Sitwell's death being a murder.'

'That's because the only witness was Judith Ainsworth, an upright member of the community. She said Clara fell; not the truth – that she pushed her.'

'But how would killing Clara help her with the school fees?' Andrews asked.

Cressida took a breath, then explained. 'That letter we found in the *Anthology of Modern Poetry*, it was written by Clara, was it not, Andrews?'

'Yes, we had the writing compared to a sample of hers. It was written by the late Clara Sitwell.'

'And I found it in a book being sold by Mr Bell, who lied about where it came from, not knowing that I had already discovered its provenance. So, it was Clara's book, with a letter written by Clara, in it. But who was that letter to? Judith.'

'How can you tell?' Andrews asked.

'It's the only explanation that makes sense. Clara knew everything going on within the cathedral, and she'd discovered that her maid, Nancy, was a petty thief.'

'Her hairbrush had gone missing,' the dean murmured.

'Yes, and several of her cherished books. And I should imagine that Clara confided her suspicions to Judith, perhaps asking if she'd noticed anything go missing from their lodgings. If only she'd shared those thoughts with Aunt Mary instead, none of this would have happened, but telling Judith that Nancy was most likely a thief gave her an idea. She used it to distract from the real theft that she and her husband were planning – that of stealing the bones.'

'How did Clara Sitwell know about the bones? How did Judith, for that matter?' Andrews asked, while Kirby held his pencil poised.

Cressida paused. But Geoffrey Sitwell, the dean, filled the silence. 'I don't know how Judith would know, but if she did, then Clara would have done too. She had a way of finding things out, and she and Judith were always nattering over a sherry, or two. I remember one evening I came upon them arguing in the parlour, and Judith left in quite high dudgeon. That was only a few days before Clara's accident—'

'That wasn't an accident,' Cressida reminded him.

Geoffrey sighed and nodded. 'Poor Clara. She must have

needled the information out of Judith, she was awfully good at that.'

Cressida carried on as the dean removed a handkerchief from his pocket and blew his nose. 'Hence the letter written to Judith warning her; pleading with her not to carry out her plan, of how unchristian it was. But Judith was determined, and couldn't trust Clara not to do the "right thing" and turn her in to the Church, or legal, authorities.'

'Clara...' The dean looked wobbly and Dotty rushed over to him to take over from Cressida, who moved over to where the precentor was standing, head bowed as if in prayer over his cuffed wrists.

Cressida thought for a moment longer, then spoke again. 'Ha, of course. No wonder Judith was so upset when we saw her talking to Mr Bell. She knew she'd left that letter in the book she'd borrowed from Clara and now it was gone. Casting aspersions about Geoffrey being responsible for his wife's death was a low blow, but I think she was getting desperate. If anyone found that letter – as I did – well, questions would be asked. Mr Ainsworth, am I right? Did Judith somehow find out about the bones and then want to steal them from Anthony and sell them to the highest bidder?'

The precentor raised his head from the ground to the heavens and sighed.

'The game is up, Mr Ainsworth. You're in cuffs and Judith will be arrested now too. I don't think we'll have to look too hard for evidence to convict you of Anthony's murder, and your wife for that of Clara Sitwell.'

The precentor drew himself up to his full height and then deflated again, his shoulders sagging. Finally he spoke. 'My conscience is finally getting the better of me.'

'Better it had before you killed Tony,' Nancy spat out, though Andrews and her father shushed her.

'But yes,' Michael Ainsworth, the precentor, carried on, 'it was me. Judith wrote the note luring Nancy to the crypt so that there would be someone to take the blame. I hadn't reckoned on you and your aunt being taken on a tour. It was meant to be me who found Miss Biddle by the dead body. I also hadn't reckoned on her using the passageway. I had only just left when she entered.'

'I told you I saw the Silent Friar... Oh...' Nancy furrowed her brow as she realised who it had been that she'd seen. 'I couldn't say it was from the tunnel door though, I didn't think it would look good if you knew I knew there was a secret passage.'

'How did you know about the passage, Nancy?' Cressida asked, almost as an aside.

'When I cleaned for Anthony, I saw the map he was studying. Such a clever man, you see, and so kind and...' She started crying again.

'There, there, Nancy,' Cressida tried to comfort her, but she was still desperate to get to the truth about the bones, and Anthony's role in everything.

'Mr Ainsworth, did you know Anthony had found the bones of St Swithun?'

'Yes. He confided in me. He said he'd found the casket, but didn't want to tell a soul. I knew, of course, that they'd be extremely valuable, and once I'd told Judith, she hit upon the plan to wrestle them from him and sell them before he could enshrine them somewhere in the cathedral. You're right in that Judith knew Nancy and her father had a small-time racket running out of the pub, due to Clara confiding in her. When Clara found out Judith's plan, she threatened to go to the police, or worse, the Church authorities. I couldn't ask Anthony more about the bones in case he got suspicious – not that he'd have ever guessed our plan, but there are as I'm sure you've worked out, petty jealousies among us here. If he thought I wanted to unearth the bones before he did, he'd assume it was because I wanted the glory for the music department or some such thing. So before we could sell the darn things, we had to find out what Anthony had discovered. Where they had been hidden in 1910.'

'So, you broke into the archive?'

'Yes. I knew Anthony had refused Mr Flint the new padlock in the latest round of budgets, so it would be easy enough. And Anthony had refused to reveal the location of the casket, but I knew he'd found it through looking at the 1910 records – Flint was able to tell me that.'

'I had no idea that was your motive Michael,' Mr Flint spoke up, the look on his face one of pure disappointment.

'So how did Nancy end up with one of the pages from that stolen record book in her dressing table?' Dotty asked.

'And Anthony had one in his pocket...' Cressida remembered. 'The page from the record book which was at the beginning of this whole mystery.'

'Once I had the right record book, I made the mistake of bringing in the help of the professionals.' Michael looked over to Robert and Nancy Biddle. 'Breaking into the archive was enough for me. I gave the book to Robert Biddle and told him where to look. We were to split the proceeds of finding the bones between us. A nice settlement for him, and enough for the boys' school fees for us. With Clara gone, Geoffrey had, by luck, offered us the Deanery, so we didn't need all the money from the relics. We're not greedy people, you know.'

Cressida almost snorted in shock, but turned to his co-conspirator. 'Is this true, Robert?'

It was Nancy who spoke up. 'It's true, miss. But, you see, Mr Ainsworth didn't know how much I admired Anthony, and I didn't want him to lose his precious bones. I tore out those pages, and when I was cleaning for him, I slipped a page into one of his spare robes. I think he found it all right, as he had an argument with Mr Ainsworth in the pub.'

'You lied, Mr Ainsworth,' Cressida accused him. 'You said it was about music and bells and your difference in how you worship? You even quoted Abbot Suger to me.' She was peeved.

'I know, I know,' Michael, the precentor, shook his head, his handcuffs rattling as he did so. 'I couldn't very well say, "oh yes, that fight, it was about the fact I was in the process of discovering where St Swithun's bones are too, in order to send them to France for a casket load of cash."'

'Well, no. But it's good to know the truth now.' Cressida arched a brow at Andrews, who in turn made sure that Kirby was getting all of this.

'What about Alfred?' Dotty piped up. 'Why was he framed, with the cloak and the journal in his room?'

'Framed is exactly right, Dot.' Cressida turned her steely blue-eyed gaze back to the pub landlord, Robert Biddle. 'And, in some ways, I can understand Mr Biddle's plight. His business partner, Mr Ainsworth, and his wife, had just set up his daughter for murder.'

Kirby broke his lead and hurriedly found a new pencil. He was poised to continue as Cressida clarified.

'Mr Biddle knew straight away that his daughter had been double-crossed. When he went to see her in the cells, she told him that she'd lied to us about being Anthony's fiancé. But she also showed him the note, supposedly from Anthony. He recognised the writing as being Mrs Ainsworth's, perhaps, or just figured out that she had been lured there by the only people who he knew could have had reason to kill Anthony: the Ainsworths. But to get them back would be to jeopardise the money. He'd already alerted his contacts – Mr Bell in the bookshop, no stranger to stolen goods—'

'How did they know that?' Andrews asked.

Cressida had it all worked out now. 'Nancy had been using him to fence the books she'd taken from the Deanery. I found a piece of suede in her bedroom too, and it was a perfect colour match to some old tomes Mr Bell was repairing.' She paused, then added, 'I'm very good at spotting colours, you see. And that shade of purple was just like a pair of shoes I'd seen... Anyway, it doesn't matter, but Mr Bell had already asked for Pierre Fontaine to come and be the go-between. He could take the bones to the Continent and sell them there for a fortune to the Catholics, who still put a huge amount of faith in those sorts of things.'

'Let me get this straight, Miss Fawcett,' Andrews stopped her. 'You've got the Ainsworths who had ascertained that there were relics which could be stolen, and they knew the Biddles were the ones who could fence them. But no one had figured on Nancy being so sweet on Anthony, who was the only one who knew where the relics were and wanted to keep them safe until the cathedral was ready for them—'

'Exactly, so when she tipped him off that his precious bones might be about to be swiped from under his nose, it caused all sorts of problems. Now, despite being cross with her for tipping Anthony off, of course Mr Biddle didn't want to see his daughter hang. And of course neither he nor Nancy realised that she would be exonerated anyway by the experts on blood splatter and all that, so Mr Biddle rather clumsily tried to create a patsy. Alfred was an outsider: easy to blame, easy to plant evidence in his room, and easy enough to get his cronies in the pub to swear blind that he was a wrongdoer.'

'Is this right, Mr Biddle? Did you kill that man merely to frame Lord Delafield and cast suspicion on him for another murder he couldn't possibly have done?' Andrews turned to the cuffed man. 'Be a man now, and own up if so. The law will look kinder on your daughter if you own up to your misdeeds.'

Biddle looked at Nancy, who hung her head in shame, or

grief, or both. Then he looked at Cressida, who held his gaze unflinchingly. Finally, he nodded.

'Yes. I'm not a fool, I knew I couldn't pin Anthony's death on him if he had an alibi, but I just needed to buy enough time to get Nancy released. Then she could hop it to France with the help of that Pierre chap and be out of the law's grasp. I didn't know she'd be let off due to not actually having done it.'

'You never thought she had, though?' Cressida quizzed him.

Robert Biddle looked at his daughter, then back to Cressida. 'Course I didn't. But I also couldn't take any chances. She was caught red-handed. It looked bad for her.'

'Where's Pierre Fontaine now?' Cressida asked, stealing a look at her best friend and rejoicing in the relief on her face. This most recent confession meant that Alfred was saved.

'Chesil Inn,' Biddle replied. 'Ainsworth, there, was here tonight to retrieve the bones.'

Michael nodded. 'You failed to get me that map though, you blundering fool,' he muttered.

'It was when I saw the light on in Anthony's house, and was attacked by Mr Biddle over the map that I knew something was about to happen tonight.' Cressida thought for a moment then almost laughed. 'But me getting the map first... Is that why you started fighting each other just now? When we thought we were done for?'

'That and all the double-crossing, I should imagine,' Dotty said.

'So where are they? The bones?' Andrews asked. 'It would tie everything up nicely if we could return them to their rightful owner, whoever that technically is.' He momentarily looked heavenward, then back at Cressida.

'I... I don't know,' Cressida admitted, but she uncrumpled the map of the crypt that had been crushed in her hands as she and Dotty had hidden from the cloaked figures. She reached into her pocket too. 'But I have a feeling this key will help us find them. I found it here, down in the crypt, when Alfred and I came in to search the place yesterday evening. The thread tied on it matched one I found in Anthony's spare robes, so I assumed it was his, and that it was thrown from his hand as the murder took place.'

'I saw him carry a box down here—' Michael admitted, though he was interrupted by Cressida.

'As did Mr Havering, who was keeping watch over the entrance for Anthony's reaction to the bells.'

'So I thought he'd have it on him when I accosted him. He'd found out too much from Nancy about our plan. I'm afraid he had to die, else he'd reveal it all. Then I heard voices in the nave and had to make my escape before anyone found me there. I never found the casket.'

Silence fell on the crypt as this was considered. A silence broken only by a small dog sitting next to one of the pillars panting happily. One of the police lanterns spread a warm golden glow over the floor where she was sitting, and the shadow cast by an uneven flagstone was more noticeable in the light. Ruby panted harder, then sort of snorted.

'It's that thing she does,' Dotty reminded Cressida. 'The wolf in her coming out in a very minor, puggish, way.'

'She's found something,' Cressida agreed and hopped over a couple of puddles to where Ruby was sitting, looking pleased as punch with herself. Cressida smiled at her. 'Come on, shift off, you gorgeous little thing, you.' Cressida shooed her away and grappled with the flagstone. Due to it being moved not that long ago, it was easier than it looked to pull up. Moving it to one side, Cressida reached down into the cavity and carefully lifted up a golden casket. She recognised it – she'd seen it before. She glanced at Mr Flint, who nodded. It was identical to the one from the medieval painting of St Swithun's burial. These were the bones.

Dotty, Andrews, Kirby, the dean and Mr Flint splashed

their way over to her as she gently fitted the key from her pocket into the lock. The catch sounded and the lock clicked. Cressida slowly raised the lid of the casket and as the bells of the cathedral pealed above them, she looked upon the bones of Winchester's very own saint. St Swithun was safe.

50

Cressida pulled her coat around her and, arm in arm with Dotty, hurried through the chilly streets of Winchester towards the Guildhall and the police station within it. Ruby was trotting along at their ankles, and Dotty was the picture of happiness, as she had been since they'd been able to persuade DCI Andrews of Alfred's innocence.

'We knew he couldn't have done it. But to think it was the pub landlord himself, and him so embroiled with all the thefts too.'

Cressida squeezed her friend's arm. 'With Robert Biddle now under lock and key, that petty thievery ring will be quashed too. And that might have just saved Aunt M's life, as well as Alfred's.'

'But Nancy would never kill your aunt, surely?' Dotty's expression changed back to one of concern.

'She was happy enough to drug you both, and Cook, to get away with some more thieving. And don't forget the rumours about a house clearance at Priory House.'

'Oh, you give me the shivers, Cressy.' Dotty shook herself down. 'Thank heavens they've all been brought to justice.'

They clasped each other close as they crossed the green and then ducked back into the well-lit cobbled streets that led to the police station.

Andrews and Kirby, with their prisoners, had gone on ahead and, despite the lateness of the hour, had promised to start the paperwork for releasing Alfred. And they'd sent constables off to find Henry Bell, the bookseller, to bring him in – he had been a vital part of the gang of racketeers, the fence with contacts on the Continent who could sell the stolen items from places like the Deanery or Priory House without being suspected.

'I can't wait to see Alfred,' Dotty said, as they neared the corner of the road the police station was on. 'Mama has been beside herself and I don't think even Papa knew what to do. That it was all a horrible mistake, a plot against him even, and he'll have no tarnish on his character is such a relief.'

Cressida just squeezed her friend's arm again. It was a relief. A relief that Alfred would be free, and a relief that, despite it all, her investigating had managed to save him; even if it had put him in jeopardy in the first place. It was all very well being a hothead and letting herself get into all this, but that she'd endangered Alfred... she couldn't bear the thought of it.

'Evening, ladies,' Sergeant Kirby greeted them at the door of the station. And behind him, looking tired, cold and unshaven, but otherwise well, with his pipe stuck nonchalantly out of his mouth, was Alfred.

'Alf!' Dotty ran towards him and enveloped her big brother in a hug.

'Steady on, sis,' he said, almost bowled over by her. But she hugged and hugged him and, when she finally released him from her tight grip, she still held his arms and looked at him.

'Oh Alfred,' she said again. 'I was so worried. So was

Cressy, of course...' Dotty looked behind her to where Cressida was standing, suddenly unable to decide where to put her hands. She had them in her pockets, then folded them across her chest, then finally scooped up Ruby and held her to her blushing cheeks.

Alfred pulled Dotty off him and walked up to Cressida. 'Look here, old thing,' he touched a hand to her upper arm. 'Thank you for getting me out of the hot water.'

'I... I think I might have been the one to get you into it, Alf, and...'

'Well, hot or not, it's all water under the bridge now,' he said, and smiled at her.

She thought back to the list of fun things to do she'd found in his bedroom at the Wykeham Arms. Did Alfred really love her? Despite all the young heiresses he was always being introduced to, and the fact that Cressida had always been just 'old thing', his sister's best friend. His friend.

'I'm sorry, Alfred, for getting you into it anyway. I'm not proud of myself. I think maybe it's time I listened to your Uncle Kingsley and let Andrews alone.'

'What rot. Uncle Kingsley's just been on the blower. Got filled in on the case. Said it was only because of your ingenuity in following all the clues that the relics have been found. Said something about medals and possibly a reward. Definitely a place at the top table at the annual policeman's ball.'

Cressida grinned at him and Alfred looked at her quizzically.

'What's got your goose, Cressy? What's so funny?'

Cressida moved Ruby in her arms so she could look into her snub-nosed little face. Addressing her dog, and Alfred at the same time, she replied, 'I just think it's funny that your Uncle Kingsley has just offered top honours, and a ticket to the policemen's ball, to Ruby. It was her that found the casket.'

'I guess it takes a dog to find some bones,' Alfred chuckled.

Cressida looked indulgently at her pet. 'Even if that dog is just a pug.'

Within a few moments, Alfred was signed off and out and ready to leave with them. Dotty had threaded her arm through his and was walking alongside him, her head leaning on his arm. Cressida walked beside them, lost in her own thoughts and letting Alfred by turns both scare and scintillate his sister about his time in the cells.

Cressida could only think of how lucky she was to have them both in her life, and that they could all now head home to Priory House, where Aunt Mary, now she'd found the linen cupboard, promised to make up a bed for Alfred, despite once more being without a maid.

'... Of course the trick was to eat the stuff before the whiskered and long-tailed beasties got there first...' she over-heard Alfred telling a squealing Dotty as they crossed the small park in between the great west front of Winchester Cathedral and Priory House. The street lamps gave off pools of golden light that illuminated the fallen leaves all around them but left the shadows dark as night.

Cressida glanced back towards the cathedral and then stopped in her tracks. Alfred and Dotty didn't seem to notice, but Ruby snuffled a concerned snort or two in her arms. Cressida held her breath. *Surely not...*

There, between the lamps, just for a second, she'd seen something.

Tall as a lamplighter, and just disappears into the ether...

But with Robert Biddle now locked up and the Silent Friar, as seen by Nancy the day of Anthony's death, none other than the murderous precentor... who was the cloaked figure who was moving in the shadows towards the cathedral?

Cressida watched, paralysed, as the figure moved into a

circle of light closest to the cathedral. Then it turned, and Cressida froze. Across the darkness of the park, she saw the cloaked figure nod his head at her and she found herself dipping hers to him in return.

And then, in a moment, he was gone.

A LETTER FROM FLISS

Dear reader,

I want to say a huge thank you for choosing to read *Death in the Crypt*. If you did enjoy it and want to keep up to date with all my latest releases, just sign up at the following link. Your email address will never be shared and you can unsubscribe at any time.

www.bookouture.com/fliss-chester

I really hope that you're enjoying reading about Cressida Fawcett and the mysteries she and her friends solve. If you love our amateur sleuth – and Ruby too, of course – I would be very grateful if you could write a review of *Death in the Crypt*. I'd love to hear what you think. Reviews from readers like you can make such a difference helping new readers discover my books for the first time.

And I'd love to hear from you – have you ever been down to a cathedral crypt? Or seen caskets of relics and wondered what their history was? Let me know! You can get in touch on my Facebook page, through X, Instagram or my website.

Thanks,

Fliss Chester

KEEP IN TOUCH WITH FLISS

www.flisschester.co.uk

 facebook.com/flisschester
x.com/socialwhirlgirl

AUTHOR'S NOTE

Death in the Crypt was a really fun book to write. I loved exploring Winchester and going to the cathedral and can highly recommend buying a ticket, which includes a tour and entry to the crypt – when it's not flooded – and can be used multiple times over the course of a year. There's a stunning Antony Gormley sculpture, *Sound II*, in the crypt close to the spot that my fictional Anthony is murdered. 'Atmospheric' is certainly the word for it! Thank you to my friend Louisa Scarr (a brilliant author of suspenseful thrillers and police procedurals) for coming with me and being encouraging as I asked random cathedral volunteers about vestry doors, entrances to the crypt and learned all about the heroics of William Walker. Fact really can be stranger than fiction, and the cathedral *was* sinking and Walker *did* spend months in a diving bell shoring up the foundations... with bones and bodies floating past him. Grim!

I've tried to keep the cathedral, and the city of Winchester, recognisable to those who know it, but, of course, as this is an entirely fictional work, I have also changed certain aspects and place names to fit the story. I really don't think there is a secret passage to the crypt... or is there?

My thanks as always to my brilliant editor at Bookouture, Rhianna Louise. I don't think anyone has ever come back from maternity leave and had to hit the ground running as fast as she has with this manuscript, which, thanks to her guidance, has become the fun and pacy book it is. Also, thank you to my agent Emily Sweet at Aevitas who is always a huge support and my own personal cheerleader. I don't think I could have got eleven books in without your help over the years.

Writing for a living, though an absolute privilege, can also be lonely at times, and the days would seem emptier without my writing buddies. You all know who you are, and you also know that you're responsible for the Silent Friar almost being called the much less mysterious 'Mr Biscuits'. The name still tickles my funny bone and makes me smile when I think about it. Thank you all for being on the end of a WhatsApp whenever needed.

Last, but certainly not least, thanks as always to my lovely husband, Rupert. Your enthusiasm and support of my work is limitless and appreciated. I'm very lucky to have you, old thing.

PUBLISHING TEAM

Turning a manuscript into a book requires the efforts of many people. The publishing team at Bookouture would like to acknowledge everyone who contributed to this publication.

Audio
Alba Proko
Sinead O'Connor
Melissa Tran

Commercial
Lauren Morrissette
Hannah Richmond
Imogen Allport

Cover design
Debbie Clement

Data and analysis
Mark Alder
Mohamed Bussuri

Editorial
Rhianna Louise
Lizzie Brien